Fitz Hugh Ludlow

Little Brother

And Other Genre-Pictures

Fitz Hugh Ludlow

Little Brother
And Other Genre-Pictures

ISBN/EAN: 9783337140311

Printed in Europe, USA, Canada, Australia, Japan

Cover: Foto ©Andreas Hilbeck / pixelio.de

More available books at **www.hansebooks.com**

LITTLE BROTHER;

AND

THER GENRE-PICTURES.

BY

FITZ HUGH LUDLOW,

HOR OF "THE HASHEESH EATER," "REGULAR HABITS,"
"AMONG THE MORMONS," "SEVEN WEEKS IN THE
GREAT YO-SEMITE," ETC. ETC.

"Maxima reverentia pueris debetur."—JUVENAL.

BOSTON:
LEE AND SHEPARD.
1867.

IN MIND OF A COURTESY TO WHICH THREE PICTURES IN THIS

CABINET OWE THEIR PRESENT SETTING, AND A LARGE-

HEARTEDNESS WHICH FROM THE BEGINNING OF

HIS CAREER HAS AFFORDED INNUMERABLE

HELPS TO THEIR ARTIST, THEY ARE

INSCRIBED TO

THAT WISE AND GENEROUS FRIEND OF LETTERS,

FLETCHER HARPER, Esq.

CONTENTS.

———◆———

LITTLE BROTHER.

———◦◦◦◦———

I.

A BOY TOO MUCH.

T was of no use to tell Kate that Augustus — of the same surname, and aged seven years — was a sweet little fellow. He *ought* to be, considering the number of paper-bags, labelled "Stewart's Assorted Candies," he consumed per week. Of as little use to say he was a child: there were some children who didn't put newspapers on the strings of their sister's piano, and play it was a banjo. Oh! he would outgrow it, would he? Then, why wasn't he sent away somewhere till he did? Or put into something, and locked up? Or put under somewhere, — a large barrel, for instance, with the head knocked out to give him air, as they do with young tomatoes and pieplants till they arrive at an age when they can come to the table?

Then Kate Jones's mother — just like a mother, as she was! — assumed the part of a tenderer variety of Judge-Advocate; and while she acknowledged that the little Augustus *did* almost exhaust her patience on occasions, recalled **a number of very** pretty ways he had, nice things he had done, affectionate words he had said, and the truly good heart that the child possessed beneath all his boy-mischief!

For instance: Did not Kate remember how, when the family was boarding at the St. Jiminy, — that gilded cage, where families not yet able, in their own estimation, to be happily domestic in a house of their own at a moderate price, were accommodated with facilities for being very fashionably miserable at an exorbitant one, — the dear little fellow had once shown such an affectionate solicitude for his mother and sister? How, when, after wondering all one Friday why the washerwoman didn't come home with the clothes, — because they wanted to darn the stockings and see the shirts all right, — they found, in the evening, that she *had* come in the forenoon, while they were shopping down-town, and that Gus had taken all the clothes out of the basket, and put them away in all sorts of inconceivable drawers, presses, and trunks, before the two ladies returned; and when he was asked if he had anything to say why the sentence of being spanked until he was red should not be passed upon him, he sobbed, and put his little fists into his eyes, and faltered out something which led them to understand that the "Song of the Shirt," read by his father to them all, three evenings before, had left such an impression on his young mind that he had hidden the clothes, to prevent his mother and sister sewing

on them and dying of consumption ? Didn't Kate remember that ?

Yes; Kate *did* remember it. And she remembered
also another occasion, since they had rented their present house in Twenty-third street, when the *dear little
fellow* drove away from their connection one of the most
aristocratic young gentlemen in all New York society,
— young Schumakers Fyndings. To be sure *his* papa
did business down in some awful place that *her* papa
called the Swamp; but Kate didn't believe *he* ever went
there, or knew anything about where it was, even. Both
directly and indirectly his papa might have furnished
the calf-skin for his delicate polished boots; but there
was not the slightest suspicion of the ancestral leather
about him otherwise. No, not in the least ! And he
would have been such a desirable person to know, — but
for that little pest ! And Kate went on rapidly to re-
cite how Master Augustus, contrary to her own mature
advice, had been permitted to " sit up " at the party,
and had the little Misses Blummerie invited over to
make it pleasant for him; and yet, ingrate that he **was,**
when the gentlemen were all out in the hall, ready to
go, after the breaking-up, and Harold Fitz-Blacktease,
the son of the China trader, came downstairs, and said,
" Fellahs ! who's got a cigar for me to smoke on my
way home ? " and no man gave unto him, how that
wretched Augustus, leaning over the balcony at his
side, with slow, unmoving finger selected young Fyndings out of the throng, and said, in a voice distinctly

audible to all present, "*He's* got some; *he* has: I saw
him take six out of papa's box up in the gentlemen's
dressing-room, and they're in the inside pocket of his
Raglan !" And how young Fyndings turned the color
of his papa's boot-top morocco, and, in a humiliated
manner, extended one of the said six to Fitz-Blacktease;
and how *she* nearly dropped with mortification; and
how young Fyndings never came to make his party call
— nor, indeed, a call of any description — afterward.
Did her mamma remember *that* ?

And, only to weary her with one instance more:
Could she recall the time when Master Augustus turned
to that distinguished foreigner, M. Pâté de Perigord,
who was dining with them previous to taking Kate to
see the performance of " ze inimitable Sharl Mattieu "
in the " Critic," with Brougham, Burton, Walcot, and
Lizzie Weston, at the Metropolitan, and asked him,
" Have you got a large salary ? " and upon the distinguished foreigner answering, in his pretty, broken way,
with a disguised surprise, that he had " not ze salaire at
all," the *enfant terrible* bent a severe gaze upon him,
and demanded, " How can you afford to take my sister
to Burton's *then* ? " And, in general, was it among possible remembrances that, on New-Year's days, the formidable infant stood sucking innumerable consecutive
oranges at the foot of the front-steps, and shaking with
juicy hands the lavender kids of the gentlemen who
came to pay their compliments; or, tiring of that
amusement, ascended to the parlor, borrowed the visit-

ors' hats, asked them where they got them, what they paid for them, and, with the same succulent hands, brushed the nap the wrong way?

In fine, was it on the record how *that* Augustus never ceased to behave himself in the most heart-rending and peace-dispelling, odious manner, at all times and places, universal and particular? Was it, or was it not? That was all!

At this moment the angel spoken of showed his wings. A harbinger voice in the entry cried, "Porgies! Here-er yer fresh **porgies!** Here they go-o-oh!" **The** door opened, and the terrible child came in. His head, which just reached to **the** door-knob, was covered with a thicket of corn-silky curls; and, having parted from the comb on bad terms before breakfast, had not made up with it since. His cheeks were plump as mellow Spitzenbergs, and quite as red, with overmuch shouting of his imaginary wares. These — to wit, the porgies — consisted of **a** selection from the valuable annuals and vases which **ought to have occupied the** drawing-room centre-table, and were borne in **the hollow bottom of an** embroidered footstool, turned upside down, its floss and worsted suffering undesirable attrition with the carpet; and the whole establishment, thus improvised, was fastened to his waist by an elegant groseille silken cord and tassel from his mother's morning-dress, which cost at the least twelve shillings at Peyser's. His eyes were a mischievous twinkling hazel: young as he was, there was an air of old waggishness about him, a sense of the

2

ludicrous, which promised the true man of humor
when a few more **years** in this mixed world should have
added pathos **to his** fun. But, at present, he was only
the dear, naughty little rogue, — one of those children
that you are forever wanting to whip at one end and
kiss **at** the other.

Kate had worked the footstool which this lad was
desecrating. With a fateful sternness and an agony of
mind which did not express itself in words, for these
had proved useless long ago, she put down the under-
sleeve she was crocheting, and marching up to her
brother, began disengaging the cord and tassel from
his waist.

"Take care, Kate," said the child, with a shake of his
head: "I'm a horse. You're afraid of horses, you
know, **and** this one is a very bad one. He kicks, and
bites, and runs away, and does everything that's bad.
Oh, he's an awful horse! Porgies! here-er yer fresh
porgies! here they go-o-oh!"

And he burst away from the young girl to career
around the room faster than Kate's offended dignity
chose to follow him.

"My **son,** take off that cord and sit down for a moment. I want to talk to you." This was said very
calmly by the mother of Augustus.

"Yes, mamma, I will. I'm a good horse to people
that treat me kindly and don't make me shy; so I'll just
take my harness off and listen. May I stand up,

mamma, while you're talking? Horses never sit down, you know."

"Yes, my dear, come and stand up by my side and let me take your hand." Augustus obeyed, with very good grace. Kate resumed her crocheting in silence, and the mother said to the child: —

"My son, do you love me — very much indeed ?"

"Yes, mamma, I love you — six bushels."

"Why do you love me, Augustus ?"

"Because you're good."

"Don't you want to be loved, my dear little son ?"

"Yes, I want people to love me, if they wont call me a monkey, and an owl, and good-for-nothing, and say I ought to be whipped, and sent to bed, and have my hair brushed, and everything mean." (This with a glance at Miss Jones, who did not appear to hear it.)

"Don't you think I love you, Augustus ?"

"Yes, you do, mamma."

"Why do I love you, Augustus ?"

"Because I'm naughty."

"Wouldn't you like to be loved because you were good ?"

"Wouldn't I die if I were good ?"

"Why, what do you mean, Augustus ?"

"Wouldn't I have to be an angel, and with the angels stand, a crown upon my forehead, a harp within my hand ? *That's* what I mean: that's what little Jimmy Stilton did, and he was good, Kate said. He wanted to be an angel, *he* did. *I* don't, because he died; and he didn't know what knuckle-down was ! And he thought that top-time came before kite-time ! And if he's got a harp I don't believe he can play it, for he couldn't do anything with a jews-harp, and a harp's an awful lot harder, — isn't it, mamma ? "

" Don't say ' an awful lot,' dear; say ' a great deal.' Oh, how sorry I am to think my little boy wouldn't like to be an angel ! You can be an angel and *live*, too, Augustus; you can be an angel, and stay to make us all very happy."

" I know it; you're an angel, mamma. Give me a *great big* kiss ! "

" There, dear ! there are two instead of one for you ! But let me talk to you a little more; did you never read the pretty books you get at school, about being good ? "

" Yes, mamma, and that's just it ! Don't all the good children in books die ? Don't Nathan Dickerman sit on a chair in his picture, with something very bad the matter with his back, and don't *he* die when he's only ten years old ? And don't little Mary Lathrop die when she's eight ? and didn't she turn round when her brother slapped her, and say, ' Hit me on the other cheek, *dear* ? ' I'd ha' *deared* him ! I wish I'd been there; I'd ha' *lammed* him, *I* would ! "

" But don't my little son remember that all the naughty children in the books get terribly punished for it, — say, my little Augustus ? "

" Oh, yes, *they* die, too ! they go out in boats on Sunday, and get tipped up; and in the pictures you can't see anything but their hands sticking above the water, and nobody comes to pull them out. Or they go up into trees to hook birds' nests, and the limb always breaks, and then they get it! Oh, cracky! *don't* they? Everybody dies, in books; good boys die, and naughty boys die!"

"What are you going to do, then, Augustus, if the good boys and naughty boys both die?"

"I — I — I —" Here Augustus stopped and scratched his head in deep meditation. Finally he brightened up with the discovery of a capital idea. "I guess," said Augustus, "that I wont be *very* naughty, nor *very* good; I'll be *half-an'-half!* and then I'll keep alive fornever and never!"

"O Augustus! Very well! half-and-half is better than very naughty; and I'm afraid that my little boy is *that*, too, sometimes."

"Yes, I am; I'm very naughty to-day; for I've been playing porgies with the books, and the vases, and the footstool, and your cord. But I wont do it any more. And I'm very naughty to Kate, too, to-day; but I always *am* naughty to *her*, because she's so naughty to me, — and, besides, I do hate that Spindle-shanks!"

"Augustus! I shall punish you, if you call your sister names!"

"I aint a-callin *her* names; *she* isn't spindle-shanks."

"Who do you mean, then, Augustus?"

"I mean that old thing, Mr. Lilykid, who is all the

2*

time coming to see Kate, and drinking papa's Champagne, and dancing polkas with Kate, and taking her to the opera, and calling me 'sonny!' Just as I was coming upstairs with the porgies Johnson let him in, and asked me would I tell Kate that a gentleman was in the parlor; and he's been here ever since, cooling his **heels while** I was up here talking, — that's what Johnson calls it when he has to wait. What does 'cooling his heels mean, mamma?'"

"Good Heavens!" ejaculated Kate; "and you never told me of it, you wicked, wicked boy! If you don't whip him for *this*, mother, I shall think you mean to let him rush headlong to destruction!"

So saying, she jerked the bell-pull, as if it were Master Augustus's ear, and communicated with some faintly tintinnabulating conscience in the basement of his system, instead of merely sounding an alarm to Johnson in the kitchen, who straightway knocked at the door.

"Go down immediately to the parlor, Johnson," said Miss Jones, in a tone whose sternness was just enough smothered to fall short of the guest below, "and tell Mr. Lilykid that, by a mistake, I was only informed just now of his being here, and will see him directly. And remember, Johnson, never, on any occasion when you have a message for me, to give it to Master Augustus, but **bring it** *yourself.*"

"Directly" is an idea of such wonderful elasticity that, in the seventh sphere of the spiritual world, where Mrs. Hatch informs us that we shall be clothed with

ideas in lieu of matter, it will probably answer to the
India-rubber of this present gross life, and be manufac-
tured into all sorts of ethereal overshoes, belting,
shoulder-straps, water-proof coats, and stretchable ar-
rangements whatsoever, by some Horace Day of that
stage of existence. "Directly," with the soldier and
sailor, means as long as it takes to turn on their heels;
with the waiter at the eating-house where I lunch, it
means as soon as the fat man in the next box has ceased
to be hungry, thirsty, and morning-paper-ivorous; with
young ladies in general, it signifies any conceivable time,
from half an hour and rising, in which a lovely mauve
barége robe may be put on, its skirt, under-skirt, and
over-skirt shaken down, so as to lie airily over those
magnificent thirty-spring skirts, with tapes woven in
and adjustable bustles, created by the wondrous Mrs.
Peddie, of Bowery, just below Bleecker street. This
was what "directly" meant with Miss Kate Jones in
particular.

With a sweet smile upon her pretty mouth, — which
was *not* the result of saying "papa, propriety, poultry
prunes, prisms," but of a still better recipe, — the banishment of all thoughts concerning that dreadful Augustus,
— she descended to the parlor, and met Mr. Lilykid
with a voice from the "Young Lady's Behavior-Book"
and a bow from the third figure of the Lancers. Mr.
Lilykid, being a gentleman who ran entirely to the small
and well-polished toes of good society, either had no
heels to cool or ignored them completely, reciprocating

the greeting as if he had only come in within the last three minutes.

" Did any one ever see such a contretemps ? " warbled Kate, with a light-hearted laugh. " Here you have been kept waiting, so rudely, I don't know how long, — it must be ten minutes, **I dare say."**

" Oh, h-a-a-adly ! ha-a-adly ! " murmured Mr. Lily-kid, in gallant deprecation. " What's that pwetty thing the poet says ? — ' How softly falls the foot of Time that only tweads on flowahs ! ' And to expect Miss Jones, — oh, that is to twead on damask woses, — otto of woses ! Weally, I feel as if I were not only on an ottoman, but an otto-man myself, now that you ah heah ! Ha ! he ! he ! he ! "

" You are very kind, I'm sure, as well as very witty ! You must have thought you were going to be fastened to your ottoman for a thousand **years, like the** King in **the Palace** of Sleepers; but it's **all** that darling **little** rogue of a brother of mine ! Johnson very improperly confided his message to him, and he went off to play, as children will, and forgot all about it. What do you find to amuse yourself with now, in town ? It's so dreadfully dull, and everybody's leaving for the Springs, or New-port, or Europe. We're going out next week; we would have gone this, but papa always likes to go with us, and he wanted to stay for the Bremen steamer. What *do* you find to do ? "

(Mr. Lilykid will excuse me for translating his *bon*

ton-ese into English hereafter, as its drawl is painful to vulgar ears.)

" My dear Miss Jones, a man devoted to good society always has enough to do! I sometimes see friends of mine feeling quite miserably, — *blasé*, in fact, — and I always say to them, ' Eustis,' or ' Ainsley,' or ' Belle-mountain,' as the case may be, ' really, how can you ? Do you know your duty to your set ? Do you reflect **that** you'll be called on to be an ornament to it next winter, — to exert yourself for its benefit, — to make yourself agreeable in every way ? And yet you are idle ! I declare it's a shame !' **For** there are so many things a man devoted to good society can do to keep himself in practice, **you know. Dear me !** I could not excuse myself to my conscience if I were idle ! "

" You say I know, but I *don't* know. Tell me, for I feel a sincere interest in knowing. I really supposed that all that gentlemen found to occupy themselves with, after the winter was over and before the summer **season began, was to lie on a sofa and** color their meer-**schaums !** "

" Aw, really ! I confess to the meerschaum; but then, that's only my relaxation.   I never permit myself to take it up unless my mind has been on the stretch for some time, and wants unbending, you know. Business first, pleasure afterward; and I have so much to keep me busy every day that **I** don't think much of mere selfish gratification, — till evening, at least."

" But you don't go down-town, like poor papa, into that dreadful Wall street ? "

" Ha-a-a-adly ! When I say business, I don't mean stocks, and rents, and dividends, and all that: my lawyer attends to those things for me. Left an orphan at a very early age, with a large property, consisting almost entirely of real estate widely scattered through the rural districts, I don't know what I should have done, young as I was, and careless of my own interests, — as I still am, — if it hadn't been for my having a capable business man, who was faithfully attached to our family, and who comes between me and all my tenants, and others who want to talk about money. My business is something quite different, I assure you. You see, Miss Jones, from my youngest days I have been devoted to good society. I live for it. I may say it is my meat and my drink to do my duty to good society. And at this season, when everybody else is voting it dull and lounging about, I say to myself, ' Lorenzo Lilykid, no lounging for you, my boy ! What are you going to do to-day for good society ? ' That's when I rise, you know. Well, you see, something always presents itself. Take to-day, for instance. I reflect, while I am taking my morning coffee, that there's serious danger of my billiards getting down. I'm startled by remembering that the last time I played was with little Tom Tibbits, — fortnight next Friday, — only pocket-game, — excuse me for being technical, — know it's very shoppy, — gave him thirty points, — beat him easily, — no sort of prac-

tice in *that*. If I lose my game, there's one duty to
good society gone, — dead smash ! So I walk down to
Phelan's, take the cue, and play a carom game, even,
with Frank Toler, — splendid cue, he ! — and just beat
him by three points ! There's one duty to good society
fulfilled, — feel happier, stronger, — conscious of not
giving way to loose habits. That lasted half an hour;
and when it was over, I began to reflect again. A man
devoted to good society *must* reflect, — can't rush headlong, you know, — it seems quite unprincipled for a man
with duties, and we all have those, of course."

"Of course !" assented Kate, deferentially, awe-struck
by the moral grandeur of the individual.

When I reflect, I call to mind that next winter I
shall be expected — if I am spared — to perform various
other duties to good society. The Chasseurs will, perhaps, be as necessary to a man devoted to its interests
as the Lancers have been hitherto. Shall I be ignorant
of them ? Shall I be the one to bring confusion into
my set by going to the right when I ought to go to the
left, and bowing when I ought to chassez ? No! I know
my duty better. I whistle the Chasseurs, and go through
the figures by myself for an hour. I know them well.
I can take my place when duty calls. That brings me
to lunch, — deviled chop and mushrooms, at the St.
Germain. There I have an opportunity to study the
manners of the best men. Major Totbury, of the Seventh, sits at the next table, taking fricandeau of veal
and sherry, followed by quail *sauté aux truffes ;* 'pon

honor, most accomplished luncher in New York; eats
by science; might be a lesson to anybody. I learn from
him, — he doesn't know it; but I honor him, and shall
remember his order next time I lunch there."

" Oh, you satirical man ! " said Kate, elevating her
pretty eyebrows.

" Oh, not at all ! I entreat you, don't think so ! If
a man devoted to good society lunches, he owes it as a
duty to good society to lunch well. Declare I respect
him for it. Very well, lunch finished, what next ? Reflect again. Lunch suggests suppers, — suppers in general, by a natural train of associations, bring up suppers
in particular, — evening-party suppers; and then, with
the greatest remorse, I find, oh, such a horrible piece
of last winter's reminiscence staring me in the face !
What do you think I was so wretched as to do to Miss
Arabella Dubblezeppher at the Snugfittes' Fancy Dress
Ball, in January ? "

Miss Jones blushed an apocalypse of all the many remaining proprieties which good society had not subdued
to their right proportion. Young gentlemen did so
many ardent things beyond squeezing the partners of
the bosoms a trifle too tight in the Deux Pas, — when
the Champagne was not prudently toned by pious education and a bottle of cooling Chablis or Sauterne in the
dressing-room ! " Kissed Miss Arabella Dubblezeppher " was in her mind, and her mind — untutored soul
that she was — being so near her tongue, therefore did
Miss Jones blush.

" Really, I can't form the slightest idea."

" You were not there, — to my great desolation having received **Mrs.** Tambour's cards first, as I remember, — and, **therefore,** Miss Dubblezeppher was the Houri, **at** least of Snugfittes' Fancy Dress Paradise. **And I — *me voici l'étourdi !*** — spilt a whole table-spoonful **of** melted chocolate ice on her wings, when I was helping her."

" **Oh,**" said Kate, visibly relieved, and thinking of the dozen or so rich silks **hanging** in her wardrobe, fraught with similar remembrances in various **colors** differing from the original, which never more would flutter to **the** wooing of Dodsworth's pipes. " **Oh !** is that all ? "

"*All*, my dear Miss Jones ? It is enough, and far too much. Since I first devoted myself to good society I never but once before committed a piece of similar maladroitness. How did Miss Arabella receive it ? Ah ! admirably. In the Dark Ages, in a castle on the Rhine, for example, had I been guilty of such a crime against a lady of rank I should have forfeited my life, — been **immediately run through with a** sword by one of the gentlemen **present,** — and, perhaps, should have died feeling that I was but a just sacrifice to the indig- nation of what then was good society. But Miss Ara- bella only looked at me with the sweetest smile of the evening (again because Miss Jones was not there), and in answer to my humble apologies, said, —

" ' Oh, I beg you wont think of it, Mr. Lilykid ; it is not of the slightest consequence.'

" I could not stop my ears, however, to the fact that

3

immediately after she turned to the lady next her, Miss Millefleurs, and made use, in an undertone, of that very disagreeable word from the French, ' *Bête !* ' Very well, to-day, as I said, that came painfully to my memory; and, 'pon honor, I vowed it should never take place again, or I would doom myself **to** voluntary exile from the society to which I am devoted."

"O Mr. Lilykid, don't talk so dreadfully ! You are the very life of our circle ! "

" *Mille ringraziamenti, donna bellissima !* I hope that exile will not be necessary. Don't laugh at me now, really, I beseech you, if I tell you what was my employment for the next hour after that regret awoke in my mind. I happened to remember the means I took when first, at a very early age, I resolved to devote myself to our good society, and trembled to think of doing all the gaucheries which I saw committed by other gentlemen upon ladies' dresses with glasses of Champagne and plates of cream and salad and cups of coffee. I returned to my quiet lodgings. I locked myself into the privacy of my apartments. I took all the chairs and placed them in a row with intervals of a foot or two between. Then, with a saucer full of water in each hand, I practised vaulting over them, one after another, until I succeeded in accomplishing it without spilling a drop. This morning my success was admirable; at the end of an hour I was able to take one, **two,** or five at a spring without losing a single globule from the saucers. It is arduous, I know; it requires resolution, patience, perseverance, but a man devoted to good society must, in conscience, have all these. I shall do it daily for some time, and I shall be abundantly repaid, **my dear Miss** Jones, if next winter I see the fruits of my labor in not offending against society as I did at Mrs. Snugfitte's."

"How few gentlemen ever think of us ladies and our comfort **as you do,** Mr. Lilykid! Let me return you my thanks on behalf of our whole sex! Do you know that at that very party at Mrs. Tambour's, which you spoke of, I had such a love of a rose-colored brocade, with point lace Bertha *à l'Imperatrice,* utterly ruined by a plateful of oysters spilled right into my lap? And such a curious coincidence! I made the very same remark as Miss Dubblezeppher to the lady next *me!* Oh, that lovely brocade! it was *too* bad!"

"And *I* never saw you in it! It would have ravished me! You are so beautiful in rose color, — pardon me! Rose color is so beautiful on *you!* Have another one next winter, **and dub me with your** *bouquetière* its guardian chevalier. I'll hover around it! It shall attract me as the flower does the bee! I shall watch over it as the angel guards the moss-rose till it blossoms! And Jove! I'll call out the man that desecrates it with a particle of anything to eat or drink!"

"Ah, faithful knight! you deserve worthier occupation for your bravery and your vigilance than one poor maiden's party dress."

"Not at all. The old knights, we hear, devoted them-

selves to the *redress* of fair ladies, — I will devote myself to the *dress* of one; he, he, he, he ! only a difference
of two letters in favor of brevity. And if the true
Queen Rose shall smile upon her chevalier from above
the false rose, which shows her beauty better, the happy
man will then only feel that he has a worthier commis-
sion, and will dare to look up and ask to be dubbed
again *her* knight."

As he said this, Mr. Lilykid bowed reverently to the
lady, whom he had been gradually drawing nearer as
he waxed eloquent, and taking her fair, soft hand in his
straw-colored Jouvin, pressed its rosy finger-tips to his
mustache.

Irresistible sweet tingling that shot through Kate's
young form from those electric points ! What rare,
delicate politeness ! what an original **grace has** such
a demonstration as this to the heart of **a young Ameri-**
can maiden, **though the women of** the Continent take it
as such a matter of fact, receiving it as the most formal
compliment fifty times a day ! This Mr. Lilykid was
such an unusually charming man !

Mr. Lilykid drew nearer. He still held the hand with
which he had been so rapturous in **his** own; it fluttered
like **a** little white mouse that is very much frightened;
and Mr. Lilykid pressed it tighter to keep it calm. **Mr.**
Lilykid laid his glove upon his watch-pocket, and
exhibited symptoms of getting down upon one knee, —
which light-infantry movement, thank Jove and **the**
Brooks Brothers, was much facilitated by the roomy

cut of pantaloons then fashionable. The trembling extended from Kate's hand to her whole little frame; she
blushed again, and the rosy sky of her face disputed
possession with the down-dropped twilight of her eyes;
she heard the clock and her own heart tick audibly.

"Come right along; they're in here, and *he'll* be so
glad to see you. Come along, papa !"

Heavens ! It was that horrid Augustus right at the
door. Mr. Lilykid's symptoms took a turn; he released
the little hand; he returned to a position which did not
bring in play the peculiar advantages of the peg-top.
And just in time; for the door opened, and lo ! a stout,
good-humored man, with an abundance of whiskers, and
a jolly, play-ferocious style of countenance, like a Lam-
bro converted to the domestic virtues, loomed up
through the opening, preceded by the *enfant terrible*
tugging at his right little finger.

"Come right along, papa. They'll be so glad to see
you. They're both in here. Come right along !"

"Mr. Lilykid, how d'ye do, sir? Hope I see you
well. Pleasant weather we're having."

"Aw! yes, de-cidedly ! How de-do, Mr. Jones.
We were just speaking of you a moment ago; quite op-
portune, — he, he, he !"

Mr. Jones, according to his cheerful domestic custom,
kissed Kate affectionately, not having seen her since
breakfast, perhaps not at breakfast, as he went down-
town early; stripped off his immense Raglan, — like the
sun coming out of a cloud, or a gigantic orange-peeling

3 *

itself, for the purpose of feeling nice and easy, — gave it
to Augustus, who staggered out into the entry in entire
eclipse under it, and hung it up on the highest peg he
could reach, and then sat down in the most good-natured
manner to be the gentleman of whom John Crapeau
says, —

"**Deux,** c'est la compagnie — *trois,* c'est une **foule.**"

If I should record the conversation it would not assist
the progress of this story. How could it assist the
progress of anything to bring together three people,
two of whom suppose Panama **to be a** manufactory **for**
large durable hats, **and the** remaining one of whom tells
said two that **Panama has gone up** to 117, **as if it were**
a piece of information **calculated to excite the** liveliest
emotions **of pleasure; but left them ignorant** whether
Panama had floated to that degree of latitude, now
numbered so many **souls of** population, or **had** risen on
its hats to that shameful price in specie ? How could it
assist the progress of anything to bring **together** two
people from one world and one from another, **sympa-**
thizing with and contiguous to each other about as nearly as the Earth and **Le** Verrier's last-discovered planet,
unless, perhaps, they **wished information; and** who
wants *that,* in good society ?

So that the only progress which *was* assisted was **Mr.**
Lilykid to the front-door. With another bow, — this
time from **the fifth figure** of the Lancers, where the

partners meet, the music lulls, and the hands linger, —
Miss Jones stood in the parlor entrance, and said, —

"Good-afternoon."

Mr. Lilykid had the parlor-door between himself and
the intruder from the broker's world. Once out of
eclipse from that gross body, he became ardent again.
A second time he pressed the little trembling hand to
his lips, and murmured, —

"You asked what I could do to keep New York from
seeming dull, and yet *you* will be here for nearly a week
longer ! My morning was spent in duty ; my afternoon has been, — oh, *such* a reward ! *Al rivedersi !*"

And, accompanied by Kate, the broker ascended to
the blissful domestic regions, where his wife was telling
Scripture stories to little Augustus, who sat, listening
intently, in her lap. The history of Joseph, the good
boy who let himself be put in the closet rather than do
anything naughty, was interrupted by Kate's enthusiasm on the subject of that delightful man, Mr. Lilykid,
— much to the little brother's disgust, who wanted to
know whether the sacred character kicked, and how
long he stayed before they opened the door; and finally
ended by muttering, with his thumb in his mouth, —

"I wish Spindle-shanks could be locked up where
Joseph was. You're always plaguing me. It's *mean*,
— that's what it is !"

"I wonder," said Mr. Jones, in an absent-minded
manner, "who this Mr. Lilykid is ? "

"He's a most charming man ! " answered Kate.

" He's a big monkey ! " said the pleasant child.   And
the ringing of the dinner-bell prevented any arrival
at a compromise between these slightly differing
opinions.

II.

A BOY TOO LITTLE.

THE next morning, at nine o'clock, **Mr.** Jones — having finished his **omelet, rolls,** and coffee, **kissed his wife** and daughter, and entered **his** Raglan like a brave **man** investing a small town all by himself — stood **on his front-door** steps waiting for **a** stage. **A** ruddy glow suffused his wholesome, energetic face; the morning was cheerful and warm all around him; the fine stone pavement, everywhere fresh from its morning libation at the hands of hose-holding footmen of opulent families; the air was clear, and all the purer for being mingled with pleasant suspicions of Liverpool coal **smoke; instead of the morning birds** which warbled far up in country woods, **the stronger-voiced, but none less** sweet, melodious sweeps poured their matin lay along **the** street as far **as** ear could hear, **echoed** back by portly free-stone fronts that, in lieu of hills and crags, stood bathed in the golden flush of the early sun-glory. Now and then a person with Hebrew features trudged by, with a narrow slat-box strapped upon his back, uttering a single mournful dove-note, which might be variously construed as meaning that, by his aid, there could be "glass put in," or that he carried some choice comestible called "glass-pudding," **and** pleasantly toning with this pensive cry the joyous music of the morning. All was calculated to inspire a man who had just had his breakfast with the most benevolent emotions. **Such** city mornings confirm cockneyism. **I do not wonder that** it is hard for gentlemen to get **out of town, when** there is such an air of civilization and nature mingled before his very face, — that birds and rivulets and dewy meads seem mere fanciful superfluities of life, — and the country means littler rooms, damper sheets, vulgarer people, and coarser fare than he has at home. When the country means Potter County, Pennsylvania, or White **Lake,** in Sullivan, a deer coming down the runway before the mouthing dogs, and yourself lying at the bottom with a trusty **rifle; when it** means a yacht on **the Hudson, off Fire Island, or on the waters** around **Cape Cod;** when it means John Brown's Tract, or the Adirondacks, or the Green Mountains, with one of Crook's best rods, two spare limber tips, a book of flies, and, better yet (with an apology to the shade of Herbert), a tin box with cullender lid full of active groundworms, — then the country is something to be sighed for, set store by, and travelled toward, *via* the very first lumber-wagon that can be obtained at the wildest point **of tangency which Man's** railroads make with Heaven's woods. But between **New** York and any country which means something short of these, there is no choice worth a toss-up, — except in favor of Gotham. And, alas ! who

can get to these with a fashionable family ? Who can
persuade his wife and daughters to camp out with him ?
Nobody, — since the **old** Hebrew times, when, with all
their wives and their little ones, Israel's gentlemen bade
adieu to the brick of the city, and went out for a **day's**
merry-making that stretched through a season of forty
years.

By this time the stage is within a block of Mr. Jones's
curb. He is getting ready to point his finger at it when
the door opens behind him, and Master Augustus — just
risen, red and triumphant, from his morning bed of
martyrdom, the bath-tub, his morning crown of martyrdom, the comb — leaps out and grasps him by the
skirts.

"Where are you going, my dear papa ? "

With a heart mellowed by the golden suffusion of the
morning, the immense Raglan clasped its little son in
its arms ; and the good-humored, rosy mouth of the
broker above exclaimed, with a hurried kiss on little
Mischief's Spitzenberg **cheeks,** —

"*I am going* **to make** *bread for my dear little boy !*
Whist ! Hello, stage ! "

And Mr. Jones the next moment was climbing into the
writhing mass of morning-paper-reading business-men
who, through much tribulation to ribs and toes, were
jolting down-town.

"Going to make bread for his dear little boy ? "
Master Augustus stood on the door-step until the stage
went out of sight around the St. Germain, pondering

these paternal words. In spite of what Mr. W. Cowper
has seen fit to remark in derogation of

> " The child who knows no better
> Than to interpret by the letter
> The story of a Cock and Bull,"

I must stick up for the opinion that childhood is an age
of literal interpretation. Cream-tarts, at seven years
old, mean nothing more nor less than cream-tarts, — just
so much flour, sugar, vanilla, and whip, — and not an
allegory of any kind whatsoever. So that the more
Master Augustus reflected, the more did the image suggest itself to him of the burly, fatherly figure, denuded
of the Raglan, standing — with sleeves rolled up, a
white smirch on each cheek, and whiskers well powdered — over a gigantic bread-trough, kneading with
pugilistic earnestness a glutinous mass of the veritable
staff of life for the beloved family. On little Mischief's
mind the first idea of what his father did down-town was
now dawning. He made bread for his little boy.

Augustus shut the door and went into the house. A
greater antipathy than usual to words of three syllables
came over him: he threw the spelling-book under the
bed; yet there was a restless craving in his soul which
was not satisfied by nine-pins, and the young voluptuary
found only an aching void in his box of builders'-blocks.
He had caught a glimpse of more elevated happiness
than was ever dreamed of before, and that portion of

the world which had hitherto satisfied him was now hollow and unreal.

He descended to the kitchen. He marched up to his **former terror,** the **cook,** a fierce Welshwoman, whose habitual aspect toward a fiery range had given her cheeks a permanent rouge, sanguinary to look upon ; and who had, at an early period of her engagement with the family, relieved herself of Master Augustus's onerous acquaintance by informing him that the reason of her leaving her last place was the dissatisfaction of the lady at having her bad little boy chopped up into a hash one day. But, emboldened by the consciousness of a high aim, Master Augustus advanced three steps into this formidable person's domain, and in a meek but firm voice requested to be allowed to make bread. This praiseworthy demand being met by no more encouraging reciprocation than the frenzied charge upon him of the red-faced woman with a large rolling-pin, the boy retreated discomfited, and sought his mother in the sitting-room.

" Mamma," **said he, eagerly, " don't** you want me to be like papa ? "

" Yes, my son. If you grow up and become such **a** man as he is I shall be very happy."

" Well, I want to be like him, too. He's gone downtown to make bread for his little boy ; and that **nasty** cook wont let me do it in the kitchen. Can I do it up here ? "

Mrs. Jones laughed. But she **had** an inventive

4

genius, and was pleased with any direction which Augustus's inquiries took, diverging from that broad road so much dreaded of mothers, — mischief. So, in a few moments she improvised. a baker's apparatus for her son, giving him an old valise for his kneading-trough, **two** or three pillows for dough, an empty sand-box for a dredger, and **a** couple of unoccupied **shelves** in a clothes-press for his oven. Seeing him sedately arrayed for work, with one of her white aprons pinned around his neck, and his little blouse-sleeves tucked up to his shoulders, she returned to her writing-desk, secure, as she thought, of at least ten minutes' undisturbed attention to the letter she was busy with.

Master Augustus had worked away at his trade with such laudable assiduity as would have raised him to the side of Ephraim Treadwell, — had made a dozen batches of pillow-bread and baked **them,** and made them **over and** baked them **again, when he began to** feel that something was wanting to his happiness. There was a lack of verisimilitude about pillows, — they did not brown nicely, — and he felt he was *playing* bake after all. Still he was a good boy, and did not trouble his mother with requests for any new suggestions.

In fact, Augustus was so quiet that, after the quarter of an hour which Mrs. Jones had counted on had flown by, — and another quarter after that, — she looked up from her writing-desk, of her own **accord,** to see what miracle had caused this unparalleled peacefulness. To her surprise Augustus was gone. The last batch lay in the valise unkneaded, the sand-box dredger was on the floor, her white apron hung on the back of the chair, and baking-day was evidently over. The mother went **to the** top of the stairs and called, "Augustus ! **Au-**gus-tus ! " No answer was returned. She looked **down** at the hat-stand, — the little wide-awake, like the Panjandrum " with the little round button at the top," was not on any of **the pegs.** Perhaps the child was on the front balcony, engaged in his favorite amusement of letting miners down a shaft, — performed with two cats, **a** basket, a piece of string, and the front area. She looked out of the window, — no Augustus visible. And then the thought struck her that the naughty little boy had gone out to play in the street with other naughty little boys, contrary to her express command, and to the manifest violation of the fifth commandment and his clean trousers. His having stolen away so quietly from the sitting-room certainly looked like it. Mrs. Jones rang the bell, and Johnson appeared.

"**Go** out," said his **mistress,** "**and look up** and down **the** street **for Master Augustus. When you find him** say that I want to see **him directly.**"

Johnson obeyed; and Mrs. Jones **sat down at her** writing-desk again, with a sad maternal sigh.

She had finished and was sealing another letter when Johnson knocked again at the sitting-room door.

" Come in ! **Well,** have you only just found Master Augustus ? "

" No, mistress; hi 'aven't honly just found 'im; hi

honly just 'aven't found 'im hat all, ma'am. **Hi've been
hup hand down** street hin hevery direction, hand looked
heverywhere with hall my heyes, hand **hi've** hasked
heverybody hif nobody 'aint seen **nothink of no** such
young gentleman nowheres, **and nobody 'aint.** Hif
there vos somebody **with a** bell 'ere **has there his in the
hold country, somethink might be done, but** " —

Here, at the end of the catalogue of familiar **means,**
Johnson, like most routine-trained Englishmen, came
to a dead halt, invention being in its embryo stages
with him; and at **the** same moment Mrs. Jones's heart
stopped also, and the blood forsook her face.

"O Johnson! **You** don't mean to say you think
Master Augustus is *lost!* "

" Hi can't say ma'am. 'E might **be** ; then 'e mightn't.
Children his different: **sometimes they** his ; sometimes
they hisn't. **Shall I call the perlice, ma'am** ? "

"**The perlice** " — **which, to be** nationally bigoted
again, **is the** British sovereign remedy and veritable
Morrison's pill for every social distress, from the hissing
of a Puseyite intoner down to the settlement of canine
difference **of** opinion in an alley — did not strike Mrs.
Jones favorably. She did not like **to** appear arresting
the poor little fellow, — which was the only use she
knew **for** those estimable citizens **in** blue, led to
victory by Mr. Pillsbury. She **had** the idea that **it**
would make **him feel like** a rascal, which **she eccen-
trically** considered **the front-door to being one. So she**
asked, —

"Is Miss Jones in, do you know, Johnson?"

"No, ma'am; she went out 'arf 'n 'our ago, **ma'am.**"

"**Ah!**" said Mrs. Jones; "**very** likely Master **Augustus** may **have** persuaded her **to** take him **with her.** Nothing more for the **present, Johnson; only wait in** the kitchen, — don't **go out; I may ring for** you **again.**"

Mrs. Jones knew she was deceiving herself. It was *not* very likely that **any amount of persuasion** from the **lips of the most honey-mouthed orator** could have **induced** Kate **to take Master** Augustus **down-town with her under the most** favorable **circumstances of re-splendent bib,** tucker, and behavior; **and** nothing **short of an** Arabian Nights' imagination **could have pictured** that event taking **place** under the conditions of the play-day suit and style of manners in which he had been invested when his mother last saw him. Still, all that was most motherly in the mother clung to **the hypothesis as the** sole alternative **to wringing of** hands, utter **dying down of heart, and that dreadful dissyllable in** a city's vocabulary, — "*Child Lost!*"

Probably Kate would **be at home in an hour or two.** Within that time Augustus **might return of his own accord; at the** end of it **Kate might bring him back.** The **mother would** wait an hour **longer before she** let herself **be alarmed.** So she said. Yet how could she keep her promise? She resumed her seat to write another letter. She set the "New York" down mechanically at the top of the page; **and before** the date

4 *

could follow it, her mind was wandering through painful, misty mazes of speculation, her ear was listening to
every roll of wheels or ring of footsteps in the street.
Then her eye grew faithless to the work before her: it
was drawn by a resistless magnetism to the deserted
bread-tray: it was fixed there; and a cruel, motionless
fog appeared to rise before it, out of which sometimes
the child's image peered for a moment, kneading away
quietly at the batch of pillows; and then, in its place,
the dreadful absence of the child seemed taking a visible shape in the question, " Will he ever stand there
again ? " She shut her desk, walked restlessly across
the room, opened a closet-door as if he might be hidden
there,— the little Mischief ! — then came back to the window, lifted the sash and peered long-sightedly up and
down the street, with a wistful hope of being surprised
by his far-off voice or figure. Then she sat down again,
resolutely saying to herself, " I will *not* be alarmed ! "
The very earnestness of the resolution alarmed her all
the more. She left her room, mounted to the garret,
searched its crannies, descended to the basement and
the cellar, with all the servants following her, and carrying out their peculiar ideas of being helpful by holding
candles where there was plenty of light, and saying,
" Oh dear ! " and " Bless my soul ! " like responses in a
service. She sought behind barrels and boxes and bins
for the boy who was not there. Then the back-yard
was ransacked, as if it had been a very Titantic labyrinth, instead of a small, frank-faced open space, without

a hole where an errant cat could hide itself; then every room and closet in the first and second stories was invaded, to its very wainscot crevices. And thus the mother spent the hour in which she would not be alarmed until Kate got home.

At last that young lady came back. She had been to Stewart's and Thompson's. I write that last word with a tear trickling from my nib tributary to departed worth. Thompson's, the extinct but not forgotten! And of course Augustus had not been with her. She calmed her mother, assured her that it was only another of that boy's pranks, and, without manifesting a heartless *insouciance*, still took his absence so coolly, and was so sure that he would be back presently, that Mrs. Jones began to distrust her own fears, and, for a time, was composed and hopeful.

Let us see what has befallen the little brother. Growing dissatisfied with his pillow-bread, this young baker became irresistibly fascinated with the idea of going to see how his father made **it**. Watching **his** opportunity, when his mother **was most absorbed in** her letter, he slipped out of the sitting-room, downstairs, out **of** the house. Almost all the way to the St. Germain **he** ran or skipped as·fast as his little feet could carry him. **He** took this direction because it was that which he saw the paternal broker follow every morning, — this gait, because, as I have noticed, it seems to jolt the conscience and keep it from crying "Stop!" — at least in little boys running away, — with whom that organ bears the proportion to the specimens taken from the mature individual **of 10 : 1.** Perhaps **even** this little brother may grow up, under kindly fostering influences, to be a brisk Bear-Papa, making time sales of Michigan Southern, 600 shares more than there **can be in any** possible market, seller 30 days, and a **very amiable** man in his family and the church of which **he's** a pew-holder.

When Augustus came to the St. Germain, he stopped **for a** moment and looked up toward Worth's monument, **then** down toward the steeple of Grace. For a moment **he** felt inclined to turn **in the** direction of the former, — it was mightily like a big granite chimney of some uncouth shop under ground; but just then one of the stages which his **papa** patronized came around the corner and **took its way** down-town. **This** settled him, **and he joined the great tide** that sets to the bottom of the **island. He was a sturdy little boy, and walking did not easily tire him. After several** alarms **of** voices calling **behind him,** which his fancy, always assisted by the organ we have before mentioned, kept shaping into "Augustus, come back!" or something of the same reproachful import; — after numerous distant visions of black whiskers and big Raglans of the paternal cut, but sadly disappointing him **as** they drew nearer; after sundry hustlings from ill-humored urchins, hurrying men, spacious lounging ladies, and busy workmen whose white **overalls** suggested to him **the supposed** trade of his father and fired anew his young ambition, — he reached the lower end of Union Square. Here he

made a natural mistake, — followed the straight line,
and thus losing the Broadway trail, kept on down Uni-
versity place. In the quiet of that street he first saw
people disengaged enough, as he thought, to answer
questions. A rosy-cheeked servant-maid was on her
knees at the door of one of the houses, diversifying her
labor at scrubbing the freestone steps with occasional
remarks of an animated character to a person who was
shooting coal through **the sidewalk and letting the** dust
scatter to counteract her soap.

" Do you know where Mr. Jones lives ? "

The maid stopped scrubbing and leaned upon her
brush; likewise the coal-heaver, putting his shovel in
rest, and propping himself as deliberately on its handle
as if he had selected that attitude for the day, and both
of them surveyed the little estray from head to foot.

" What do you want of Jones, sonny ?" finally spoke
the man of coal.

"He aint Jones ! he's *Mister* Jones; he's my father.
And I aint sonny; I wish you wouldn't call me it. I'm
Mr. Jones's little boy, and I want to find him. Say now !
do you know where he is ? "

" What does he do ? " **said** the maid, in a brisk manner, and fixing her black eyes resolutely on the child **as**
if he would like to deceive her **if** he dared, but she
wouldn't have any of it. " What does he do, now ? does
he take in washing ? "

" Washing ! " ejaculated Angustus, with a smile of
supreme scorn. " We've got a girl like you who does

our washing; I guess *he don't* do that! He does something an awful lot better than that, — and I'm going to
see him and ask if I can't do it, **too."**

"What is it he does do, then?" said the coalman, and
both he and the maid regarded the child with increased
curiosity, mingled with somewhat of respect.

Master Augustus drew himself up to his **full** height of
three and a half **feet, and** replied, **in a dignified** manner, —

"He makes bread; that's what Mr. Jones does!"

"Oh," said the coalman, visibly relieved from the
strain on his bump of reverence, "he makes bread, does
he?" And simultaneously both he **and** the maid broke
into a loud laugh very disagreeable to Master Augustus,
and uttered the words " Jones the **baker,"** as if **it were**
the richest joke of the season.

"He don't put no alum nor sody into his bread, does
he, sonny?" suggested the coalman, pleasantly. " He,
he, he, he!" said the housemaid. To all of which Master
Augustus replied, sullenly, "None of your business!"
and continued on his unassisted journey down the street.
For a long time his wounded pride prevented him from
asking any further questions. He passed the Parade
Ground, and University place was University place no
more, **but** Wooster street, — a thoroughfare unlike any-
thing he had ever seen before, and growing stranger **and
stranger** with every step. **Smells** intensified, **and his**
childish nose waxed more and more *retroussé* as **it** grew
acquainted with adjacent stables **and** cabbage nearly as

old as himself. He had seen dirty little boys before, and
played with them, **to the utter horror** of his sister and
her **renunciation** of his acquaintance till he **was** new
scrubbed and clothed. He had even wished he could **be**
like them in their emancipation from soap and combs;
but he had never seen *such* dirty little boys as he met
now, and he was cured of all pining after their inherit-
ance. In the country, in summer, he had loved pigs,—
had, on one occasion, captured **and** brought **a very** little
one into the parlor; **but his heart went not out to** *these*
pigs, — **the pigs** of **Wooster street,** — **foul,** dissipated
beasts, with blear, besotted eyes, who ever and anon issued from yards where they seemed to have been getting
intoxicated for the **last** twenty-four hours on fermented
potato-peelings, and staggered in a half-vicious, half-
imbecile manner toward the gutter, attempting to force
a passage on the way between the little legs of Mr. Jones's
littleboy. There were truculent, cowardly dogs that ran
off a little way with a **snarl** and then turned to see if there
wasn't a chance of getting **a nab at** his plump little
calves **before they** betook themselves **utterly into ·the**
dirty, open entries of their owners; there **were women**
with gin-reddened eyes pressing dirty torn **shirts on**
boards behind broken windows, who seemed to be considering the question of throwing their irons at him;
and a one-eyed man, who sat on the rickety steps of an
old crow's-nesty, mouldy, tumble-down tenement house,
smoking a black pipe, two inches short, looked so remarkably like the ogre in one of his picture-books that

Master Augustus dodged around him into the middle of the street, and when he cried after him in a hoarse voice, "Where'er ye goin', bub?" took to his heels and ran, with his heart beating like a baby trip-hammer, for at least two blocks before he dared to stop and look around.

What with fright and the natural emptiness of interior which periodically attacks the species at an age when the affinity for pie and bread-and-butter is still dominant, Master Augustus was now reasonably enough in somewhat low spirits. Add to these influences the fact that he was now doing the longest distance in the shortest time that he had ever performed in his life, and we can excuse him for feeling the bricks move up to meet his feet as he went — for wanting to sit down somewhere and take something solid. Still he did not give way to tears. The idea of New York in all its wild, labyrinthic bigness had not yet broken upon his mind, and he consoled himself by believing that his father must be very near, and that that bread-making individual would doubtless, like the parent of the other prodigal son, "have bread enough and to spare," with very likely a cream-tart or two to compensate for the absence of butter. Moreover, he was a child of sturdy pluck, without much water that he ever cared to throw away except that which he had to be washed in; and when his heart billowed up towards his eyes, the grand notion of seeing how his father made bread, and learning to do it himself, choked the refractory organ down, and cheered on his tired feet.

But at last he **must rest.** A hospitable-looking **door-step,** with no Wooster street pigs, adjacent stables, cross dogs, or children with dirt on their faces of more than three days' antiquity, allured him, and he sat down. A good, motherly-looking Irish woman saw him from the window, opened it, and said, compassionately, —

"An' where is it ye're sthraying, me poor little bye?"

Augustus took courage and answered that he was going to look for his father.

"An' who's that, thin?" continued his kind interlocutor.

"His name is **Mr. Jones** — and — and" — Augustus hesitated, remembering **the** coalman's impudent disregard **for the** profession ; but the affectionate, interested, face, in its white frill cap, won his confidence.

"And he makes bread, that's what Mister Jones does."

"An what's his first name' darlint? There's a dale of Joneses hereabouts, and some of thim has a way of bein' called John, — faith, most of thim, indade; is your father John Jones?"

"No ma'am, his name's Augustus, and I'm called after him ; and I'm going to see him make bread, and to learn how myself. And if you'll tell me where he is,—'oh, I'll be so much obliged to you!"

"Poor little darlint ; and are ye a great way from home, sure? Ye're a very dacent little gintleman, and it aint from these parts ye are, I'll go bail."

"**I** guess I am a good way from home. I came

5

through an awful lot of streets; but I must be pretty near papa now, and when I find him, oh, Jiminy ! wont it be jolly though ! "

As his heart warmed towards the good woman, Master Augustus became more and more at ease and inspirited to a degree which **quite made** him forget his hunger and fatigue. It did not have that effect, however, upon the kind soul who talked to him. She saw the dinnerless look in his eye, and asked him to come in for a little while, — an invitation which he willingly accepted. Then she brought out the "cold pork and praties," and the hard, sweet home-made loaf which a good woman will always make good, and which everybody not utterly demented would rather have than the best of baker's bread, and Master Augustus made a kingly meal. This over, he thanked the kind woman, and, in **spite of** her **utmost persuasions,** started anew in search of his father.

It would take too long to trace through all his wanderings this poor little journeyman baker, — mentioning every street that successively and progressively he got more and more lost in. It is enough to say that **twi-**light came on and found him in that dreary kennel known as Thomas street. Broadway, with all its splendor and **its publicity, is** close at hand; Thomas street, with its filth and its secret dens, where all sorts of corruption of soul and body lurk and fester, in spite of its magnificent neighborhood to the king of streets, is as grim and pestilential as any alley or morass miles away. I

believe its very nearness to Broadway makes it worse :
it is a sort of gutter just over the fence of Splendor's and
Decency's back-yard,— a sort of rubbish-heap, where
Christian Respectability throws all its outcast parings
of Humanity that are too foul to be beheld in front and
in daylight. I have seen such beautiful women and children, nevertheless, in Thomas street, looking out of
black, filthy entries ; the boards of the threshold rotten
under their feet, the dews of corruption trickling down
on them from the slimy eaves above, as in a charnel-
house, and they themselves having such a look of fierce
despair on lips and foreheads which a gallant may once
have kissed reverently, passionately ! What strange,
wonderful jewels, thrown out of their setting to the
swine for one small flaw, sometimes get cast into Respectability's rubbish-heap ! When I have gone from
Broadway, where I have seen beautiful women walking
or riding in glory, into Thomas street, where I have
seen those other beautiful ones, and have thought my
thoughts about **Thomas** street and its suggestions, it has
become the hatefulest street in all New York to me.

As I said, in this horrible street poor Augustus found
himself at nightfall, with his little feet a couple of the
sorest burning blisters, his whole body exhausted by
fatigue and the recurrence of hunger, his heart sunk to
zero, and his mind a perfect chaos of bewilderment. He
had asked questions about " Mr. Jones who made bread "
of so many men, women, and children, within the last
two hours, and in such a broken-hearted carelessness as

to whether the answer were impudent or not, and had
received so much varied information upon the subject of
different members of the Jones family, that he began to
feel himself going crazy in a great wilderness of Joneses,
in which every separate tree, as in a vast forest, is like
every other, yet different also, and none of them familiar,
homelike, or in any way reliable as a guide. If he **had**
been older and metaphysical, the poor child would have
described himself as losing his identity. In this horrible
Thomas street, among the huddled negresses and white
women painted **and** blowsy, — the hustling, drunken
white men and strapping buck-negroes, — the vicious,
shrieking children, the universal array of horrible sights
and sounds, animate and inanimate, in this horrible
Thomas street, — Augustus came to a stand-still, and for
the first time long-menacing despair **now** ascended the
throne. Tears of fear, contrition, bodily distress began
to flow without measure. **He thought of** the mother
whom he had left to go after his father, and his tears
became still bitterer. As he realized the agony she
must be in, and the impossibility of his ever finding his
way back to her over the great distance he had come,
the *bigness* of New York, the cruel, hopeless *bigness*, for
the first time in life broke upon him, and he sat down in
abject misery on the sidewalk as any dirtiest of the little
boys in Thomas street would have done. No longer
did he hope to **find** his father; he knew that good man
was at home hours ago, sharing the family distraction;
but still to every ruder or kinder soul that questioned

him as he sat with his feet in the gutter, weeping, he replied, mechanically, —

"My papa is Mr. Jones, and he makes bread."

We leave the poor child to the tender mercies of Thomas street, while we return to the distressed household who are mourning for him.

Gradually even Kate became alarmed when an hour had elapsed after her return from down-town and no signs were visible of Augustus. She accordingly advised her mother to adopt the following plan, and helped her carry it out: Johnson was to take a certain list of their acquaintance, she and her mother a certain other, and they were to call and inquire if anything had been seen, at the several houses, of the little brother. This idea was accomplished, but, of course, with no success.

Kate then thought she had better become hysterical; but upon her mother's representing to her how much more useful she could be by retaining her self-possession, and how very much she would be in the way if she didn't, the young lady denied herself the pleasure, and came out in such character, — such admirably womanly strength and helpfulness, — that her mother was perfectly astonished, and couldn't sufficiently reverence her never before appreciated daughter.

The next thing they did was to dispatch Johnson in a carriage for Mr. Jones; and then Kate sat down on a sofa, and laid her mother's head upon her breast.

"Darling, darling mother!" said the young girl,

5*

"perhaps this trouble is only to punish me for having been so often unkind to little Augustus, and to teach me that I ought to conquer my selfish heart, and aid you a great deal more faithfully in taking care of him. I *will* learn the lesson; and then brother will be brought back to us, and we shall be a much happier, more loving family than we have ever been before. Don't despair, darling; the Lord will not take the dear child away from us, I am sure, if I try to profit by this trouble."

Such things, and many others as good and noble, did Kate say, in a broken, feverish voice, but with an attempt at being very cheerful, — stroking her mother's fair, hot forehead, and kissing away the tears of unspeakable distress that kept welling up into her beautiful eyes, while she hurriedly wiped away and hid those that came into her own.

In about **an** hour — for **the carriage had** orders to **drive as fast as possible** — **Mr.** Jones **got** home. He had not been in his office, and **Johnson** had found it necessary to seek him at the Brokers' Board. He took his darling wife and daughter into the bosom of the vast Raglan, and kissed them again and again with the redoubled tenderness of great trouble, too choked to speak. When, at length, he found words, they came from his heart all wet, — as if they had just struggled ashore, half-drowned, from the great sea within him, and were dripping with the brine that still heaved and shook his great, broad man's breast.

"Dearest wife, — dearest Kate! don't you cry, my

larlings," he uttered in a trembling voice, falsifying his
loctrine by his example. "We'll find that precious boy,
if we have to take all the detective police into pay, and
get broke or die doing it. **I'll** go directly to the police-
station of this precinct, and have the little fellow's description telegraphed all over the city, with offers of a
reward of five hundred dollars to the officer that brings
him home."

No sooner said than done. The carriage that had
brought the father up from Wall street was at the door,
kept in waiting. He leaped into it, and was speedily
at the elbow of the telegraph operator of the nearest
station.

"Don't alarm yourself too much, my dear sir," spoke
that person, sympathizingly; "these things are happening every day, and they always turn out well in the end.
This little brass jumper at the end of our wire saved
forty children last month; and in all the time that the
telegraph's been working we've only lost two out of
several hundred children who got astray. Three of the
forty we saved in April were gone a couple of days,—
one, a whole week. He got on a train going **up the**
Hudson River Railroad. Mother went nearly crazy, —
not expected to live from day to day; but we found
the little youngster, and brought him home safe and
sound. Mother recovered in about ten minutes, — then
nearly died again for joy. First day she was able to be
out, came up here, and wanted me to take a hundred
dollars. Much obliged, but rather not. Duty was its

own reward. Then *she* fell to kissing everything,—
kissed the machine,— kissed the policeman who brought
the boy back,— actually kissed *me !* " And the operator smacked his lips as if the taste of the grateful tribute
still lingered; then fell to work, — went click-click-click-
click-click-click-click-click for **a** few assiduous minutes,
— **and lo** ! every police-station in New York was intro-
duced to Master Augustus Jones, and bent its multiplied energies to the work of finding him.

Wonderful, beneficent, omnipotent telegraph ! What
marvel that mothers kiss thee ? And though the grace-
less, ungrateful tribe of intellectual prigs, and the hair-
splitters of the Supreme Court who back them, harass
with endless patent cases the siver hairs of our noble,
thrice-beloved Morse, — though America leaves to for-
eign powers the graceful privilege of recompensing the
last years of **a** life of unselfish **genius, as fully** as the
mere money-tribute of a **hundred** thousand francs can
do it, — does not every click of his offspring's electric
tongue that brings home a wandering child throb a
sweet note of reward in the great philosopher's loving
heart, — does not the whole nation of thankful mothers
bless him and kiss him a thousand times a year ?

Mr. Jones made an arrangement with the telegraph
operator that the moment that any news came to the
station of the child, or the likelihood of the child, it
should be immediately sent to No. — West Twenty-
third street; and then went home to do what he could,
poor man! for his broken-hearted wife and only less

broken-hearted daughter. There was no resource **left** for them but to wait; and waiting, when a child **is lost,** is the bitterest mode of prolonging **misery.** To be sure **all the resources of the** great police system **of the great** city of New York were concentrated on that one little **boy. The** original use of the system — rascal-hunting —could **not have so** brought it to **a focus;** if Master Augustus had **been a noted** bank-defaulter, **or a** swindler of stockholders, he would have **had** less personal attention to boast of. Everything that could be done was doing for him; and yet, as that **father, mother, and sister** sat still in their distress, they were full of the keenest self-reproachings, — **of** a sense of inertness which seemed to them, **by** a strange paradox, the **more** unfeeling **in** proportion as their feelings were more harassed by it.

Hour after hour dragged on, and still no word came from the station. The poor mother began wandering about in a frenzy. From room to room, wherever Augustus had played, she strayed with her eyes full of a dreamy, misty pain. **When she** came **upon** some little toy with which he had **played, she** snatched it up, kissed it passionately, **and her** tears **came pouring** in torrents. Standing before a little pastel picture of the child, taken in his fourth year, she grew transfixed, and remained motionless, gazing at it in such an agonized silence that she could hear every beat of her own heart. And then she knelt at the little bureau where his tiny clothes were kept,— drew out, one by one, the manikin suits which her motherly care had proudly embroidered for him, —

examined his small stockings, and, as she saw the places
where his little, restless feet had called her needle into
play, asked herself, with a fearful sinking of the heart,
whether she should ever mend them for him any more;
and again the passionate tears blinded her poor eyes.

Kate had thrown herself upon her bed. She could
not cry, for her self-reprovings were too stern. She
buried her hot face in her pillow, pressed one hand
against her aching heart, and with the other ceaselessly
pushed away her long dark hair from her forehead, as if
it were hated evidence of the pride and accomplice of the
selfishness which her bitter mentor now told her had so
often done wrong to the poor little lost brother she
might never see again.

The father paced all the rooms where his wife wandered, with a stern wretchedness in his once cheerful,
buoyant face, hardly ever able to speak a word, and
chiding himself when it had been spoken; for it always
sounded so cold, so hard to his burthened heart, that it
seemed a cruelty rather than a consolation to the suffering woman whom he loved.

At last they all came together at the side of the bed
where Kate was lying. The husband and the wife both
dropped on their knees, and the strong man poured forth
his soul in this one prayer of agony, —

"O God! save our child, and take away all our
worldly prosperity if thou wilt!"

Clasping each other's hands the three bowed there in
silence, each thinking the continuation of this prayer

which they had no voice to speak. For several minutes they remained there, and then the mother arose.

" My husband," she said, " I shall die of this suspense. Let us go up to the station again."

Johnson once more called a carriage. Father, mother, and daughter got into it; the driver was ordered to hurry to the station-house at his utmost speed. When they reached there they ran up the narrow stairs to the telegraph room with a lightness like that of the strongest, most refreshed feet. **As** might have been expected, there was no encouragement there for them, except the repeated injunction of the operator not to despair, and his recital to the mother and sister of the statistics in favor of finding lost children, which he had given to the father three hours before.

" We have news of several boys and one girl, already this afternoon," said the operator; "the girl was lost last night, the boys this morning. It takes a good deal longer to find girls than it does boys, because a girl is more helpless when she's astray, — so's more pitied, and often gets taken in somewhere and sheltered, instead of being left for the policeman to bring to the station. That makes it a harder job to find her. You feel **bad** enough, mum, about your boy, I know; but it's a great deal better than if it was a girl. We'll find him for you any way. Lord bless me ! there aint a chance as big as that of his being lost permanently;" and the operator fillipped away a piece of string that he had been toying with as he talked, to represent the very small chance indeed.

Then **the** distressed three returned home again. Six
o'clock and dinner-time came, but nobody touched **a**
mouthful. Bearing the agony of suspense as strongly
as they **were able,** they passed the hours of growing
darkness till nine o'clock; and then, from sheer ex-
haustion, the mother and sister of the wanderer were
compelled to lie down. The father sat and watched by
their bedside, or paced the dreary rooms, whose emptiness of the one absent seemed to make them echo to his
tread, " Lost ! lost ! "

To return to the curb-stone where we left Master Augustus sitting. About ten o'clock there issued from the
tenement in Thomas street, just behind him, a young
man, whose general appearance was strangely at va-
riance with the surroundings of the place. He wore a
black Kossuth hat, neat dark pantaloons, well-polished
boots, and a light surtout; for the evening was cool,
though toward the end of May. His face was refined,
manly, and resolute; his eyes and hair black as jet, **and**
his beard strong, curling, and abundant; and he seemed
about twenty-six years old. A squalid woman, very
much draggled and torn, lighted him, or perhaps smoked
him would be more accurate, to the rotten threshold,
with a malodorous, half-penny tallow-candle, that stewed
and **dripped in its own ruins,** like everything else in
Thomas street. In a strong Milesian brogue she asked
him, as he was passing **out, —**

" An' what may yer bill be, docthor ? "

" Nothing," said **the young** man, **" except** to promise

.

me that if that baby lives, — which I hope it is likely
to do now, — you wont get drunk again till it's over
teething."

" Houly Mother **bless ye, but ye're a dacent gintle-**
man; and may ye niver want a friend in disthress ! No
more I wont, and that's thrue for me: an' if I does it,
may the divil " —

" Never mind the devil, — you've had enough to do with
him already, **Mrs. Murtagh**; only remember not to
drink."

" Good-night, thin; angels bliss yer sleep, honey ! "

" Good-night ! "

He was about **turning up toward the hospital, when**
the strange little object on the curb-stone attracted him,
and he stopped, bent down, and looked intently at Master Augustus. " It can't be possible, even in Thomas
street," soliloquized the young doctor, " that a boy of
that age is lying here drunk at this time of the evening." He shook the little fellow gently by the shoulder,
and roused him from **his sleep against** the friendly hy-
drant, which had been his pillow for **the hour and a
half past.** Augustus awaked and looked at him dream-
ily, not realizing where he **was. The young man im-**
mediately saw that he hailed from none of the **Thomas
street houses.**

" What are you doing here, my little fellow ? You'll
be lost if you stay out so late; you had better go home
to your mother; she's frightened about you now, I've
no doubt."

Augustus stared in surprise.

"Do you know my mother?"

"No, I don't, my boy."

"How do you know I've got one, then?" asked Augustus, triumphantly, in spite of his sleepiness, and true to his native fondness for always "putting in a clincher."

"I think you look as if you had one. She made that little pair of pantaloons which you've been getting so **dirty** on the pavement by sitting down and going to sleep here, instead of saying your prayers and climbing into your pretty little crib."

"Crib!" muttered Augustus, scornfully; "I guess I aint a baby! I sleep in a *great big bed*, — all alone by myself. Who are you, anyhow?"

"My name is Doctor Morris; and I'm a good friend to you and your mother, for I'm **going to** help you **to** get home. Where do you live? — what's your name?"

"Augustus Jones."

"**Where do** you live, Augustus?"

"I live at my papa's, — he's Mr. Jones, **and he** lives up in Twenty-third street."

"Do you know what the number is?"

"No, sir."

"What does your papa do?"

"He makes bread."

"Oh! we'll find him very easily, then. Are you too tired to walk? You must be if you've come with those little legs all the way from home to-day. Let me carry you."

"No, I can walk."

"Well, come along, then. We'll go and get a Directory, and see the number where your papa **lives,** and then it will be all right in a very short time."

By his kind yet not too patronizing manner, he won Master Augustus's confidence to such a degree that the boy took **his hand, and** the **two** went slowly together into West Broadway, talking as they walked.

"Do you like oyster-pie, Augustus?"

They were just then passing a restaurant, and the doctor noticed that the boy looked **in** eagerly **and** snuffed its savors with high appreciation.

"I *guess I do!*" responded Augustus, enthusiastically.

"Well, I am glad to hear that; for I know a great many boys, and all the good boys are very* fond of oyster-pie."

"Are they?" said Augustus, delightedly. "Mother says I'm a *very* good boy sometimes."

"Well, then, I'll try you, and see if she's right."

The pair, still clasping hands, went into the shop, **and** the doctor ordered as large a piece **of oyster-pie as a** boy of seven could eat; and, when that amount had **been** ascertained by actual measurement, paid for it, and went out, leading his *protégé.* Master Augustus's confidence in his new friend rose several hundred per cent. He began to be communicative. Speech never flows freely when one is hungry, because the up-train of words is **loth** to move, knowing, as it does, that the **right** of way on that single track, the throat, belongs to a bread-and-butter train down.

"I want to **ask you a** question."

"**Ask me as many as you** please, Augustus. I like to show off what I know."

"Well, then, do you *really kill people ?* "

"No, indeed. **What in the world do you mean by** that ? "

"**You're** a doctor, — that's what I mean. I've heard people **say, a great** many times, that all doctors kill people. There was Jimmy Stilton, — he was a good boy, Kate says, — and I heard her say, too, that the doctor killed him with too much oil and such nasty things. But **I** guess he'd have died any way, — he was awful good. Now tell me honest, *do* you kill people ? **I wont tell anybody !** "

"**No,** Augustus, — honor bright ! — **I don't** kill anybody at all, except **old Mr. Fever, and** cross old Mrs. Stomach-ache that plagues little boys so, and **ugly little** Miss Cold-in-the-Head, and such naughty people **as** that. I shoot *them* with pills, and smother them under plasters, and drown 'em in drops; but I don't hurt good people at all."

"Then, by hokey, I'll like you very much indeed, old fellow ! I didn't ask you if you killed people because I was afraid of you. I only wanted to see some of the people you killed, and see how they looked, and how you did it. I wish you'd like me."

"**So I will, Augustus.** I do like you **now;** and we'll

have many a nice play together, I hope, after I get you home to your mother."

"I've got a sister, too, — she's an *awful* pretty girl: don't you wish you knew her ? "

"Yes, indeed, I'd like to know her very much. You'll introduce me to her, wont you ? "

"Yes, I will. Her name's Kate. She's got great big **eyes, — almost as black as the** ones you've got, — and curls, too, — Jiminy, *such* curls ! **Wont you** tell anybody if I'll tell you something ? "

"**No**; I'll keep as still as a mouse about it."

"Well, when I was a little boy, — that's a great while ago, before I was big, like **I** am now, — she was very nice to me, and never called me bad names, like monkey, and mischief, and plague. And when they used to ask me who was going to be my wife when I got to be a man, I always used to say Kate was going to be it. Wasn't it funny ? I guess it was ! I didn't know that little boys couldn't marry their sisters, you know. And **now** there's **an awful mean** old Spindle-shanks that comes to see Kate, **and he thinks I don't know what he** is up to; but I do. **He wants to** have her for his wife; and I hate him like **poison.** He calls **me** sonny, and he makes her not like me; and he aint nice at all, like you are. I wish doctors did kill somebody sometimes ! Couldn't you kill him, just once, without being caught, so that Kate wont marry him ? "

"I'm afraid not. Isn't there any other way of stopping her ? "

6*

Augustus did not answer for some time; but walked along, biting his little nails in deep thought. At last he brightened up, and gave the friendly finger he had hold **of a** violent joyful twitch which nearly dislocated it.

"Yes, sir-*ee*, there's one way of stopping her **without** killing old Lilykid! Will you do it? Say, old fellow, will you do it?"

"What's your plan? Let's hear it, Augustus."

"*You go and marry her yourself!* Wont that be nice? You'll be my brother, then; and I'll never plague you when you come to see Kate, and you can have the parlor all to yourself! Say now, wont you? That's a nice old fellow! Say yes. Come now, say yes, wont you?"

Dr. Morris laughed heartily at this ingenuous proposal, then replied, —

"But how do you know I aint married now? And what if *she* shouldn't say yes, too? Then I'd be 'up a tree,' as the boys say."

"I know you aint married; you dont look married. You're so good to me I don't believe you've got any little boy of your own to be good to. And I know she'll say yes." Here Augustus lowered his voice to a tone of reverent piety, most laughably incongruous with his general naughty-boy bearing, and continued: "When I say my prayers I'll ask to have her say yes, and then she's got to, haint she? *That'll* fetch her!"

The doctor, overwhelmed by the strength of the child's mountain-moving, or woman-moving faith (which misogynists assert to be the same thing), had to lean against an adjacent tree-box until he could sufficiently recover his gravity.

" Very well ! you can try it," he replied; " **and if I** find out you aren't making believe when you say Kate's such a pretty, good girl, — why, perhaps we'll see what **we can** do to kill Lilykid in a decent sort of a way. But here's the Girard House: let's just step in and look in the Directory to see where your father lives."

" What's that big word ? " ejaculated Augustus. ·

"The *Directory.* **It's** a big word, and it means a big book that a good man wrote to help people to find **out** where little boys who get lost ought to be taken home to."

" And did the man know I was lost ? And has he written all about it in the book ? I think he's awful mean ! He aint a good man at all ! I'll bet they've got the book in Sunday school, and little Tommy Jenks, **who** reads all the big books he can get hold of, will find it, and make fun **of me ! How did** they know about **me ?"**

" Oh ! **it** don't tell about *you;* **it only** tells about your father, so we can find his house and take you to it."

" Oh ! " said Master Augustus, once more drawing **a** long breath, " that's all, hch ? Well, you look into it, and read me how my father makes bread."

By this time the doctor had opened the Directory, and was turning it over on the counter of the registry-clerk. He came to the Joneses, and began sailing over

that illimitable sea, with no helm but the Christian name
Augustus, and no chart but the general idea that that
Augustus was a gentleman who devoted his energies to
baking, **and spent his leisure in** Twenty-third street
somewhere.

No such combination **of circumstances could be**
found. There were Joneses enough to erect themselves
into a ward, — Augustus Joneses enough to form a pri-
mary meeting in that ward, — but bread-making Augustus Joneses, who lived in Twenty-third street, were
nowhere visible.

" You're sure his name is Augustus ? " said the doctor, perplexedly.

" Of course it is ! " replied the stray youth, with
marked emphasis. " If it isn't, what is it, then ? "

There was cogency in that argument. Doctor Morris
did not dispute the question further.

" But aren't you mistaken about his making bread ?
Isn't he a tallow-chandler, — or **a** broker, — or a minister ? "

" He *makes bread*, I say, — that's what my papa
does ! He told me so this morning when he was going
down-town."

" Well, then, Augustus, I must say I'm puzzled what
to do with **you, my boy.** Your papa's name is left out
of the big book, and I must say *that* is very mean."
The doctor stopped, and thought for a moment. " Well,
there's only one way left. We'll have to go to the station-house. That's the place where **boys** that get lost

have to go when they can't get found in any other way."
And, with his young charge, Doctor Morris took as
straight a line as possible for the nearest rendezvous of
our municipal protectors.

They reached the station, but found some difficulty,
for a moment, in getting in, as a crowd of all the un-
soaped sight-seers in the neighborhood obstructed the
door, with shoulders and elbows in various stages of
tatter, from ragged sleeves to no sleeves at all. That
pleasant spectacle, an arrest, had just taken place, and
its cheap frequency did not seem to derogate in the
least from the zest with which it was attended by the
congenial spectators. A policeman, like the circus elephant, kept going around " to make a ring," with his
billy for a trunk, and prevented the patrons of the show
from seeing more than they bargained for. He knew
·Doctor Morris as a benevolent *habitué* of the lower
slums of the ward, nodded to him, and, upon his whispering to him that he had a lost boy in tow, opened a
way for him among the throng, and let him into the
sanctum of public protection.

Here the object of interest became apparent. A gentleman, dressed in the height of fashion, evidently for a
little evening party slightly different from the one ·to
which he here found himself invited, stood between two
other gentlemen in blue, — like a bridegroom in charge
of his groomsmen, except that they appeared rather
more anxious than usual lest their principal should bolt
before the ceremony was over. His whiskers and mus-

tache were of the most *recherché* Young England cut; his gloves were as close a fit as if by some triumph of art kid hands had been grafted on a human stock; and his voice was subdued to the most mellifluous accents of the drawing-room, as he gracefully debated the question with his attentive friends. *The* question, I say. A fragment of his little address will reveal what it was: —

" Weally, my fwends, I haint the least doubt in the wo-ah-ld of youah pwopah intentions; but you labah undah an errah of judgment, — that is all. It is a devilish inconvenient thing for a gentleman, having an appointment to meet, to be detained in this way on such an absu-yd cha-a-ge as this ! Weally ! Obtaining funds on false pwetences ! Ha, ha, ha ! Damned amusing, 'pon honah ! I am so unfawtunate as to wesemble the weal man, I suppose. Dooced funny ! Nevah knew I wesembled anybody; if I had, I'd have made every endeavaw to altah my puysonal appeah-ance ! Good joke, — 'pon my soul it is ! " ·

" You'll find it's something else than a joke before to-morrow morning ! " said defender of our *American* interests No. 1, very grimly.

" I'll be dommed if ye aren't afther finding it's a divilish sarious matter ! " corroboratorily added defender of our *American* interests No. 2.

" You may pe sure of dat, mit all yer kid kloves and de colt vatch-chain ! " still further assisted defender of our *American* interests No. 3.

(All of these defenders, with others of still varying

attainments in the Anglo-Saxon tongue, were selected
for the office of policemen, on the ground of their acquaintance with the *American* interests they had in
charge. One of them could not speak a word of English.
I remember having seen him at a fire, where the sagacity
of the municipal authority which selected him became
particularly evident, in his being unable to converse
with the outsiders, who might otherwise have hampered
him in the discharge of his arduous duty.)

"I only ask a few moments' delay," continued the
gentlemanly prisoner, with his former graceful com-
posure. "I have sent for one of my fwends, who will
not hesitate to go with me before the magistwate
and become my su-wety to any amount for appeahance
to answah to this most widiculous cha-a-ge; and I shall
then be able to keep my imp-aw-tant appointment!"

"What's the nature of the prisoner's accusation?" said
the doctor, in an undertone, to the Hibernian defender
of American interests.

"Shure and he's an embezzling rascal, that's what
he is," answered the defender; "and he's arristed for
swindling **a poor divil of** a bootmaker out of a hundred
and fifty dollars. He's got about tin or a dozen names,
— now he's 'Lord Divil-knows-who,' with a large property in Ireland, — bad look to the black mouth that says
he ivir saw the light o' that blissed island! — now he's
'Mr. Pennyroyal Pike,' a rich Amirican from the South,
and then agin he's 'English Jimmy the Gintleman;'
but Hivin knows one name is plinty good enough for

the likes o' him, an' that's Andrew Redding, an' bad
enough it is, too, the skoonk ! "

All this time Augustus, hid behind half a dozen blue
coats, the opacity of whose tails caused him the most
lively indignation, was tugging to get a look at the
object of interest, but with signal unsuccess. Unable to
contain himself any longer, he pulled the doctor's finger
savagely, and exclaimed, —

" Lift me up, wont you ?   Don't you think a fellow
wants to get a squint at him, too, hey ? "

Doctor Morris good-humoredly obeyed, and elevated
the *enfant terrible* by the waistband to a position highly
eligible for the squint desired.

" Jiminy ! " exclaimed the youth, — all symptoms of
ten o'clock and sleep leaving his eyelids, — " if that isn't
the nasty old thing **himself !   It's** *Spindle-shanks* —
that's what it is.   How de do, Mr. Lilykid ? "

The gentlemanly prisoner turned round **with a** start,
but, quick as thought, the **doctor dropped** the bad boy
to his native level; and Mr. Lilykid failed to discover
that member of the detective service who had played
this ventriloquist trick on him.

" Hush ! " said the doctor, whispering sternly into
Master Augustus's ear.   **" If** you don't keep still **I**
wont marry Kate !   Is that the Lilykid you were talking about ?   Speak softly ! "

" Yes, it **is,**" said Augustus, half-offended and half-
awed by the peremptory manner of his friend.

" Then don't you open your mouth to anybody about

it till I tell you, or he will run away, and **we** can't kill him, don't **you see ?** Will you promise me ?"

" Yes, if you wont let him get my sister."

" Well, keep your promise, and he shan't have **her.** Good boys, who like oyster-pie, always keep their word; and I know *you* will."

" Yes, sir," answered the little brother, in a low whisper, feeling confidence restored.

Just at this juncture Mr. Lilykid's friend, very **much** like him in personal appearance, and answering to the name of Buckingham, appeared, signified his readiness to go bail, and went away with Miss Jones's admirer and the groomsmen in blue, to visit the magistrate.

A quarter of an hour afterward the frantic family in Twenty-third street received the following despatch: —

" *To Augustus Jones, Esq.,* —

" A boy has been found, and is now at this station, answering description of this **P. M.**'s telegraph from **you.** Says his name is Augustus **Jones ; but as** he firmly **asserts, with** apparently perfect intelligence, **that his father is a baker, we** do not wish to hold out any strong **hopes of his identity. Come down directly.**

"BULROCK, *Telegraph Operator.*"

Within thirty minutes longer, **as may well be** supposed, Mr. and Mrs. Jones and Kate were at the door of the station-house where their terrible suspense was to be removed, or left to grow worse, to linger forever. So strongly did they realize this fact, that they faltered **on** the threshold, hesitating to go in.

7

"The boy is asleep now," said one of the policemen; "he seemed so fagged out that we laid him on a cot, and he was off in no time."

He led the way, as he spoke, into a room furnished with comfortable but plain cot-beds, — where all the sleeping took place that was ever performed in that centre of public vigilance, — and turned on the gas more brightly to let them see the stray. Like a little cat, with his legs curled up against his stomach, and his head on **his** soft paws, lay the child sleeping. Yes, his hair was the true curly corn-silk! Turn the gas up a little higher! All the three rush around to the side of the bed and turn down the corner of the quilt from his face. It is *he!* It's that darling, darling, naughty little brother!

Had Augustus **died from the** effect of that rapturous **meeting, the policeman** would have been able to testify **on** the inquest that **it was** murder, for the boy's little **ribs** cracked audibly. He was smothered in the Raglan, like a performance of "the Babes in the Tower," with one babe scant; his nose was flattened against the bones of Miss Kate's corsage; last of all his mother got him, not **to** let him go. He was hugged, he was deluged with kisses and tears, he was called several dozen epithets **which** the wildest system of moral philosophy **would have** failed to **make** consistent: an angel, and a little monkey; a darling, a naughty wretch, a beauty, a dear little dirty pig; a wicked, wicked boy to break their heart so; a cherub, and a rascal. **All** of which

blandishments were equally ravishing to Master Augustus, — aroused as he was out of a sleep of utter exhaus-
tion, — only enough awake to feel a general sentiment
of vindictiveness toward the human race, and wondering, like Mr. Pickwick on the occasion of his celebrated one-horse act, whether it was not all "a horrid
dream." When he came to sufficiently realize his position, his first remark was directed to **the** large Raglan
and Whiskers, who stood alternately laughing and crying at the foot of the bed.

"How *do* you **make** bread, anyhow ? *Say !*"

But as the reality of things still further broke upon
him, — as he remembered all the mortification and **the**
pain of his weary day's wandering, and felt what a
heavenly thing it was for a poor little lost boy to have a
mother's and father's and sister's loving hearts to come
to when the dread and the danger were at their highest,—
he softened like a little tough snow-ball in April thaws.
He wept on **one** bosom, and laughed on another; he
hugged them all passionately **as far as his** small arms
could reach around; **he** asked forgiveness in choked,
inarticulate sobbings, and made innumerable **prom-**
ises, which, if kept, would have put him in the category
of those boys who *want*, at least, to be an angel and
with the angels stand.

Everything having become ordinarily placid once
more, Augustus looked all around him anxiously, and
not seeming to find what he wanted, called out in a loud
tone, —

"Doctor! Doctor! Where are you, you good old fellow?"

The gentleman sought, with a proper delicacy, had taken himself out of the way when the carriage arrived, and was now talking with some interesting specimen of **character** he had found among the policemen in the outer room. He never liked to be idle; and he knew that blue uniforms do not cover uniform natures,— human nature being the same, that is to say, the same in no two cases, wherever you find it. Hearing Augustus's voice, he joined the party in the cot-room.

"Here he is!" exclaimed Augustus, triumphantly. "That's the man that knows what a good boy I am, and gave me a big piece of oyster-pie! Come here, old fellow! You found me, didn't you? *That's* my mother, and *that's* my father, **and** *that's* **Kate!** Isn't she an *awful* pretty girl,—just as I **said she** was?"

"O Augustus!" exclaimed the young lady, blushing and holding up her finger.

"This is a proud and grateful moment of my life. I'm honored by seeing you, sir!" said the Raglan, with the warm heart inside of it, shaking the doctor's hand warmly inside the privacy of a giant sleeve.

The mother clasped the other hand, and looked the eloquent thanks that mothers know, but on such occasions can seldom speak.

"I might have had a less eccentric introduction, but certainly not a more **favorable one**," said the doctor, returning all his salutations with a frank smile. " You, who are so happy, can feel how happy I must be in the accident which connects me with this little fellow's recovery. Indeed, I wish all my patients were recovered as quickly."

The doctor's manner was very manly, self-possessed, and polished; his smile showed a beautiful set of white, regular teeth, and the impression he made upon Miss Jones was altogether favorable. She looked at him with considerable interest while he **spoke;** and the quick eye of Master Jones did not let this fact **go** by unobserved.

" Look-a-here, old fellow, I want to whisper to you ! "

" No whispering in company you know, Augustus."

" But I *must,* just this *once !* "

" Well," said his mamma, considerately, "just this once, then. I guess we must excuse him, doctor." The doctor bent his ear, and Augustus uttered eagerly: —

" You can do it; she's a-going to like you; mayn't I just pitch into **her** about old Spindle-shanks just one little *wee* **time ? "**

" **No, my dear boy; if you do, you wont be** keeping **your word, you** know. **And** good **boys** always do that. Wait till **I tell you you may,** and then you can. I'll tell you why sometime, — and till **then be a** little man; stand by your promise. **You** *will,* wont you ? "

" Yes," said Master Augustus, with a deep sigh, — feeling that one of the principal gratifications of life was inscrutably denied him.

" **We** shall hope to see you at our house whenever you

can run away from your professional duties," uttered the Raglan, ardently.

"You will always be most welcome," said the mother.

And **the** daughter smiled a bewitching invitation, which was full as cordial as if it had not been silent.

The restored little brother was then lifted into the carriage, — enthusiastic thanks and good-bys repeated to all who had been engaged in the good office of finding the lost sheep, — and the wheels rattled away.

Between the station-house and Twenty-third street Master Augustus had his inquisitiveness on the subject of the parental bread-making relieved; but, to his bitter disappointment, only by finding — as is the case with so many, alas! of our earlier roseate visions — that it was not literal, but figurative.

III.

JUST ENOUGH OF A BOY.

GOING into the country for **the** summer ! There is crash upon the wide surface of the parlor-floors; but it thinks of the kisses it had last winter from glancing kid and satin toes amidst the delirium of Redowas and the spheral sweep of the German, and sighs knowing that for the sweltering months to come it must do Lenten penance for its carnival, — abandoned to dust, and silence, and darkness. The gay fauteuils, the ottomans, the sofas, in monastic shirts of rough Holland, are ready **for** their summer repentance likewise. Till the house-cleaner, and the upholsterer, and the footman, forerunning the **family in October, shall** come **again to shrive** them and unbind their sackcloth, they **must sit in the** gloom and mourn for the flirtations they have aided and abetted, **in corners and behind** brocatelle curtains. **The** piano is **a** sarcophagus: Sphor and Thalberg, Chopin **and** Schubert, the whole grand army of Mozart, Bellini, and their operatic brethren, lie silent beneath that coffin-lid of mirror-bright rose-wood, side·by side with Glover, Foster, and George Christy. They do not crowd each other; but if they did, they could not speak to complain of it, for they are ghosts that cannot answer till they are spoken to, and **the** cunning fingers that once broke their spell are in a pair of **pretty** little Lisle-thread travelling gloves toying with a parasol. Miss Kate is all ready to go, and in time, **too: a** fact which the satirical **assert to be of** such rare occurrence in a lady's lifetime, that, whenever it does happen, a monument should be raised to commemorate it. Such a monument *is* raised in the present instance, just inside the hall-door. Its pedestal is a Saratoga trunk of a size which could not have existed at the time of Noah, or other families than that gentleman's would have survived the deluge; its shaft gradually rises in successive courses of smaller baggage, and its capital is a hat-box, marked " Miss Kate Jones." It is not quite as high as Worth's **monu**ment, but full as handsome, and a great deal more truthful, as Miss Jones *has* been at Twenty-third street, which is inscribed in several places on *her* column, while **Mr.** Worth, I understand, was *not* at a few of the war-localities engraved on his.

Mr. and Mrs. Jones are lovingly talking over their plans for the summer, as they promenade the hall with their arms around each other's waists: the wife so glad that the husband is able at last to get out of town with her; the husband so proud and pleased to think he has **a** wife who does not look upon him merely as **a** money-machine **kept going in** Wall **street to** manufacture the basis of her independent summer-pleasures, — who waits for him rather than go anywhere without him.

Master Augustus **was** wound up last night like an alarm-clock, by the information that they would all start to-morrow. It was, however, impossible to set his striking-hand at any particular hour; consequently he has been going off all day. He **was** wide awake at three o'clock this morning, insisted upon being dressed at four, took his cap in his hand as soon as he got down stairs, ate breakfast with his gloves on, spent the interim between that and lunch in standing on the steps to see whether the carriage was coming, and passed the remaining time until it actually did come, in requesting exact information, to the very minute, of the time of day, at intervals of a quarter of an hour. It is historical that, for the last three hours of suspense, he did not once sit down; but when he received his little boots, after they had been blacked for the journey the third time that day, he put them on by a Blondin feat of balancing, standing on one foot, and altogether did enough running up and down stairs, in his anxiety to get on, to have carried him to the Highlands of Navesink (the family's destination), had that point been attainable **to a** pedestrian.

While the family were awaiting the carriage the door-bell rang. Augustus happened to be making a broad jelly of his little nose at that moment against the hall window-pane, and thus being convenient to the door-knob, turned it without waiting for Johnson. To his great delight Dr. Morris greeted his eyes.

"Come in, doctor ! come right in !" cried Augustus;

" we're all a-going away, and I'm so glad to see you I don't know what to do !. Are you going away, too ? "

" No, Augustus. This is the first day I've had any time to come and see you, and now you're going to run away and **leave me. Ah ! Mr. and Mrs. Jones, how do** do ? Miss Jones, I hope you are well. I'm sorry to be so *malapropos*, yet not exactly either, for otherwise I should have missed you entirely."

" Sit right down, and excuse the plight we're in ! " exclaimed the broker, shaking the young man's hand warmly inside of the gigantic dust-coat sleeve that now replaced the Raglan. " Yes, do I don't think you're detaining **us**; the carriage wont be here for half an hour yet; " and Mr. Jones handed him one of the penitential chairs.

With Augustus on his **knee, Dr.** Morris sat conversing with all the family until the carriage came. Then, with most cordial invitation to visit them at the Highlands during the summer, and be their most frequent guest on their return home, they gave him those pleasant, earnest shakes of the hand which leave a grateful memory on the touch, corresponding to that of fresh clover on the sense of odor; and the hearty souls, carrying innumerable little morocco bags, black wicker baskets, satchels, umbrellas, parasols, shawls, books, dusters, together with four *Harper's Magazines* for the current **month, that no one might** be **tantalized by** witnessing the perusal of such an interesting periodical when he or she had it not, entered the carriage, and the door was shut. But just before the driver tightened his reins, Augustus, as if by a sudden premonition, exclaimed, —

"Doctor! wont you tell a fellow where you live? **Mamma's going** to teach me to write, and my **very first letter** will be to *you!*"

Doctor Morris took a card from his pocket-book, and handed it to the little brother through the window. It bore his name and address: —

M'GREGOR MORRIS, M.D.,

Physician and Surgeon.

NEW YORK HOSPITAL, 10 P. M. — 7 A. M.

OFFICE AT OTHER HOURS, No. -, CLINTON PLACE.

It was no doubt a premonition which induced Augustus to obtain this, — a very remarkable and providential one also, as afterward appears in the course of this narrative. He put it into the pocket of his little summer-cloth jacket; **the doctor** hailed a stage going down, and the carriage, with its joyful **Joneses, set** off at cheerful speed for the foot of Robinson street.

It reached the slip about **twenty** minutes before the good little steamer *Highland Light* was to start. Mr. Jones took his wife and children to the promenade deck; found stools for them, and left them near the pilot-house, while he returned to the wharf to attend to the little matter of baggage that had come down in a cart behind the carriage. By the time that it was all on board the

second bell began to ring, and Mr. Jones ascended once
more to rest from his labors in the family bosom. At
least so he congratulated himself, for he had cast his
eye upon one particular stool when he went down, and
hoped that it would not be taken before he got back.

He was disappointed. His sweet Kate was already
in the meshes of an apparently most charming conversation, the amiable ensnarer being none else than Mr.
Lilykid. Close by them his wife sat where he had left
her, fully occupied with diverting the vindictive attention of Master Augustus from the mutually agreeable
pair. With the maternal assistance that youth was
vigorously combating the fiery temptation to " out with
it, and call him Spindle-shanks to his face."

" Mr. Lilykid, father," said Kate, looking at the gentleman's hands as if she expected them to shake one another. This did not happen, however, the father feeling
a share, slightly modified, of the son's sentiment, at the
intrusion upon his family party. He bowed gravely,
Mr. Lilykid gracefully, and Kate continued: " Mr. Lilykid has given us quite a pleasant surprise; he has taken
rooms at the same house with us for the next month,
and will be there till he accompanies us to Saratoga."
Such an ominous scowl overspread the face of Master
Jones, at hearing of this delightful prospect, that his
mother feared he was going to say something, proposed
a promenade to her husband, and, in company with him
and Augustus, left the two to their *tête-à-tête*.

In two hours, as is usual, the little steamer had

squeezed up the narrow channel of that estuary inside the Hook, known as Shrewsbury River, as far as the landing from which the craft takes its name, —the Highland Lights. This beautiful place is one of Nature's composition pieces. She has taken Butter Hill from the Hudson just below Willis's, with all its measureless depth of great, free, wild wood clinging to it from foot to sky, and set it on the resounding sea-border; from the neighborhood of Philadelphia she copies one of the most charming bits of her own fairy Schuylkill and winds it around the mountain's base; with her whitest pencil she draws the long glistening stretch of narrow beach with a single stroke from Sandy Hook to Deal, and sets that as the other boundary to the stream; and then her grandest inspiration wells up upon her from the Atlantic caves, and the tameless sea, hiding its further fury under the very eaves of the eastern heaven, surges into the picture to tell her that her completest work upon our American coast is done ! On the mountain we may stroll all day and ever find new endlessness of fragrant shade, **or seat** ourselves at night beneath the twin light-houses on the ridge, watching the misty-golden rays of the revolving lantern creep with slow rhythm, like the shining antennæ of some vast lightning fly, upon the dark bosom of the league-broad sweep of sea; in the river the timid stranger may lave himself as in some shallow inland pool at home, — on it he may row or sail; while the brave, and the brave fair whom they deserve, find a tumbling surf to meet

8

and conquer in laughing wrestle, just across that shining sand-strip on whose hither edge all is so calm. This is the Highlands of **Navesink**. Yet there are a few people — a few **thousand only — who steam** past it serenely, for the most part, it is to be hoped, **with their** eyes shut, and go to that barren waste — shared with them only **by the** fisher-hawk nesting **in grim** dead **trees whose** struggle with desolation lasts **till they reach** forty feet at the utmost — that grassless strip **of** powdered glass known **as** Long Branch; **and there,** where there **is** no boating, nor sailing, nor fishing, nor wandering in woods, but only surf for the bravest, rides in sand hub-deep for the most eccentric, billiards, ten-pins, perpendicular imbibition, a mad repetition of last winter's fevered Pyrrhics, and a sleeping in **hot** closets for the most fathomless of pocket, **these few** thousands actually pass more or less of the summer.

But the Joneses — and Mr. Lilykid, because of the **Joneses —** got **off** at the Highland Lights. In the arms of the indefatigable Mrs. Jarvis, that dauntless woman who, like a landlady variety of the Phœnix, still arises and keeps boarders above the ashes of her Sea-View House, we leave the Joneses for the present. Mr. Lilykid, with carpet-bag **and** umbrella, strolls up **the** steps **with them.**

The climate is heavenly at this place, — the diver-sions innumerable. Without the slightest misgiving, therefore, we leave the party to entertain themselves, and pass over the space of three weeks. At the end of that

time the postman of Clinton Place left a letter at Dr.
Morris's office, which that gentleman opened and found
to read as follows: —

"Joon thee 20 Furst, shrooseberry litowses.

"**dere** doktur — Thare is Krabbs hear. Tha goe side 1st.
Wen **itt is lo** tyed and runing fast itt is esy cawtt. We ete them &
boyl them **til** tha ar read. **tha ar cawt** inn a nett, which is a
grate **menny holes** maid **ov twain an wove** intow **a** bagg, too lett
out **thee watter. kum up bear rite of.** spindel Shanez is aboot
To Runn a wa with kait Thee da after Tomoro, n sed ude Stopp
Him. now Dew it ore ile brake Mi Wird. Thee Bote Sales from
robison strete. this is thee wa tow git thair — al thee Stag **Lions**
thatt runn doun brodwa goes as fur ass mury strete. Taik **cnny**
1 ov them an git owt att mury. then goe strate doun tow Thee
Doc. if u dont i shall lern how two Sware fromm 1 ov thee
nawty Men which opins Oistors hear fur thee hotell and dew it
verry much. johnson is riting fur me Becaws i amm sich a Pigg
with mi Penn that evn Iff I shud Beginn nise & clene ide Sune
git Inc on my Close Becides i dont no how tow rite enny wa & i
Hop ule xquze me, doktur **moris** fur Takin Thee Libburtey on
Bein A Sirvant & ritin tow u fur master agustis Without noe
**Iuterdukshun, which evn Speckin Wudent Bee aloud inn thee
Old Kuntry,** which things is diferint **Inn thee noo, ware al Men
is Fre & Equill an noe** kweshuns **Ased —** which Sirkumstanses
Halter kases & soe noe mour noose fromm ures affekshinilley
willam johnson i mene toe sa Mastir **Agustis.** pee ess. iff u
kum i wunt Lern toe Sware ass a Matir **ov Curse.**"

Having finished the perusal of this remarkable epistle,
the doctor wrote a note to a brother physician, asking

him to take **care** of the few serious cases, of which he inclosed him **a list, marked on** the slate which hung **at** his door, " Called **abroad on** consultation: back in a week," — and **performed his** bachelor packing by the usual method of cramming a dozen **shirts into a** valise constructed for **five, completing the process by sitting** down on it till it would lock. This was two **o'clock in** the afternoon of the day before the elopement was appointed. At six o'clock he **was** on the wharf of the scene of action. There **are two** places in the United States where the **arrival of** a steamboat is still **as** thrilling a fact to the pulse of popular life as when Fulton ran the first **trip** on his *Chancellor Livingston.* One of these is Newburgh, on the Hudson, where the whole town, **from** its corporation-officers down to the small boy with molasses candy for **sale, and the still** smaller boy that spends **his** cent with him, is poured upon the **long wharf in one compact,** surging mass of human cocoa-nuts at every **arrival of the** *Thomas Powel.* The other is Highland Lights. Here, everybody is always expecting somebody, or in spasms of anxiety to buy a New York four-cent daily for ten cents.

But while **the doctor is** elbowing his way through the crowd, **climbing** over trunks and getting involved in the **legs of the** black **porters who** carry them, a little hand **pulls him by the finger, a** little face, **the very one he is** looking for, peers up into **his, and** Master Augustus exclaims, with frantic pleasure, —

" You dear, *dear* old fellow ! I'm so glad to see you, I don't know what to do ! "

As they emerged more from the crowd, it became apparent how much interest the child had really taken in the arrival. He had been engaged in his favorite pursuit when he saw the boat coming up the river; and just as **he** was, without a moment's compromise with the social amenities, had run to meet it. A covered basket, evidently, from confused bubblings and scratchings heard within, full of the spoils of crabdom, hung at his waist suspended by a strap; his pantaloons, rolled as far as possible, displayed a pair of fiery-red, sunburned little snipe legs; and he directed his own and the doctor's steps to the spot where he had thrown his net down for greater ease in running. This being secured, Augustus exclaimed that he was ready to go to the house, and proposed the following programme:

" Now," said he, " we'll walk right into the parlor, and I guess Kate and that old Lilykid are alone together. I'll go straight up to him and say, 'Old Spindle-shanks, you sha'n't have my sister !' and then you come close up behind me and say, 'No ! *that* you sha'n't, you wicked man !' And **then we'll** call him all the names we can think of, and tell him just what he is, and if he tries to run away, you can knock him down; and if Kate faints, why, you can bring her to, can't you ? "

" Not quite so fast, my dear boy ! everything in time. I want to look around a little this evening, and " —

" Look around ! Thunder ! Why, old Lilykid's going

8 *

to try and run away with my sister *to-morrow!* I heard
him telling her that **they'd take** a sail up to Red Bank
and do it, and then come back and ask mamma to ask
papa to feel all right about it; and she didn't say she
wouldn't! They were down in the grape-arbor, and
they didn't know I was up on the top of the steps and
heard it all; but I did! What do you want to look
around for? Don't you believe *me?* There aint any
time to look around; mamma puts me to bed at eight
o'clock, and he'll have Kate to-morrow!"

"No he wont, Augustus, my boy! I've been getting
all ready for him. Before your letter came I had gone
to the station, where your mamma found you, and heard
enough said and got enough papers — they're here, in
my breast-pocket — to stop all that very suddenly! Be
patient, now; don't say a word **to anybody, not even of
my being here, till I say you may; and we'll attend to**
the matter **just as it ought to be done.** You shall be
with me, too, when it happens; only don't spoil everything by being in too much of a hurry."

Thus he pacified Augustus, and persuaded him to go
up quietly to tea, while he took his valise to the Pavilion
next door, and, as he had said, looked around during the
evening.

At eight **o'clock the broad full** moon rose out of the
**far border of the sea, and began to compete with the
rear-guard** of the sunset in making that whole American
coast heaven as gloriously beautiful as **any sky** of Italy.
In that mixed light the rushing, booming surf on the outer

edge of the sand looked like the breaking upward into
a freer air of some great genii-troubled mine of molten
gold and silver. On their terraces toward the river the
luxuriant trellised grape-vines, fanned in the fresh **salt**
wind, turning now the dark green surfaces of **their**
leaves, and now the snowy under-side toward the light,
and seeming thus to come and go like the ghosts of little
children, or white-breasted birds who loved the sea
border and dallied around **it, unable to fly quite** away.
At the dock the Shrewsbury fleet of yachts, sail-boats,
oyster-crafts, and fishing-yawls lay, sharing on all their
hulls, spars, and the sails of such of **them as had not**
been furled for the night, the beauty of the universal
chastened silver, — rocking gently between the sway of
the down tide and the east wind, and all lifted out of
their fairer or their meaner uses to one common level
of a moon-glorified, fairy-lake flotilla. And already far
out on the measureless waters the golden feelers of the
revolving lantern began to creep vastly, flashing now on
the marble spread **of** distant ships that seemed motion-
less, but were really **bowling gayly** on a scupper breeze,
— **now on the pathless** field of the hillocked sea, — now
athwart, and losing themselves in the causeway of silver
which ran straight from the beach **to the** front portal of
the moon. With **a** hundred and fifty other gentlemen
smoking their cigars on the Pavilion terrace, — two
hundred ladies dreaming or chatting with no covering
on their heads but the tiara of the moonlight, — a hundred children of all ages frolicking away the thought

that that kill-pleasure, bedtime, was sooner or later inevitable, — Dr. M'Gregor Morris sat in his wicker arm-
chair, and agreed with Nature that she was beautiful.
His eye wandered to the other house across the ravine:
presently there sauntered forth upon the porch two figures
that he knew, — a lithe girl's form, a tall whiskered cavalier, — and the minute-hand of Destiny seemed to run up
suddenly to striking-point. It was time to "look around."

The doctor cast one lingering glance on the beaming
earth, ocean, and heaven; sighed, threw away his cigar,
and repeated the words of the Missionary Hymn, —

" 'Every prospect pleases, and only man is vile!'

Moon, I'd like to pay my respects to you a little longer,
but really I haven't time. *Au revoir* for the present!"

Only a narrow ravine, wide enough to admit the passage of a steep cart-road down to the river-beach, sepa-
rates the terraced lawns of the two houses. It is cus-
tomary, of course, for gentlemen at the Pavilion to
stroll as near the boundary fence of that resort as they
please. Dr. Morris availed himself of this fact, and, putting up his collar for an incognito, lit another cigar, to
appear as nonchalant as possible, and began pacing up
and down the grassy border of the lawn that looked toward the porch of the next house. There was nothing
in this act to awake suspicion in the two who sat there
side by side, half in moolight, half in shadow; they paid
no attention to him whatever, as much because the sight
of unknown gentlemen next door was usual as because

they were preoccupied. Privacy in publicity is one of the many attainments easily acquired by the flirtations, to say nothing of more earnest affairs, of watering-place life.

Before the doctor's cigar was smoked out, he had come to the following conclusions : That the beautiful young girl on the porch was in the toils of the neighboring rascal, by force of one of those strange delusions which affect the simple and the high-minded alike. She believed she loved because she heard that she was loved. Her nature, in its first ardor of womanhood, feeling out into the new world for that necessary something to expend its powers of growth upon, to cling around, to climb **up to,** had unfortunately touched a villain. **She** was not to blame: in society, a man's true self is such **a** deep down substratum, so overlain by successive layers of constitutional caution, educational reserve, handsome physique, elegant manners, tailor-skill, and innumerable deceptive conventional circumstances, that it is hard for any one, however world-sharpened, to penetrate the **crust and** get at the basis **of** the human geological system. Much **less for a young girl, utterly innocent,** pure-hearted, **unread in the book of man's hidden badnesses,** who, moreover, had **a father and mother** as frank **and** unsuspicious of evil as two people could be and live in a handsome free-stone house in an eligible city street, a lot necessarily attained, as times go, by some slight measure of worldly keenness. She had not really loved yet, — something within him made the doctor particularly willing to believe *that ;* she was only measuring the depth of her heart, and, striking on a big slimy sea-snake that lay basking a little way down, thought her lead had touched the bottom. The doctor was assured of this, and, in corroboration, he perceived that the gentleman was the chief actor in the *tête-à-tête* across the way. He gestured, he talked, he bent down over his beautiful victim, and altogether seemed putting forth his utmost power, live a travelling magnetizer exerting his will to get and keep his subject " *en rapport.*" Kate listened to him, looked at him motionlessly as a snake-charmed bird; she was under a spell, which the doctor was also willing to believe could be broken by some resolute third person with a will as strong as the fascinator and moral force a trifle greater.

Having " looked around " to his satisfaction, the doctor retired to his room to refresh himself by sleep for the exigency of the morrow. Immediately after breakfast the next morning he despatched, by one of the waiters, the following little note to Mrs. Jones: —

" MY DEAR MADAM, — I am staying at the Pavilion for a few days, and would have taken a still earlier opportunity than this to pay my respects to you, but for the fact that I am arranging a little surprise for one of my friends, and accordingly wish, for a few hours longer, to preserve my incognito. May I entrust the secret of my being here with you until I am able to call in person, and at the same time ask that my little friend Augustus may be permitted to spend the day with me, and, if it is pleasant, take a sail up the river with me this afternoon ?

" Very truly your most obedient servant,

" M'GREGOR MORRIS."

In twenty minutes, the boy brought back **this** answer: —

"**My** VERY DEAR SIR, — Your incognito is perfectly safe with me. It will give me the greatest pleasure to accept your very kind invitation for Augustus, and nothing, certainly, could be more delightful to him. I am afraid the child has very little to amuse him here ; he is compelled **to** seek most of his pleasures alone, as **it is, perhaps,** hardly to **be** expected that **a** boy of his age and somewhat too roguish tendencies could prove very congenial company to a young lady like my daughter. His father is compelled to be a good deal in New York during the day, and **I** am not as vigorous a playmate as he needs. This afternoon, Kate, with a friend of hers staying here, is expecting to take a sail **on** the river, and I have been puzzling myself all the morning for some plan to interest my little boy, in case, as is probable, it would be too much trouble to make him one of the party. Your invitation is, therefore, both extremely kind and *apropos;* and as soon as Augustus can be discovered, recalled from his crab-fishery, and put into presentable condition, he shall **be** sent over to your **room.** We shall make haste to give you a cordial welcome as **soon as you find it** convenient to make **your** promised visit.

"Sincerely and gratefully your friend,

. "CATHARINE JONES."

This note was followed, in about an hour, by Master Augustus. The doctor and he then descended together to the little wharf where all the pleasure-boats of the Shrewsbury fleet still lay moored, it being morning bath-hour, and all the lovers of "a wet sheet and a flowing

sea" disporting themselves in the surf on the other side
of the bar.   The doctor, therefore, had his pick of the
flotilla.

Leading Augustus by the hand, he went up and down
the wharf, surveying with critical eye the different crafts
in respect to their points **for** fast-sailing, and at length
stood still above a cat-rigged boat, clinker-built, clean-
sparred, compactly and sharply modelled, which bore on
her stern the name *Shanghai.*   For the benefit of those
who do not go down unto the sea in cock-boats and behold the mighty wonders that are done, not only on
the deep, but on shoals, with vessels drawing one foot
water, I say, episodically, that the cat-rig boat is one
which carries a mainsail only, and is a favorite on the
Shrewsbury **river,** where the channel, in places, **is so**
extremely narrow that the short tacks one is **o**bliged to
make **would be much** additionally **shortened by** the pro-
jection of a bowsprit, with the alternative of running
that delicate piece **of** timber into the bank on either
side.   Moreover, **the** cat-boat can be managed by one
man, in trolling for blue-fish or Spanish mackerel, with a
wind on the bow; he can man his main-sheet with one
hand, feel his squid-line with the other, and tend his tiller between his knees.   If he carried a jib a second hand
would be necessary to mind the fore-sheet; or, in going
about quickly, it might foul, put him in the wind's eye,
and set him drifting stern-first, with an eight-pound
blue-fish to help himself off the squid with natural
alacrity.

" Do you know anything about the *Shanghai ?* " asked the doctor, of his companion.

" I guess I do ! " answered the youth, enthusiastically.

She's the fastest boat on *this* little river. I'm going **to** buy her when I'm a man, and peddle clams, if mother'll let me,—that is, if I don't be a lawyer or saw wood."

" Then you've given up the idea, since I saw you first, **of** going into the bread business ? "

"Shut up ! What do you want to plague a fellow for ? I was a little boy **when I** said *that*, and I've travelled a good deal since. There's such an *awful nice* man sails that boat ! He showed me how to find soft crabs, and he's given me ever so many sails **in** the *Shanghai.* His name's Van Brunt, and I like him better than all the other captains put together."

" Well, Augustus, I guess, to please you, we'll take Van Brunt's boat for this afternoon."

So they hunted up the master of the *Shanghai,*— were modestly corroborated by him in their opinion of the craft's fast points,—**and** engaged her from dinner-time until they got tired **or through, which, in the** opinion **of the doctor and** Augustus, **would occur about** simultaneously.

There are too many sources of amusement at Shrewsbury Highlands, from which the two could have extracted pastime until three o'clock, P. M., for me to chronicle here. At that hour, as the doctor sat smoking his after-dinner cigar on the Pavilion terrace, and Master Augustus stood at his knee learning how they cut

9

people's legs off, for *his* post-prandial sedative, and very much disappointed to hear that the doctór could not also add any description from eye-witness of the amputation of heads, Morris, who had been all the time watching the wharf, "out of the tail o' his eye," saw **Mr.** Lilykid assist Miss Jones into the vessel known as *My Own Mary Ann,* and take the tiller in his hand. The captain of the craft proffered his assistance, — seemed even disposed to come on board and sail the *Mary Ann* for them, — but the man devoted to society waved him off with a courtly gesture of the hand, and signified his ability to manage for himself.

As soon as the *Mary Ann* glided from the wharf, the doctor told Augustus to follow him as quick as possible, and started with all speed for the *Shanghai.* **Van** Brunt had her ready for him, and, **without losing a moment's time, the two tumbled aboard, and the** lithe little **cat ran out into the stream.** Her captain, from the wharf, watched her for a moment, to be sure of the seamanship of the doctor, and then retired, perfectly satisfied, to the little oyster and soft-crab stand at the foot of the Pavilion steps, where his cronies most did congregate. The wind was blowing frésh down the river,— that 'is, toward its mouth at Sandy Hook, though Shrewsbury people persist in calling that direction *up,* referring all motion to New York as the head of things, — but the tide was at the first quarter of a particularly strong flood, and it was very easy for a skilful hand to beat up as far as Minturn's Point, — a bald promontory of the Highlands where the river divides, one branch bending at right angles westward to Red Bank, and the other keeping straight on to the southward to Branch Port, the point of debarkation for Long Branch. Once around the point, and a boat could lay her course, taking the southerly wind abeam and the favoring tide all the way to the Bank.

The boat that Mr. Lilykid had **was** a good sailer in good hands, but still not to compare with the *Shanghai*, which was of lighter model, from her clinker build "lifted quicker," spread more mainsail, and trimmed closer to the wind by several points. At the present time the *Mary Ann* was *not* in remarkably good hands, made her tacks irresolutely (on the second one from the wharf nearly missing stays as she went about), and did not take advantage of the flaws, but luffed when she ought to keep on. Morris was a good sailor for an amateur, and possessed what is an advantage to all but practised professionals, a small pennant to steer by, while the object of his chase had none, and was compelled to watch the leach **of his sail.** So that the *Shanghai* overhauled him rapidly.

Still the old saw, that "a starn chase is a long chase," might have come true but for one little fact which Mr. Lilykid did not know, and whose knowledge the doctor owed solely to that keen-eyed young observer of men and things, Augustus. About ten rods out from Minturn's Point a weedy shallow commences and runs in a south-easterly direction almost entirely across to the

bar, compelling those who prefer the channel to getting
aground to hug the point as closely as possible. The
doctor, being put in possession of this bit of information, made his last long tack completely across from the
bar to the point, and then luffed up a little to pass
through the narrow channel. Mr. Lilykid, being ignorant of it, kept more away while he was still to wind-
ward of the *Shanghai*, expecting to make a clear run up
the north bend of the river which now opened straight
before him.   So that, just as Morris passed the point,
Lilykid's ears were greeted by that ignoble and re-
pulsive sound, the grinding of the sand upon his keel,
and the next moment, with a prolonged groan and a
dead thud, the *Mary Ann* became an unexpected guest
in the eel-grass and mud-bowers of the treacherous
Shrewsbury amphitrite.   Augustus gave a prolonged
crow, and stood up on the centre-board to the imminent
danger of his little shins' more intimate acquaintance
with a jibing boom.   The doctor pulled him down directly, and told him to keep out of sight for the present,
at the same time putting the *Shanghai* right into the
wind's eye to drift slowly with the tide, till he " looked
around " a little further.

For the first time he now saw Kate plainly. She
thought something dreadful had happened, — feared
that the *Mary Ann* had been stove in, — and was leaning over the gunwale, very beautiful but pale as death.
Mr. Lilykid, for his part, did all that was possible for
a man to do; standing on his quarter-deck and calling

with his might and main to the unknown crew of the
Shanghai to "come *heah !*" **Ah** ! he little knew how
ready they were to answer that hail. The next minute
the *Shanghai* had backed out of her narrow channel
by the utmost exertions of the doctor with a long sweep,
and stood over to their shoal. Only the bows of the
Mary Ann were grounded; her stern lay in such deep
water that the *Shanghai* run her bow close up without
danger of sharing the catastrophe. With a loose coil of
the main-halliard Dr. Morris quickly made fast, and
then in **the calmest possible tone said,** —

"Miss Jones, permit me to **assist** you on board our
craft."

She looked **at him** searchingly, recognized him, and
the marble whiteness of her face changed to an intense
crimson flush; but she leaped on board the *Shanghai*,
and passed to the stern, where she sat down, just noticing Augustus, and hid her face in her handkerchief.
With a cheerful, graceful step, acquired probably from
practice **in the** Chasseurs **during his** life-long devotion
to society, Mr. Lilykid next advanced, and was about to
step upon the bow of the *Shanghai* when the hand of
the doctor gently kept him **back.**

"Excuse me, **sir, but there is no room** for you on
board this boat."

"Weally, Mistah, I don't know your name, but this is
most extwa-awdinawy conduct ! Not woom ? Why,
I've known that cwaft of youahs to cawwy twenty-
five !"

9 *

" Really, Mister, I *do* know your *names*, — this may be true, — but were you ever cognizant of its carrying Mr. Lilykid and Lord Rocamblebury, and Pennyroyal Pike, and English Jimmy the Gentleman, **and Andrew Redding** ? I put it to your good sense whether so many of you wouldn't sink us ? I object, my dear sir, to the *Shanghai's* having anything to do with your transportation: this is *not* a convict ship, and *I* am not a police-officer. Though I have had the pleasure of knowing **some who** were intimately acquainted with you, and recollect being present on one occasion at —— street station, where you were detained from a little party, but found bail it seems. However, in going, let me advise you to keep clear of the Highlands, as soon as the tide rises, for there *may* be gentlemen here to see you by this evening's boat. **I** just drop the hint. Good-day."

As the doctor concluded this **long speech,** — somewhat *too* **long to be put among the terse** and remarkable sayings which have become immortal, but not too long for his object, which was delicately to enlighten Miss Jones as to the character of the man her innocence had trusted, — he shoved off the *Shanghai* and sprang to the helm just in time, for, as the little craft swung around on to the wind again, a puff came which nearly brought the water up to her lee combings. Just then the mute astonishment and rage of the devotee of society gave way to a fierce and undisguised expression of the same emotions; he uttered language which it is to be hoped he had never practised in the depth of his elegant solitude, and wrenching out an awning-pin which stood at the bow of the *Mary Ann*, sprang for the deck of his foe. Sprang, but fell about three feet short, and as Kate cried out in terror not to let him drown, took that trouble for himself, wading back to the stranded vessel, a very wet but by no means a cool gentlemen. To conclude forever this fragment of the Lilykiddian biography, let me say that as the tide rose the *Mary Ann* floated again, and, putting her before the wind, her unfortunate captain sped for the coast that is nigh unto Keyport, and there running her ashore, departed for quarters unknown to those gentlemen of **the** detached service who came up to visit him on the evening boat. And the rest of the acts of Lilykid, are they not recorded in the unwritten imprecations of Jem Conkrite the craft's owner, who, with much expense of " hallowed sweat " and unhallowed breath, reclaimed the *Mary Ann* from the waters of Raritan Bay, with a broken gaff and a splintered centre-board, and after repairing the same got out a writ with innumerable aliases for his **absconded debtor,** which remaineth unserved unto this day ?

In ten minutes from the shoving off of the *Shanghai* she was moored again at the Pavilion wharf. During that short trip the doctor, yea, even Augustus, did all that lay in their power to arouse Kate from the terrible dream in which she seemed immured almost from all outer help. Morris, by the most assiduous, unobtrusive attention, — by speaking, without apparent intention, of other things than those just present, — attempted to make her feel that he could not possibly be in possession of her secret. And Augustus — if not yet quite fit to be an angel, and with the angels stand — proved himself worthy of belonging to quite as good a class of spirits, for our earthly purposes at least; namely, those who run about instead of standing among our human sinners and sufferers, and make them as comfortable as possible with all sorts of faithful kindness.

As the doctor lifted Kate ashore, she spoke almost for the first time, —

" Is that man really all you told him he was ? "

The doctor bowed, and put into her hand a little package of papers containing the data of the police-office.

" Then God bless you ! " said she, pressing his hand with a look of unutterable gratitude. " **You** saved Augustus; and now, — you will never know on earth what good you have done *me !* "

IV. BEING A FEW FRAGMENTS FROM THE LIFE OF THE BOY AND HIS FRIENDS.

But the doctor *did* know, and on earth, too (though his feet did not seem to be exactly touching it at the time), the good he had done, and was to do, for the little brother's sister.

During the same summer, toward its close, a little bird, swinging on the twig of one of those trees which, at the upper point of Goat Island, look toward the Niagara Rapids, caught this little bit of a talk and brought it to me.

"And can *you* really, — with all the jealous, unsharing, rival-hating **heart of** a man, still *love me ?* *Me*, whose heart **once** went so bitterly astray, and was nearly **wrecked forever ? "**

"Not your *heart*, Kate ; your *head* only ! You were merely feeling your depth, — or, better still, merely trying your strength to mount. **If** you thought you **had** reached your full height, is not that what many do, and then sit sadly on the lower stairs, unsatisfied, pining, miserable; looking with despair through a whole life on the bright blessed height, far over them, to which they might have scaled; knowing that not their heart at all, but their young, untaught head, has brought this spellbound wretchedness upon them ? And shall I love you less for remembering **the ladder** on which **you** climbed **up to a true** man's **soul,** — **believing in my** heart **of hearts that you have now reached your height ? "**

"Yes, I *have* reached it."

"God bless my darling! "

There was a wedding in Twenty-third street. Little Brother sat up to it, without doing the most trifling thing that was disagreeable. Indeed, the little Misses Blummerie said he was charming ! And he did both

look and act as handsomely as any youth who longed
to put away the *enfant terrible* part of boy character
possibly could. His chief amusement, when not bringing up little girls by the hour together to kiss the bride,
consisted in poking with his small finger the side of the
groom's white satin waistcoat, and whispering, with
most amiable inaudibleness, —

" *Didn't* we dish him, old fellow ? — *say !* "

About one o'clock, A. M., when the little girls had
gone and the big ones were going, Master Augustus
yielded to Nature's kind restorer, and was surrendered
to her in a state of most unreserved capitulation.

Just before the lights were turned off for the night,
the new bride and bridegroom stole into the little bed-
chamber where the little brother was sleeping, as he
was wont to brag, " all alone by himself."

They both bent down and kissed the rosy cheek
which, under its curly corn-silk, was lying on the little
open palm; looked tenderly at him, and then at each
other.

" Once you thought he was a little imp."

" And now I think he is a little angel."

And what they both thought was, that it was not
such a bad thing to have a little brother after all.

FLEEING TO TARSHISH.

.

FLEEING TO TARSHISH.

I.

OR three years Jonas Moddle had been a daily student of Greek and Hebrew. He was just out of the Theological Seminary — Reverend, and thinking himself reverable. He not only knew the original for the contested passages in St. John, but what Moses has said on a subject which interests nobody except the Cohoes Mastodon. He was a splendid Hebrew geologist, and a noble fossil minister. In Greek he needed no lexicon. In Hebrew he found more trouble on account of the left-hand-way of reading; but still knew enough to dig out an ingenious derivation in support of an accepted theory. (Grecians and Hebræans will know what I mean.)

He also knew some English. In exegesis he was unrivalled. On a single passage he would say more than any other member of the class on the four gospels. The wonderful sermon, in which he electrified all the brethren, by proving the whole plan of salvation from the text, "Og, King of Bashan," will never be forgotten by the alumni of St. Elymas.

So promising a **young** man could not be without "calls." Almost simultaneously, and within a week of his ordination, he received two **invitations to** become a settled minister. **One** from the Church of **St.** Simon Stylites, in New York, another from a **feeble** but struggling organization in a small town **of** Western **Missouri.** On the very day he received both these invitations, **he** attended a missionary anniversary, **and** heard a Western rector give some account of the state of religion in his section. Christianity, out there, seemed at a low ebb. Six weeks previous, he had lost one of his wardens-in a knife-fight with a Presbyterian deacon upon the subject of free-will. The survivor retained too much sectarian prejudice to come to the funeral. Some people, to attend his service, rode twenty miles over the **worst roads** in Christendom, — the women, like the men, **on** horseback, and frequently astride. **His parochial income** last year amounted to $420. He had repeatedly preached to an audience of but a dozen whites; though, he added with some hesitation, — as if apologizing for the fact, and not feeling entirely sure but there was something political in it, — a humble variety of piety prevailed rather widely among the negroes.

After the meeting was over, Mr. Moddle sought an introduction to Mr. Bowers, and inquired of him if, in his peregrinations through his section, he had ever heard of such a place as Muddy Creek. "It is the next parish to mine," replied Mr. Bowers, "and dreadfully in need of an able man it is! I sometimes run across when the roads are passable, and I've not got too tired through the week, to hold an evening service there. **But** there's astonishing little interest there about church matters. The few people that know they've got souls to save come pretty regular, and the very chief of 'em, Binks, is an earnest Christian man; **but, dear** me! they can hardly get together enough congregation to take the loneliness **out of a jury-room in the court-house.**"

"**Ah, indeed!**" replied Mr. Moddle; and then he went home to look over his letters. The one from Mr. **Binks was upon half a** sheet **of** commercial bill-paper, and, although not a remarkably fine specimen of **a** churchman's hand, made up for it on the margin by **several** very accurate impressions of his thumb. It was sealed with a red wafer, and this is a correct transcript of it: —

"Muddy Creek, Mo., May 9.

"Rev. J. Moddle: Dear Sir, — Making a tower to the eastward this spring, I went to New York. While **there, I heard you preach.** It was in that white church up Broadway. **I hadn't for a long time heard a sermon so able as that was; by it my soul** was enlargd. Now there are two things we want out here to Muddy, — an able man, and a place to praise God in. If we can get the former, I'm sure we can get the latter. We are a mighty little flock now; but we're all of us faithful and our hearts is set. Even while we have to worship in the court-house we don't forget the assembling of ourselves together; and if we had a good strong man to help us

we'd put our shoulders to the wheel with him; and, my
dear sir, it's in my heart **to** believe we could get the
Lord's charriat out of this slew.   The **whole country**
round about seems given up,—if we didn't know **the**
Lord never gives anything up.   **There's but few reapers
out** here for the harvest, though the field is **white with
it.**   Such lóts of men and women and little boys and girls
that don't know anything about the gospel, and havn't
nobody to tell 'em—**my** heart does feel for 'em too !
If you'll come to us, **my** dear sir, we're ready to shear
our best with you.   **We** can only pledge six hundred a
year for the first year; but till we do better, there's a
home in my family for you, and welcome.   The salary
is not much, but time will raise it.   We'll all of us feel
as if we could live better when the church is built up.
So that **will** change; but **there's one** thing never will
change, my dear sir, and that is the sureness **you** may
feel of finding us to your back **whenever** hard pushing's
wanted in the work of the Lord.   Please consider, and
write to direction of

"Yours resp'y,

"Robert Binks."

The other note was much briefer,—had at its head a
monogram in mediæval letters of bright scarlet,—smelt
of cedar-lined secretaries,—was sealed with a coat of
arms, and read thus:—

"New York, May 15th.

"Rev. Jonas Moddle: Dear Sir,—I am instructed
by the vestry and wardens of St. Simon Stylites to an-

nounce that at their meeting on the 12th inst., you were unanimously elected to the rectorship of their church. Should you gratify us by accepting that mark of the high regard in which we hold you, please grant me an early reply. I have only further to say, that we have at your · disposal a rectory attached to the church, and the parochial income of our clergyman is $4000 per ann.

"**I** remain, Rev. and Dear Sir, resp'y yours,

" M. CATESBY SPROULL,

" *Clerk of Vestry.*"

Mr. Moddle read both letters with profound attention, — laid them on the table, — clasped his hands across the back of his head, and tipped back his chair. The balancing attitude of his body was only symbolic of the posture of his mind. Poor both in its style and its proffers as was the letter from Missouri, there was no denying that it moved him. After that, and the testimony of the **Rev.** Joseph Bowers, it was impossible to doubt that Muddy Creek **needed a** highly able man, and was a vast **field of usefulness.**

Nobody familiar with his own nature can need an enumeration of the arguments which St. Simon Stylites pleaded in its favor to a human heart. But apart from the worldly splendor of the position, was to be considered the question whether a much less able man than the Rev. Jonas would not do for Muddy Creek; and the scholarly eminence he had spent so much pains in acquiring be quite thrown away in that section, though most

7 *

advantageous in New York. This thought involved
subtle casuistry. Self is a veiled client, and never appears at the bar of conscience in person. The duty of
using advantages argued on its side and that of St. Simon. If the judge granted its suit, was he acting more
through favor to it or conviction by its advocate ?

Casuistry keeps things tipped back on two legs for a
long time. Mr. Moddle's chair might have remained in
that position till tea-time, had not a classmate hurriedly
called in at the seminary room, which he was still occupying, to borrow his **valise** for a trip to New York, — a
city situated only a shirt and two collars distant from
the gables of St. Elymas.

" Just time to dump in a few things and reach the
train ! " said young brother Chawsuble. " Where is it ? "

" On the floor in the closet. When are **you coming
back ?** "

" Day after to-morrow **morning.** Where's the key ?
Oh ! here it is."

" I've a great mind to go with you " —

" Will you, though ? Capital ! You can stay at my
aunt's with me."

Mr. Moddle wanted the last volume of Alford, and
had long been intending to have his name gilded on the
back of a prize Gesenius. Besides, he might consult with
some of the elder clergy on the **subject of his** choice,
and, if he made up his mind, see the **vestry** of St. Simon
Stylites in person. His chair came down on its full number of legs; and in a couple of minutes more the room

in the valise was shared between him and Mr. Chawsuble. Just before leaving the apartment, he took the two
letters from the mantel-piece, and inserted them, at haz-
ard, between the leaves of a big family Bible, which
adorned the table under his looking-glass.

During their short ride on the cars, the noise prevented
conversation, and the studently **habits** of the two had
too much taxed their eyes to permit of their reading sen-
tences which bounced along at forty miles the hour.
Mr. Chawsuble was going to see a sweet girl to whom
he was affianced, and in view of that meeting found both
ample and satisfactory occupation for his mind in the set
and polish of a new pair of patent-leathers, favorably
placed for contemplation upon the opposite cushion.
Mr. Moddle, left to the companionship of his thoughts,
found less that was gratifying in them. If a contented
mind is a perpetual feast, an unsettled one is a supper
of the Barmecide. There is all the porcelain and silver
ware of possible advantage, but no succulent fruition in
the whole of **it.** At last, wearied out with the air-beat-
ing gymnastics **of casuistry, Mr.** Moddle laid his head
back on the neck-rest and tried to doze. The ruckety-
tuckety-tuck of the **car-wheels** seemed rhythmically **to**
carry on his cogitations for him, with their accustomed
wondrous translatability by the imagination, now saying,
" My heart does feel for 'em too; " and now " Four
thousand a — year and a — rectory. Little by little this
dactylic beat became more and more independent of Mr.
Moddle's volition, and he was sound asleep before the

next station closed the measure with a protracted spon-
dee.   Each succeeding **stop** interrupted his slumber but
a moment, and he was not **thoroughly aroused** until
Mr. Chawsuble shook him **up to join the crowd** in their
stampede for the ferry-boat.

The roar and glare **of the great city acted on him,**
homœopathically, like **a sedative.**   Having taken a
Fifth avenue stage, as that vehicle turned in at Eleventh
street, **he** remembered that one of St. Simon's vestrymen
lived right on his route up-town.   He accordingly told
Chawsuble that he would be at the house of the latter's
aunt about nine o'clock, and stay all night if she invited
him, — in the mean time making a call on Mr. Mansion.
The vestryman's parlor was a soul-entrancing contrast
to the bare and dingy primness of the scholastic cells at
St. Elymas.   It was **a warm May** twilight, and through
the open balcony window the bland sea-breeze fanned
an exquisite fragrance **from the** wistarias which climbed
to the second story.   The gas had not yet been lighted;
for the lingering purple of the western sky made **the**
room winy with its reflection.   It was like looking at
life through a medium of rich old port, and no Vandal
had come to dispel the illusion by any sallow, artificial
glare.   The room was yet sufficiently illuminated to
suggest that the Mansions possessed excellent taste **in art,**
showing upon the walls two delicious **Kensetts,** a Col-
man, a Gignoux, and one picture each, in their loveliest
vein, by Inness and Gifford.   Mellowed by the twilight,
these paintings seemed less what they were than magi-

cal windows, through which the eye could look from one
standing-place into many far and beautiful countries.
Mr. Moddle sank into one of the luxurious divans as into
a pleasant velvet grave; and as he admiringly drew
across his knee a superbly blooming afghan, which hung
there, he could realize the emotions with which a person
who has died in the odor of sanctity comes back to find
his body reposing under rich turf and daffodils.   Fresh
roses, mignonette, and daphne were in a small Etruscan
vase upon a malachite stand near the arch; in all but
perfume the exquisite flowers of the carpet were scarcely less real.   The furniture was all carven of the richest
woods, and the ceiling was panelled, with lovely faces
between the divisions.   A great rack, supported by black
walnut sphynxes, held in one corner a portfolio bulging
with rare studies and engravings.   Everywhere about
the room, in graceful disorder, were scattered articles of
vertu and reminiscence of travel; comic statuettes from
the Boulevards; chalets in orange and apple wood from
Berne; Buddhist charms **from** Yeddo; lacrymatories
from the catacombs; and bronzes **from Pompeii.**

   While Mr. Moddle sat waiting **for Mr.** Mansion, **the**
door of the back parlor opened and some one passed in
without noticing his presence.   As his own eyes were
turned toward the sky and the wistarias, he only heard
a footfall, and, having once turned his head enough to
see that it was not approaching him, pursued the pleasant devotional train which had been set in motion by his
surroundings.   A moment after and a skilful hand, in

the room behind him, was striking the opening chords
of a harp-arrangement of Lumbye's " Traumbilder."
The instrument was one too rarely found in any circle.
The circle in which Mr. Moddle had moved was so little
conversant with it, that, after momentarily taking it for
a piano, he started with curiosity to see what it was, then
bethought himself what it must be, and leaned back again
into his pleasant grave. His action evidently had not
been so demonstrative as to betray his presence, for the
skilful hand went on throwing its magic shuttle through
the warp of the strings, as unconsciously as if there were
no one within a thousand leagues to be wrapt in its web
of gramarye. Mr. Moddle was glad that the owner of
the hand had not seen him, — that Mr. Mansion had not
arrived to talk with him, for he was now able to shut his
eyes and give himself entirely up to the enchantment.
When the invisible player came to the exquisite passage,
written as a Cithara **solo in** the original, and of course
transcribed for the highest strings of the harp, Mr.
Moddle felt as if there were nothing good and lovely of
which the human soul is not capable, and experienced a
foretaste of that sweet, self-approving peace which belongs to those who have become perfected already. He
thought St. Catharine, carried to heaven by angels, must
have felt where their fingers touched her, thrills such as
these which came to his nature to blend with the twilight
and the odors. Just as the player struck the chords of
the finale, a door flew abruptly open right behind him,
and a hurried voice exclaimed, —

" Sorry to have kept you waiting, Mr. Moddle; but fact is I've had a meeting of the Ronkus River Railroad Directors in my library ever since second board. First moment I've had to see you; hope you're well: **got** Sproull's letter ? Thought likely. You'll stay to dinner, of course. Jane ! Jane ! Where is she ? Thought I heard her playing on the harp " —

Somewhere in the midst of this rapid address, Mr. **Moddle** found an interstice to thrust his hand and get it **shaken. As** Mr. Mansion concluded his sentence, a lady stepped out of the shadow and came toward them.

" Oh, here you are ! Let me present Mr. **Moddle, my** dear: — Mrs. Mansion, Mr. Moddle, — our future rector you know, Mrs. Mansion."

Mr. Moddle was about to stammer something which might politely indicate that if Mrs. Mansion did know she was better off than he was, when Mrs. Mansion came into the full illumination of the spring twilight, and stopped him, — stopped him no more by the affable hand which she extended, and the necessity of speaking **words of salutation, than by** the **unaided effect** of her visible presence.

Mrs. Mansion was the most impressive woman he had ever seen. Not that she was haughty, not that she was queenly in her carriage. She was in no wise the first, — she was perfectly the last of these; but her beauty had a powerful sympathetic quality, which gained little help from mere superior bearing. She met Mr. Moddle with **the respect of** a hostess and a lady, but she met him as if she had known him always. There was flattery to him in this appearance of having needed no introduction; there was captivity for him in that clear direct way with which she looked into his eyes. The young man felt as if he were altogether comprehended, and blushed as he had not since he rose to read his maiden sermon. The lady's *personnel* was of the most sumptuous blonde type. Her figure and face were those of perfected womanhood,— the contours all roundly moulded, the expressions all speaking of the fulness of life. Her hand and the arm which shone through the gossamer sleeve of her dress were delights of whiteness, rich curve, and dimple. Her eyes were large and of a reddish-hazel, and her hair a golden also touched with red. When her lips spoke, her face was expressive of infinite changes, and played perfect accompaniment to every tone of a wonderfully sweet, low voice.

Mr. Moddle heard her, saw her, and quite forgot what he was going to say. There was really no need of his saying anything, for the involuntary silence of youth is the highest compliment which can be paid to a superb woman; and, moreover, whatever was to be said, Mr. Mansion was quite ready to say for him.

" So," he rattled on, " you'll stay to dinner with us,— that's right. By the way, Pryng and Carmine are both here now, directors in this Ronkus business. They're both members of St. Simon's,—Pryng's a warden. I'll ask them to dinner, too. Board will rise about eight. Sorry to keep you so long, Jane."

" It's of no consequence to me, dear, if Mr. Moddle can excuse the condition the soup will be in by that time."

" Pray, madam, don't speak of it," said Mr. Moddle, wondering if she knew how often they had any soup at all in the seminary refectory, and how easy it would be for Mr. Moddle's utmost idea of a Sybarite to eat kale-brose in company with such a **woman.**

" Very well," said Mr. Mansion, "**I'll return to** the **board. Expect Pryng and Carmine, then, Jane.** Want them to see Mr. Moddle. They want **to see** him themselves, I know. Mr. Moddle, I'll leave you in charge **of** Mrs. Mansion for an hour. Show him **the** new Gérome, my dear."

After Mr. Mansion had gone, Mr. Moddle told Mrs. Mansion that he was glad to have discovered the source of so much happiness as he had received from her music

" And were you there all the time ? " asked the lady, with the same direct look as had first met him, followed by a down-glance of shyness.

" I must ask your pardon for that intrusion upon your privacy."

"**Oh, I was** only playing **to amuse myself, and if I made any one else happier, so much gained. Especially some one to whom I owe a debt of** the same kind. **I** have heard you preach."

Mr. Moddle blushed again. He had become inured to compliments from doctors of divinity, — but this was quite another thing.

" **I** supposed St. Simon's would invite you. I was

glad to hear you had been invited. I am still gladder to find that you have accepted. You'll find everything in your favor, I'm sure "—

Again Mr. Moddle rapidly bethought himself how he should express the fact of his acceptance still being a matter of consultation; but the murmur of that sweet voice had a rhythm which he could not break by saying only such awkward things as immediately occurred to him.

" Many of our principal people have heard you," continued Mrs. Mansion, " and the impression is universally a pleasant one. The Sunday you preached at Grace, I was only sorry Simpson had a cold, for the best music of the pulpit always seems to call for the best in the choir. We have a very good choir at St. Simon's."

"Do you sing as well as play ? " asked Mr. Moddle.

" Just about as well, however that may be. I love music. It is life and air and home and friends to me, and often it appears religion to me, too. Do you ever feel so, Mr. Moddle ? "

" It is, in a sense," replied Mr. Moddle.

" And you love it, I am sure ! "

" I do."

" We shall get on well together," said Mrs. Mansion. " Do you sing ? "

" I have an uncultivated tenor voice. May I hear you sing ? "

" I think we have time for a duet." She looked at the

ormolu clock on the mantel-piece, then went to the door
and listened.

"Yes, it's only half-past seven, and upstairs they
sound as busily engaged as ever. I'm glad you're coming
to be their rector, Mr. Moddle. These men do nothing
now-a-days but stupefy their souls with business. A man
of artistic, devotional tastes is necessary for their salvation. It's positively soothing to think of such an one."
And again she looked him in the eyes with enthusiastic
directness. "What shall we sing?" she continued, going toward the piano.

Mr. Moddle rose and followed her.

"Indeed," said he, "you must remember I have never
made music a scientific study. The utmost I'm adequate to is some simple song of Abt or Mendelssohn."

"Then you certainly know 'I would that my love?'
and here it is."

He was unable to deny that he had sung his part of
the duet. His voice, though untrained, had been much
praised, and was in good condition. That Mrs. Mansion
had found that out, — rather, seemed to know it intui-
tively, — was a pleasant and stimulating fact. He stood
by her side with a feeling of conscious ability to do his
best; and as she began the first sweet movement, his
voice underran and blended in with hers directly. Hers
was a deliciously rich, sympathetic, and flexible mezzo-
soprano, cultivated after Garcia's school, till every note
of it was automatically true, and entirely at her call.
Mr. Moddle could not but know that such a voice was

superior to his own; still she took away from him all possibility of feeling it by flowing into all his deficiencies and draping all his angles, — holding or accelerating for him with such ease, and everywhere chording with him so perfectly, that in a flush of happy pride he wondered how he had never sung so before, seeming to hear but one voice, and that a magnificent one.

"They are coming downstairs," said Mrs. Mansion, rising and shutting the piano upon the dying chords of the duet. "You've really a very fine tenor! I wish we could sing more."

There was a noise of good-evenings and walking-sticks in the hall; presently the front-door was slammed shut, and then the parlor-door opened, letting in Messrs. Mansion, Carmine, and Pryng. As they entered, Mrs. Mansion rang to have dinner served, and it was announced before the introductions were concluded. Though the other guests were his decided seniors, Mr. Moddle was selected to hand his hostess down. Though the honor and the soft white arm which accompanied it were very pleasant to Mr. Moddle, he had an under-sense that they belonged to the already consenting rector of St. Simon's — and was he that? It must be confessed that such questions are very *mal apropos* on a staircase, with a fine woman at your side, her dress not to get under your feet, and dinner, with its banishment of disputable subjects, close imminent. So Mr. Moddle led the way with his hostess, and only remarked to her upon the beauty of her *bouquet de corsage.*

"Did you notice it?" asked Mrs. Mansion, looking over her shoulder at the young man, her lips parting with a gratified smile, which made her quite radiant. "I am fond of wearing flowers; but dear me," — and she tossed her head slightly backward toward the solid business men, — "Mr. Mansion would never know whether I had a japonica or a bavardia here." She put her dimpled hand on her bouquet as she spoke, and plucking out a little sprig of heliotrope, arranged it in his button-hole, asking, as they entered the dining-room, —

"Is it ministerial though, to wear flowers?"

"I believe there are strictarians," replied Mr. Moddle, "who think it too gay."

"Well, this heliotrope should surely be allowed you; you know what it means?"

And once more her beautiful direct eyes looked in his. Mr. Moddle recollected reading in his sister's copy of "The Language of Flowers," that it meant "Devotion;" and, although in that exercise there was nothing for a clergyman to be ashamed of, blushed again.

Mr. Pryng was a dignified man, who affected the voluminous white cravats of the Regency, had a generous red nose, spoke with a husky solemnity, and, but for the large diamond *solitaire* set in his snowy frill, might have pardoned anybody who mistook him for a butler with a bad influenza. Mr. Carmine was a pale, scholarly person, with long white fingers, and no beard but a mustache. Nothing of the successful business man about him but the strong perpendicular wrinkle

8 *

between the cool gray eyes, and with a general look of
being accustomed to spend his up-town hours in a library, getting up costly monographs on the Probable
Locality of the first New York Pump, or preparing
speeches on the Distinguished Unheard-of, for the Historical Society. **Mr.** Mansion was, as we have seen,
what the world calls a driving man, — never late, —
never with a minute to spare ; and, like most people
who travel on high steam, compactly built, somewhat
below the medium size. His large aquiline nose and
his sandy gigot whiskers resembled him a little to the
traditional British type of the East India Major; but
the moment he opened his mouth there was no con-
founding his individuality, — he was the American **Business** Man raised to the highest power.

Each of these men, after his manner, paid **flattering**
deference **to Mr.** Moddle. Speaking of the past as if
he were already in it and had merely poked his head
over his neck-cloth as over some grand chronological
hedge to watch the present age degenerate, Mr. Pryng
compared Mr. Moddle to the lamented Bunscough, who
electrified St. Tabitha with his eloquence when she used
to worship down-town, — " when your father was a boy,
sir," said Mr. Pryng, regarding with compassion a young
man **whose** misfortune had detained him from the world
until it had passed the height of its **season, like strawberries** after the Fourth.

" **Dr. Lumper's library is to be sold,** I hear," said Mr.
Carmine. " It ought to go with the rectory. Said to

be the finest critical and exegetical collection belonging to any theologian in New York."

"Bless me, you don't say so!" exclaimed Mr. **Mansion**, with all the more enthusiasm that he was struggling to acquire some conception what manner of thing this might be.

"I shouldn't wonder if it were so," replied Mr. Car-**mine**.

"**Great** man, Lumper," said Mr. Pryng, solemnly; "always reminded me of the elder Puddon."

"Did you **ever** see your predecessor's library, Mr. Moddle?" asked Mr. Carmine. "Up to the time we lost him — h'm, that's — a year ago this June, — people came from far and near to consult authorities in St. Simon's rectory."

"And a good old man he was," said Mrs. Mansion, — "John, pass the spinach to Mr. Moddle, — only he stayed too much in that same library. A shepherd ought to be more with the lambs. But I've kept Mr. Carmine waiting **for** his answer. Did you ever see the library?"

"I called once on the doctor when I first thought of taking orders. My eye, untutored as it then was, could see that the library must be very valuable; but of course I had no chance to examine it."

"No; I remember you only stayed a few minutes."

Hearing Mrs. Mansion say this, Mr. Moddle looked up at her in astonishment.

"How do I know?" said Mrs. Mansion. "Ask me sometime!"

"You say it's to be sold?" spoke Mr. Mansion; "and it ought to be bought for the rectory."

"*En permanence*," gravely added Mr. Pryng, who had been consul to Nantes under one of the Adamses.

"I'll give a thousand," said Mr. Mansion.

"**So will I,**" said Mr. Carmine.

"And I," added Mr. Pryng.

"Three thousand already!" exclaimed Mrs. Mansion, with a smile, which to Mr. Moddle seemed abundantly worth that amount. "Now, what shall poor I do? I see, — I'll get up a fair."

The three elderly men for a moment looked queer. Perhaps they were thinking whose bank-account would **be drawn on for** the wool which **went** into the afghans, and the springs which gave elasticity to the *priedieux*.

"Jane is doing more than any of us; that's at least two thousand more, my dear," said Mr. Mansion.

"Now for Mr. Moddle; what will *you* give, sir?" asked Mrs. Mansion, smiling straight into the young man's eyes.

What would you or I have done? Was this any time to be talking about the uncertainty of Mr. Moddle's relations with St. Simon's?

"I will preach a **sermon upon Clerical** Libraries," answered **Mr. Moddle, under inspiration** of irresistible enthusiasm; "announcing that a collection will be taken up to swell your private contributions and the proceeds of the fair."

" A very original and well-chosen subject, too," said Mr. Carmine.

" It quite revives my recollections of the elder Bellamy," said Mr. Pryng; " though his wife's grandfather, the celebrated Carter, was even more striking in his selection of strong themes."

"**I think we** may safely call that fifteen hundred more," said Mr. Mansion.

" Why, you come next to me on the contributors' list," said **Mrs.** Mansion.

"That position is everywhere a happiness and **an** honor, madam," answered Mr. Moddle, — the sustained inspiration carrying him into a courtliness which surprised him.

Dessert over, and nothing but the nuts and sherry **left** upon the table, Mrs. Mansion told the gentlemen that she knew they must want their cigars, and that, **when** they had enjoyed them, they would find her in **the** drawing-room. As she **went out, she** bowed playfully toward all the **table.**

" I don't smoke," **said Mr. Moddle.** " So, if you'll excuse me, I believe I'll follow Mrs. Mansion."

" The father of the present venerable Dr. Canaster always regarded smoking as decidedly injurious to the polemic faculties," said Mr. Pryng, with the air of handing down to Mr. Moddle the approval of ancient times.

Mr. Moddle found in the drawing-room abundance to compensate him for the unappreciated luxury of a Cabaña. There were pictures to be looked at and a lovely woman to be sung with or talked to. There was a question to be asked, and Mr. Moddle's curiosity was too great long to delay it.

"Oh, by the way," said Mr. Moddle, in a momentary pause ensuing upon his praise of a delicious little serenade, — the " *Riez! Chantez! Dormez!* " of Gounod, — " by the way, you told me to remind you of something. How did you become aware of my being in Dr. Lumper's library ? "

"The door between the library and the parlor was left open on a crack, and a ladies' sewing-society met that afternoon at the rectory. I sat just opposite the crack, and saw you all the time you were talking with the doctor, — saw and heard you both."

" And do you remember anything we said ? "

" I remember that he was very brusque with reference to some convictions of yours, — inexcusably harsh, considering he had to do with a young convert."

" My views in favor of a more splendid ritual, you mean ? "

" Did you not rather abruptly close the interview on that account ? "

" Really, your memory is astonishing ! "

" It serves me pretty infallibly as a keeper of things and people I like. I casually asked Dr. Lumper the name of the gentleman who had been in his study; and

I gained a pleasure, when I heard whom our people had invited, by not having forgotten it. I agree **very strongly** with you, Mr. Moddle."

As she said this, she frankly put out her hand. **Mr. Moddle** pressed it with apostolic fervor. Mrs. Mansion **continued,** —

"You mustn't expect much sympathy from Mr. **Mansion. Neither he nor Mr.** Carmine nor Mr. Pryng **are of our way of thinking;** though that's of little consequence. **Mr.** Pryng is what you've seen for yourself, — **one of** those men that knew your great-grandfather intimately, and are sorry to find **you** so little like him. Mr. Carmine is a philosopher, and, I suppose, patronizes religion very much as a liberal-minded baker would be friendly with a candy-man. They are both generous men; so is Mr. Mansion. The fundamental lack with all of them is sentiment, — devotion, you know. I'm speaking plainly; but, if I discuss those I know so **well** to — perhaps I ought to say — a comparative stranger " —

"**Oh, no !**" said **Mr. Moddle, giving a** warmer grasp to the frank hand still retained **in** his own.

" It's only because **I want our** new rector to succeed in every respect. There are plenty who do agree with you. With discretion, we can all help each other. So forgive an officious whisper from behind the scenes. Shall we go to look at the conservatory ? "

Mr. Moddle loved flowers, and cheerfully followed his hostess into **a** fine greenhouse, extending the entire width of the house and to the height of the second story. Here, where an exiled banana found room to sprawl its enormous palms, and oranges sighed perfumed longings for their native tropics, beneath a crown of gas-jet brilliants which hung close to a dome of stained glass, they paused to pick mignonette and look at the newest marvel in petunias. Not far from them were the windows of the dining-room, which opened on a level into the conservatory. One of the windows was slightly ajar; and, as Mrs. Mansion was pointing out to Mr. Moddle the marvellous achievement of her gardener in producing a petunia with one red and two mauve spots instead of two red and one mauve, like the last one, both the lady and the minister had their attention irresistibly called to the fact that the gentlemen were not yet through with their **cigars. If** the smoke **of** well-flavored Havanas had **not betrayed** them, their voices would.

As Mr. Pryng helped himself to a final glass of sherry, he observed that he was glad to see Mr. Moddle a young man of such vigorously-correct habits, and something in his manner, — he had been puzzling over the likeness and only just identified it, — which recalled that eminently holy man, the late Mokes.

"A man of very fine, scholarly tastes, too," said **Mr.** Carmine, "which Mokes had not."

"**No, sir,**" replied **Mr.** Pryng; "but **Mokes** had foundation."

"Which I think our **new** rector also has," added Mr.

Mansion. "There was considerable good sense in the prompt way he took up the glove and proposed to preach a sermon. We're well suited, and I'm glad of **it.**"

When Mr. Moddle caught the first words of this conversation, he made a natural, involuntary movement to avoid intrusion on the right of private interpretation as directed at himself; but the lady smiled, put her finger to her lip, and laid a hand detainingly upon his lapel. Thus was he compelled to hear his own praises through.

"You know," said Mrs. Mansion, laughingly, as she led him away from the window, "that it was no fault of yours. You couldn't help obeying your hostess, and you're not responsible for eavesdropping. I couldn't resist making you aware how well they think of you."

The gentlemen now gave signs of rising, and Mr. Moddle went back with Mrs. Mansion to meet them in the drawing-room. We need not linger with them. Their after-dinner conversation was no more instructive than the average of mankind's, and when Mr. Pryng and Mr. Carmine had wished Mr. Moddle a **good-evening, he** recollected that he was to be at Chawsuble's aunt's **by** nine o'clock, and stood up to take leave of his hosts. Each gave him a hand and accompanied him to the door. As he was about going out he suddenly bethought himself.

"Oh !" said he, "I meant to talk over with you the question of that acceptance."

9

"It's of no consequence in the world.. Sproull's office is right across from me in Wall street, and I'll give it to him verbally to-morrow."

" But," — began **Mr. Moddle.**

" Hey ! " exclaimed **Mr.** Mansion, in a loud voice. This ejaculation was addressed to a **driver of the Fifth** avenue line, whose lamps were just coming abreast the house. " Excuse me for seeming to hurry you off," continued he to Mr. Moddle; " but if you've to be at Forty-fifth street by nine o'clock there's your stage."

" Well, good-night," replied Mr. Moddle, converting a momentary pause of irresolution into a hurried plunge down the steps.

II.

AT Chawsuble's aunt's, Mr. Moddle was apportioned a room with her nephew, and kept that young gentleman awake half the night with the light in his eyes,— a grievance all the more galling because he had just come home from the pretty girl's, fully determined to dream about her. When at last Chawsuble got as **impatient** as can be permitted to a divine, Mr. Moddle turned off the bracket, and lay down by his friend's side, but not to sleep till the sparrows were twittering in the silver of first dawn.

He was kept waking, not by light, like Chawsuble, but **by that** contest of mixed **motives** which is like a clash **and** alternation of light with darkness. **Oh that,** as in **old** times, God but once spoke audibly ! **He forgot that** when he **did, the** people **said** it thundered, — that even Samuel thought it was Eli, and Balaam was indisposed to obey it at all. Oh for some one to show the right way !

Before him passed and repassed the imagined form of rough old Binks, working away with his best shoulder under the Lord's " charriat weel " at Muddy Creek, and never abandoning his confidence of some day getting at least a corduroy to heaven **through** that " slew," though the only neighbors he had **to call on either were game-**sters, sots, and bullies, or lived twenty miles away **from** the **court-house, whose** loneliness, according to the Rev. Joseph Bowers, they were inadequate to remedy.

Then his thoughts floated away into a bland twilight, **where zephyrs were** fainting with music and perfume; he heard his own name spoken with admiration by the admirable; beauty and success ministered to him, and he sat in a grand gloom of old books and carved walnut. Nor were his fancies of a mere religious sybarite; he saw the dim yet many-tinted aisles of St. Simon's streaming with hearers, drawn by his solemn reading and his persuasive speech; saw his parish children gath-**ered** in bright attire round him and their Christmas-tree, and heard the low, reverent breathing **of communi-cants to whom his hand should seem** bringing bread **from heaven. He thought of** the poor, for whose sake he should be an organizing centre to all sewing-societies, fairs, and Protestant Sisters of Mercy.

And by which of these pictures was he most allured ? By which ought he to be ? If it was his duty to refuse St. Simon's, how should he explain his silence upon that point at Mr. Mansion's ? In this state of feverish un-certainty, **he fell asleep with the birds' waking. Chaw-**suble, being of a forgiving **disposition, would not** allow him to be called to breakfast. Accordingly, he slept till one o'clock, coming down to lunch with many excuses

for his laziness. After the meal was over, he started
for a walk down-town, to look in at the book-stores, and
call on Mr. Sproull or Mr. Mansion, if possible, with reference to the continued uncertainty of his mind toward
St. Simon's.

If possible! Wherever he dropped in, there were so
many new and interesting things to look over, pub-
lished **since his last visit** to town, that, by the time he
reached Liberty street, the boys were crying " Evening
Post! Third 'shun!" He bought a copy, and began
glancing at it as he continued down Broadway. The
third column on the first page was one of religious intelligence, and one of the first paragraphs that there
met his eye was the following: —

" It is now definitely understood that the Church of
St. Simon Stylites, whose pulpit has for a year been left
vacant by the death of the venerable Dr. Lumper, will
shortly receive, as its rector, Rev. Jonas Moddle, a recent graduate of the Seminary of Saint Elymas, whose
abilities are very **highly** spoken of."

The effect of such a thing upon a man who had never
seen his name in print was like a judge's sentence. People, whose **names have often been** treated by the press
with **hyperbole both of scurrilous** and laudatory com-
ment, **can** probably form no **idea of** the decisive character which a newspaper reference bears to the youthful
and uncalloused mind. There was no philosophizing
past it. The die was cast. Mr. Moddle belonged to St.
Simon's. As a reaction from the first thrill of astonish-

9 *

ment at the Post's notice, came to Mr. Moddle a feeling of strange peace.

"It has been settled for me providentially," mused Mr. Moddle. "I am glad I was not left to my own erring judgment. No doubt the Lord has seen a worthier man for the post of conflict and honor at Muddy Creek. I ought to be very humble when I think of it."

In this frame of devotion, humility, and calmness, Mr. Moddle retraced his steps to Mr. Chawsuble's aunt's. Both aunt and nephew had also read the Post, and their congratulations so overpowered him that he was forced to retire upstairs, and compose himself by writing letters; among others, the declinatory one to Binks. This last was a long one, full of the tenderest sympathy, merely stating that he had already accepted the rectorship of St. Simon's, and closing with an earnest invitation to call on him, should Mr. Binks ever come to New York. As he was sealing the letter, Chawsuble came running up to ask whether Mr. Moddle was going back to the seminary with him on that evening's train, or would stay down longer ? In the latter case, Mr. Chawsuble's aunt would gladly continue to entertain him; in the former, Mr. Chawsuble would suggest that he pack his valise at once.

"I don't think — I don't know — Chawsuble, I believe that if you'll see to having the janitor pack my things, express my books and clothes, and sell my furniture, I wont go back to St. Elymas at all, till after I'm instituted. I hate good-by's; so, say them you ; it doesn't

give the same pang to a proxy. I'll pay a visit there
after I get well started in St. Simon's."

"Well, then, I'll attend to the things for you; but
you'll leave a hole at St. Elymas, — everybody'll feel
sorry. Good-by, if you're sure you wont come along."

"Good-by, Chawsuble; **write me in a day or two.**"

The next day Mr. Sproull called on him, and took him
over to a suite of rooms, which had been specially fitted
up for him. "The rest of the house is all renovated except paper, polish, and fresco," said Mr. Sproull; "so
you wont be disturbed in your study by any din of saws
and hammers. Dr. Lumper's old housekeeper has been
living here to keep the place; she used to be **called a**
good plain cook; she'll take your orders, and, if you
don't like her *cuisine*, why Delmonico's is handy. I believe she has a daughter to wait; but, if not, my wife
will select a good housemaid at the intelligence-office."

Mr. Moddle answered that his tastes were simple and
easily gratified. Mr. Sproull told him that the institution ceremony, if he **were** willing, could take place early
the following week, shook hands with him, and left him
to examine his **rooms.** They **were** furnished with critical elegance **and extreme** luxury **of** form **and color.**
What most immediately possessed his eye was a little
altar of pure white marble, occupying the corner next
his bed, surmounted by a richly carved cross of gold
and ivory, with a long wax taper in Sévres candlestick
on either side, — a vase of flowers, and gorgeous *priedieu*
and altar-cloth of scarlet embroidered with heliotropes,

completing its accessories. Attached to the fresh-cut roses in the vase was a card, on which a woman's pen had written these words only, "To my minister." But the heliotropes showed Mr. Moddle, even better than the roses, whose hand had placed the altar and laid the offering on it.

The institution ceremony was a brilliant success. So **were** the library sermon and the fair. The sermon awakened such a flood of recollections in Mr. Pryng's mind that, wherever he went for a week afterward, it resembled general clearing-up day in a catacomb, whereat bystanders were choked by the mummy-dust of all such greatness as has been embalmed since the day of Jeremy Taylor. Mrs. Mansion's fair, — with beautiful millionairesses for bait, on a back-ground of parti-colored canopy, — was a trap which **sprung itself on many** opulent middle-aged gentlemen of well-pre-served susceptibilities, — never letting them off short of a ten-dollar pen-wiper or a hundred-dollar nightcap, and, in the aggregate, closing on nearly a thousand more than the charming vestry-woman had promised.

The auction was over, and St. Simon's had been the successful bidder for the library. Mr. Moddle was re-arranging it the day after, according to his own private plan of reading, when the house-keeper came to tell him **that an** express-box was waiting for him **in the hall. It proved to be** his St. Elymas books, forwarded to him by Chawsuble. After opening them and carrying a few armfuls into the library, he came to the family Bible which used to lie on his St. Elymas centre-table. His face flushed with pleasure at the return of his old friend.

"Oh," he thought, "if I had only had *you* in Chawsuble's room the night of that struggle, best book, I believe I should have made an oracle of you, as in the many past days when **I** have consulted the *Sortes Biblicæ!*"

He sat down in his dressing-gown at the foot of the stairs, and musingly spread the Bible on his lap. It fell open where Mr. Moddle had deposited his letters on the day of leaving St. Elymas. He put the St. Simon's letter in his pocket, sighed as his eyes fell on sturdy old Binks's crabbed direction, and mechanically glanced **to** the large clear text which underlay them. **It was the** first chapter of Jonah and the third verse:—

"But Jonah rose up to flee unto Tarshish from the presence of the Lord."

Mr. Moddle closed the book, laid his chin upon his palm, and for nearly an hour sat looking steadily away through **the crimson** panes of the hall, then **rose, put the** letters away **tenderly in** his **escritoire, and,** after **dressing himself, went off to dine with** the Mansions.

Mr. Moddle had scarcely got well underway **at St.** Simon's when the summer vacation closed its doors, and left him to refresh himself until mid-September. He had no lack of places to go to; one of his parishioners had a Hudson River country-seat near Hyde Park; another a cottage at Newport; a third cruised about in **his** own yacht with a keen instinct of all the coolest and

nicest spots to land at through the hot months. All
of these admirers and many more would have been glad
of him for a guest. But Mr. and Mrs. Mansion captured him for the season by inviting him to take a trip
with them to London, the Grampians, and Snowdon, as
one of their family. Mr. Moddle had never been abroad,
and the prospect of going under such favorable auspices
might never again be open to him. With some hesita-
tion at accepting such munificent hospitality, he joined
the party, and reached England in time for the Doncas-
ter. He hesitated again when the subject of attending
the races came up; but his good sense showed him the
value of the great national sport, and suggested that in
all probability nobody would be in waiting on the **turf**
to carry back reports of him to Vermont, where he was
born, and where such things were considered horrible.
Accompanying the Mansions, whose barouche went early
enough for a **fine stand, he** was pleasantly surprised to
see Chawsuble cantering up to them on a handsome gray
hack, by the side of a gentleman in cords and tops, with
a cutaway of pearl-gray velvet, and mounted on a gamy
thoroughbred.

"I saw you nearly an hour ago, and couldn't get to
you through the crowd," cried Chawsuble. "My Lord,
— let me present some American friends of mine, — Rev.
Humphrey Lord Davenport, Mr. and Mrs. Mansion, and
the Rev. **Mr.** Moddle of St. Simon's." **The** gentleman
in cords reined his horse and lifted his hat at one side
of the barouche, while Chawsuble rode round to the

other and shook hands with the occupants. The earl
was an elegant, though most pronouncedly British man
of about forty, and the first peer who had ever enjoyed
the honor of a personal introduction either **to Mrs. Mansion** or her accompanying fellow-citizens. He seemed
captivated at once by the American delicacy of Mrs.
Mansion's beauty, and immediately entered into a conversation with herself **and husband,** which absorbed
them so thoroughly that Mr. Moddle and his friend were
able to have a familiar talk, *sotto voce*, without any appearance of discourtesy. Mr. Moddle learned that Lord
Davenport was one of the richest noblemen in England;
that Mr. Chawsuble had crossed on the same steamer,
and become acquainted with him through having read
the service one Sunday in the cabin; that the earl was a
most enthusiastic churchman, and before the death of
his elder brother, had taken orders; that he still offi-
ciated daily in the chapel of his castle in Foxshire; that
he made the highest church speeches in Parliament, and
rode closest **to the** hounds, of any peer in the realm.
Chawsuble **further mentioned, as a point by no** means
inconsistent with his eminent personal excellence, that
he had invited **him to go down with** him at the end of
the session and stay a month. On their return to town
the gentlemen exchanged cards, and Mrs. Mansion invited the two horsemen to call where her party were
stopping in Russell Square. The invitation was no less
promptly availed of than accepted, and during the remainder **of** their stay in London there were many inter-

changes of courtesy between Lord Davenport and his
new acquaintances. Chawsuble frankly acknowledged
that he was uncertain whether he should return to America or not. He had only come across for a vacation
tour, but was so charmed with some of the men he had
fallen in with that he didn't know but he should stay and
take whatever place they might find for him. Wouldn't
they like to go with him to St. Mary Magdalen's next
Sunday morning? This invitation, having been accepted,
was followed by visits to Saints Albans, Barnabas, and
George in the East. The five Sundays spent in London,
before and after the trip to Wales, were devoted to a
very thorough study of that grand Ritual Movement
which reappears in England about the time of the meteoric shower, lasts somewhat longer, and possesses nearly
as much influence over the practical British mind. Mr.
Mansion, at first, could make neither head nor tail of
much that he saw. He clouded his wife's beauty with
pensive reproach for an entire afternoon by asking Chawsuble who was that fat man with so much red on his pet-
ticoat, and comparing the intoning to Shakers. When
the officiating clergymen crossed themselves, his face assumed a look which quite reminded Mrs. Mansion of
Mephistopheles in presence of the same sign, and she
had to tell him so before he could be overawed into not
making himself conspicuous to the congregation. A few
weeks' association with Lord Davenport greatly molli
fied his manners. Not only was the earl a generous,
whole-souled fellow, but a very capable one, — had worn

off by travel that almost Chinese ignorance of the rest
of the world which belongs to the native Englishman, —
was competent to talk with Mr. Mansion about American finance in a clear, sensible, and captivating way, —
and was a peer. If even Thackeray could confess joints
where his anti-snob harness was vulnerable by such a
personage, let us confess it **for Mr.** Mansion, as doubtless he would not for himself. Before he left London,
Mr. Mansion found himself not only taking St. Mary
Magdalen's quite calmly, but even feeling a lively interest in the proposition originating with his wife, **that a**
choir of parish children should be added to **their** quar-
tette when they got back to St. Simon's, and that these
children should be trained and surpliced like those then
before them. Through Chawsuble's and the earl's
introductions, Mr. Moddle was several times invited to
assist both at the chancel and in the pulpit. He ac-
quitted himself in a manner which made the Mansions
glow with a pleasant sense of proprietorship in him, and
got his eloquence referred to by the London correspond-
ent of the Herald. **Thrown constantly in** the companionship **of the** men whom Chawsuble had found so
charming, and prompted at every step by beauty and
enthusiasm in the very house where he lived, his sus-
ceptible nature went fluently into the new moulds, and
he returned to New York with ten copies of Keble's
Christian Year in his trunk, presented by ten several
and particular friends, and an advancement of thought
upon the sanctity of stoles and candles, compared with

which the **state in which** he left America was as one burner to **the full-orbed** chandelier.

To Mrs. Mansion Mr. Moddle owed **all** the tact by which **innovations** — or, **as they said,** restorations — **were to be introduced into** the **worship** of St. Simon's. **It is but just to him to say that he fully** realized this **fact and felt** abundantly grateful for it. **He was wrapt in admiration of that** quality of hers which in unsancti- fied **matters is called** finesse. How would his clumsy man's **hand have** managed with those **parish** children ? He confessed **to himself that** he **should** probably have poked them **all at once** in their surplices into the chancel, to have excited the jealousy and suspicion of every **im-** practicable **low** churchman **in** the **parish.** But **how** adroitly *she* began by enlisting the parents who populated the **Sunday school to join** her in a plan for having their **children taught sacred music upon two week-**day after- **noons ; and how skilfully she got one** after another of **the babies into a chorister's** gown, first **as** a reward of **merit, then on** the plea of uniformity ! What a pretty little Christmas entertainment and what a pretty little enthusiasm she got up, when they all sang carols in snowy lawn, — affecting Mr. Pryng to that degree that he shed tears, and, being unable to recollect anything **at** the time he came **on earth** which they **reminded him of,** finally fell **back upon "** cherubim " ! How wonderful also was it to see Mr. Carmine rising to express his de- light at the festival, and **proposing the** very thing most **at Mrs.** Mansion's heart, though she had never given him a hint of it in words, that this lovely choir be **promoted** to a place in the chancel and take part in the services of the church !

To Mrs. Mansion was due all the praise of that ingenuity which first presented several square feet of Salviati's handsomest work **in** mosaics **to** the church, and then had it **inserted in** the ecclesiastical East **as a** brilliant illustration to the creed and the commandments, **thus** making a background against which **the subsequent rich** altar-cloth and vivid bouquets did not stand **in** such **startling** contrast **to** stumble weak believers, **as** they would have done against the plain old panelling **of** cream and gilt. These are but a few of the instances in which that able and devoted young apostle, Mr. Moddle, was mainly succored and entirely steered by the beautiful diplomatist, who had such an influence over **men** because she comprehended them. He felt, as most men enjoying such aid and direction would have felt, something very like worship for the giver. Her presence **was a** pleasant spell ; **she lighted him always like a** lamp **of success ; she was so womanly that she could be** admired to **the full** without **the** sentiment degenerating into awe, though **her** perception of **an** end and the ways to it, her wise yet dauntless manner of pursuing those ways, might have got that poorer grade of applause, if witnessed in a man and a general.

When the Lenten humiliation succeeded the festivities of Christmas, Mr. Moddle preached his celebrated Ash-Wednesday **sermon, upon** the text, "Confess ye your sins," and concluded by inviting any sheep of his fold, whose minds, at this penitential season, were burdened with the memory of transgression, to come and talk with their true and loving shepherd in the rectory of St. Simon's. His invitation was accepted by half a dozen during the first week in Lent ; one of them a gentleman who had defrauded the revenue department; the others, people who lived unhappily in their families, and more because they desired a confidant than because they felt themselves to blame, came to let their sorrows gush into the bosom of their pastor. What with daily morning and evening prayers, two sermons on Sunday, and the Wednesday and Friday evening lectures, Mr. Moddle had his time so occupied that other burdened souls called and missed him. To meet the cases of all and economize his own leisure, Mr. Moddle, during the remaining week, set apart a couple of hours on Tuesday and Saturday afternoons, and announced from the altar that he would meet the burdened then.

At the outset he had no idea of the training which he was preparing for himself, — a training of revelation, astonishment, and consternation. As his penitential sessions became better attended, he had a hard fight not to become sceptical regarding the existence of any genuine goodness in the world at all. So many wives and husbands, who to mankind seemed models of conjugal felicity in the light of Mr. Moddle's better information became haggard wretches with aching hearts, sitting hard on nature's safety-valves for the sake of society, and tremulously expecting their rust-eaten relation to explode beneath them. So many respectable families contained one irreclaimable drunkard, and some of those drunkards were women. Such scandals of dishonesty, hushed up on 'Change, came to Mr. Moddle's ear from the lips of their socially unblemished perpetrators, that the Scriptures seemed reversed ; what was only whispered in the market-place was proclaimed in his closet. Large need that closet be which invites any average body of people to unpack in it the skeletons from their own ! Mr. Moddle seemed to have been suddenly taken round upon the wrong side of the pattern of creation. Sometimes his brain almost reeled as he asked himself whether all the beauty of the universe were only skin-deep. This private dejection, modified by the necessities of the pulpit, became a public pensiveness which sat well upon the youthful divine, and caused the pathos of his sermons to be much remarked upon. All this was well enough during Lent, but whence was he to expect his Easter inspirations ?

The last Saturday of the mournful season came, and with it a succession of the burdened. A number of ladies visited the rectory for the fourth time, — having experienced such relief of mind from their earlier confidences that they fell into the way of clearing their consciences at shorter periods, so as to keep their average burden habitually bearable. This arrangement redounded less to economy of time than the sanguine might have supposed, for although the burden which had

10 *

to be unpacked at any one time was not so great as it would have been if left longer, it consisted of much smaller minutiæ, and Mr. Moddle had frequently to restore peace of mind to lambs of his fold who had forgotten to cross themselves in the creed because they were thinking of their next neighbor's Cashmere.

He had dismissed several such cases of conscience with the absolution which the church understands to belong to people being penitent, and had become slightly weary, when a light tap on the door of the rectory study announced Mrs. Mansion. Her very presence was a sort of rest to him. Her voice was so soft, her expression so appreciative, her beauty something so exquisite to dwell on.

"Ah me!" thought Mr. Moddle: "it is I who ought to confess to that calm, all powerful loveliness, — not that to me! To me, — me, getting worldly and sceptical! Ah, if she knew! How do you do, Mrs. Mansion?"

The last sentence he spoke aloud, rising from his study-chair to meet the lady with a cordial hand.

The thought escaped her as little as the speech. Though she did not doubt his cordiality, she saw that his good spirits were assumed.

"You are not feeling well to-day," she said, anxiously.

"Only a little tired, that's all," replied Mr. Moddle, cheerily, sitting down by her side upon the sofa.

"You look so sad, lately. The other night some one remarked it at our house, and Mr. Pryng highly commended you, saying that by good rights a churchman should always be sorrowful at this season. I thought, but I did not say, that the man in you seemed to be sorrowing no less than the churchman. You know who your friends are, and where to come in any personal trial. Are you — ill, Mr. Moddle? Why wont you see Dr. Bayard? Let me give you a note to him."

"Oh, no! You're very kind, but I'm not ill, and as to knowing my friends, how could I ever forget them? How is Mr. Mansion?"

"As well as usual, thank you. By the way, he was the very person who remarked on your sadness. After the visitors were gone, he told me he thought he understood it, — you were in love; and he asked me if I supposed the young lady was Miss Brooks."

"What did you tell him?" exclaimed Mr. Moddle, crimsoning to the temple.

"That I had never esteemed myself worthy enough of being your confidante to ask the question."

"I give you full leave to state that there is nothing in the idea, whatever. Miss Brooks is a sweet girl, but neither of us ever dreamed of marrying the other."

"I wish only that I knew enough of what troubles you to help it somehow," said Mrs. Mansion, looking with eyes of womanly anxiety into her minister's youthful and fair, but weary face.

"It's no secret from you," said the young man, gratefully. "It's only those mental conflicts through which we must all pass sometimes. The Practical and the

Ideal must have a stand-up fight in everybody's nature, I suppose, at least, once a fortnight."

"Conflicts?" she answered. "You are too tired to talk of such things. I wont weary you with mine. You have surely won from all my sex your respite for the remainder of the afternoon."

She arose and brought a cushion from the arm-chair across the room, which she quietly tucked behind his shoulders, with the air of one who did no service.

"There! rest now; and let us talk of something soothing. Do you know the children have their Easter hymns beautifully; and apropos of the season, here's a little basket of trailing arbutus which I selected for you from a box sent me by cousins in Chemung."

The subtle, dreamy fragrance of the lovely pink and white buds, which Mrs. Mansion drew from her muff, seemed even more expressive of herself than the heliotrope. When he thanked her for them he looked her in the face, and could not help thinking that its loveliness was more like that of some marvellous vision than any common thing on earth. He would not let her plead his weariness for him. What sorrowed her? He clasped her by both hands, and, with the frank enthusiasm of youth, begged her to open her heart to him.

"I am not weary when I can help you," he said. "To whom should the lamb flee save to the shepherd?"

"May one be pardoned and retain the offence?" asked Mrs. Mansion, gazing into his face with a sadness which spoke more than his youth could know. "I must confess more than common penitents. I must confess that I am *impenitent*. If I sin, I love **my sin.** It may be a dreadful thing to say; but **I do !** oh, **I do !**" repeated Mrs. Mansion, in that intensest **of feminine emphases**, a low voice.

She bowed her head **on her hand;** but it fell on Mr. Moddle's shoulder as gently **as if** she had been **a** child.

"**The Scriptures and the church both represent** life as a terrible struggle," continued he, soothingly. **She** had put her handkerchief to her eyes, and he knew that **she** was weeping, though she **did not sob aloud.** "I **know** that in times of temptation it is **often hard to say which** side we stand on, — Good or Evil, — but"—

"And do *you* ever have any temptations?" **asked she,** looking up into his face with tender amazement. "**You** so good and lovely, — so like one's ideal of the beloved John?"

"Don't say so," said the minister, sadly. "I am a man, —**that** means doubt and weakness. But we always have **this sure** sign, I think, **of our** condition. **We** know we have passed **from death unto life if we love the brethren.** Now, **do you not find** encouragement in **the ardor with** which you love the church, and **work for** it?"

"What if I **had found my idol in** the church?" said she.

"In the church?"

"*In its rector*," she answered.

Her bonnet had fallen upon her neck. Her hair on **one side** becoming unfastened fell across his knee, turned into a shower of burning gold by the beam of setting sunlight which fell aslant through the windows of the rectory. To the young man's bewildered gaze she looked like an Angel of Annunciation out of some dream of Titian.

He gently laid his hand upon her shoulder and drew her face toward his.

"Sweet, wise, beautiful counsellor and comfort!" spoke he, "what shall I say to you?"

Again she lifted her sweet eyes to his, and, drawing down his lips to hers, kissed them.

"You have made me," she said, faintly. "You would have me confess." And she did not take away her face.

A tap on the study-door brought Mr. Moddle to his feet.

Answering it, he found only Mr. Binks, of Muddy Creek, who had been shown the way by the servant; then left to announce himself as standing there in acceptance of Mr. Moddle's former invitation.

Only holding parley with him as long as it took Mrs. Mansion to walk away from the sofa to the farther window, Mr. Moddle was obliged to introduce him into the study. Few people who looked at old Binks could have proposed holding interviews with him in an entry. He was not much of an ante-room subject, wasn't old Binks.

Clad in a suit of butternut homespun, unusually fine in texture and modestly dark in shade, holding in one hand not the slouch indigenous to his section, but a beaver which had graced all his complimentary occasions since the Harrison campaign, and in the other **a** glove three sizes too large for him, which he now **and** then made furtive pretence of wearing, by inserting in it, experimentally, a finger at a time, — this was the outer rind of Mr. **Binks.**

The **next was a vigorous** and sinewy body, slightly stooped by life's work; a finely-shaped head large about the crown, — the temples and the back covered with thick grizzled hair, worn long; a mustache whose gray was still broadly lined with flaxen; a pair of eyes singularly kind and honest, but **wondrously** mobile **and** penetrating; a prominent Roman nose, **a** strong jaw, but a mouth, which, when it spoke, revealed teeth as white and smile as winning as a little child's.

As to the inmost core of Binks — but to Heaven alone belongs the judgment of all true, loyal, manly fellows !

The entirety of these impressions put out his hand **frankly to** Mr. Moddle; and as the clear, pleasant eyes met his, the young minister somehow felt refreshed as if a cool wind blew on him.

As he stood explaining who he was, Mr. Binks's blue eyes glanced past the door at Mrs. Mansion. He put the Harrisonian beaver to his breast, and, bowing with the grace of a cavalier, said, —

" No, — I beg pardon, — I wouldn't think, raly, of interrupting you if ye're having a private conversation."

Mr. Moddle looked toward Mrs. Mansion, but she

studiously gazed out of the window into the ivy on the walls.

"Mrs. Mansion," spoke Mr. Moddle, hesitating, "may I introduce to you an old friend and correspondent of mine, Mr. Robert Binks, of — of Missouri?"

She turned quickly from the window, and, repressing an indescribable look of grief and scorn, became wholly the self-controlled woman, as she bowed to Mr. Binks **with the gracious** sweetness **of** some popularly beloved duchess, and welcomed him by saying that to meet any friend of Mr. Moddle's was always a delight to **those** who had been his oldest and truest friends in St. Simon's. She talked with him long enough about himself and his journey to make any man feel at ease in the presence **of** a splendid woman, and pave the way for excusing her-**self without seeming to have** suffered **an** interruption. **Then she looked up charmingly at Mr.** Moddle, and said, **"I believe I've said all I can say;** if I stay longer, I shall be late at dinner. Come to see us with Mr. Moddle, Mr. Binks. Good-afternoon, gentlemen."

Mr. Binks took a seat, while Mr. Moddle saw Mrs. Mansion to the door. He followed her silently down-stairs. At its foot she turned round, laid her head upon his bosom, and looked imploringly into his face.

"**O my own — my** beautiful Saint John!" — she spoke **in a** tremulous **whisper, — "you are my worship,** my priest! Can you **not speak peace to me?"**

Again her soft arms drew down **his** neck, and he answered, as out of a mist, "God be merciful to us sinners!"

"Can he be merciful to you, and not have pity on *me*?" she moaned, **with** her lips pressed against his cheek, clasping him fiercely as despair, yet passionately as possession.

He seemed to be dreaming **her into his** life, when a soft piping from **above** revealed that **Mr. Binks had found** the parlor **organ,** and was practising, **to the** tune of "Mornington," **the confirmation hymn,** "Soldiers of Christ, arise!"

Mr. Moddle passed his hand over his eyes like **one** just waking. He turned the knob; he clasped the beautiful **wrist** resting on his shoulder, and made **entreaty** toward the **open door.**

"Go!" He spoke hurriedly, not daring **to risk his** eyes with her own. "Quick — for God's sake — while I feel so!"

She read his face, and, dropping her veil, passed quietly out of the rectory.

Mr. Moddle, having stood for several minutes to **compose his breath which was like that of a** man who has overrun himself, returned **upstairs.**

"As you see, I've taken the freedom of trying your melodeon," said Mr. Binks. "My daughter plays ours at home and **in the** church; and sometimes, with the latter, in bad weather, I spell her a leetle. Powerful fine instrument this! How she speaks! But I don't rightly understand those square sorter par'sol handles, that shove in 'n out to both sides of the key-board. You're not feeling in very good health, I'm afeard, sir," added Mr. Binks, with a look of kindly solicitude in his eyes, and a frank clasp of the young man's feverish hand.

"No; I'm a little overworked, Mr. Binks."

"And not enough **in the open air,**" said **Mr. Binks.** "Ah, that's bad! If you could only run out for a vacation with me, now. It isn't to the end o' deer-hunting **yet,** and you kin call pe-rairie hens *prime.* What with that and rabbits and other small game, we could keep **you in** all the exercise you wanted till **July.** Then you could go out into the buffalo region as far as White Rock Creek in Kansas, where I'm a goin' myself, having some lands to locate, Lord willin'. You look as if it'd do you good; but, situated as *you* are," said Mr. Binks, glancing around the gorgeous library with honest admiration, "I suppose the idee's impossible."

A sudden inspiration flashed upon **Mr.** Moddle, and he answered, —

"**Not so** impossible, perhaps, as you think."

"No?" said Mr. Binks. "It does me good, right smart, to hear ye say so! I'd like to have you a kinder survey that field. My heart's somehow sot on that idee. Even while you stayed rector here, you could help us all the better for havin' seen us and known us. You'd be right in the way of all the fust sort of young men as went into the ministry, and, when a good man **for** us came along,—as you might judge by havin' **taken our** measure, — why, you **could ask him to come and** look at us, too, my dear sir. We're in fearful need of a first-class man at Muddy," — Mr. Binks waxed warm with enthusiasm, and wiped his brow with a soft, large bandanna,—" in fearful need, Mr. Moddle; and it's in my heart to believe the Lord's a-goin' to send him ! "

Mr. Moddle sat for a few moments silently by **his** guest's side upon the sofa. Must he go away ? **Must** he *not* go away ? Was he safe in St. Simon's church ? Was St. Simon's church safe with him in it ? He bethought himself of his old questionings at Chawsuble's aunt's; his mind **by association reverted** to the "*Sortes Biblicæ;*" and, glancing up, he beheld the old family Bible **lying on** his stand. Half-ashamed, as of leaning to the **weakness of** necromancy, yet in desperate stress as to his future course, he arose and opened this **great** volume for the first time since the commencement of Lenten exercises. Again its leaves parted where Binks's letter was left, and again had the Rev. Jonas Moddle to read from the prophecy of his namesake.

These were the passages which his eye fell on,—

" But the Lord sent out a great wind into the sea, and there was a mighty tempest in the sea, so that the ship was like to **be broken."**

Then, just across into the **parallel column,—**

" **So they took up Jonah, and cast him forth** into the sea, and the sea ceased from her raging."

Mr. Moddle, almost foundered in his tempest, looked up from the text at his guest.

" Have you still no minister, Mr. Binks ? "

" We air as we weer," said the old Missourian, sadly.

" Mr. Binks, if your invitation still holds good, I *will*

go out as you say, to give a kind of survey to your field. Mr. Binks, in confidence, I confess to you that I'm not sure but my acceptance of this rectorship was altogether wrong. I mean to resign here. I will go with you if you want me."

"My dear sir, do you think how much you're promisin'?" exclaimed Mr. Binks, with honest astonishment.

"I have thought of everything, Mr. Binks. I have weighed self and others, and found the difference between these two objects of living as great as that between the death and the life of the soul."

"It was thoughts like them which warmed my heart, the day I writ of, when I heerd you in the white church," said the old man, sympathetically.

"I have concluded upon my course without taking guidance of any lamp but duty. I will go with you, Mr. Binks."

"Well, sir, I see ye're solemn earnest, and I mayn't dispute your view of duty, but my conscience wont be quit," said Mr. Binks, looking around the beautiful room, with those same honest eyes which had ever scorned to depreciate his seller's animal in the horse-market. "My conscience wont be quit, not unless I say, this here is a powerful sight to leave!"

"I realize its attraction perfectly, and I am willing to give it all up for the right I see."

"Well, then, God bless you, Reverend Jonas Moddle! I'll never keep you to your promise, mind, — for men don't want bonds in the Lord's work, — but if you *do*

hold to it, on conseedering, I'll be unto your side as was
Hur unto Moses, and prop your elbows from sun-up to
sun-down ! "

For a few moments the two stood clasping hands
silently; then Mr. Moddle said, —

" You were talking about exercise. You'll stay and
dine with me, of course. Would you like to take a little
walk with me before ? If you're not tired — I've not
been out to-day."

" Tired ? " said Mr. Binks, as if he indistinctly remembered to have heard the word, and were trying to asso-
ciate it with some idea. " Come ahead ! I don't feel as
if I'd been out-doors for a week. I was up from the
Astor house to Union square a few times to-day ; but
bless me, that isn't gettin' out of the house ! It's houses
everywhere — it's bein' in the house multiplied by five
miles long. I'd walk smart if I could get to a little
easy breathin' distance out o' sight o' fences. I'll go
where you like, and we can talk as we go."

Mr. Moddle put on his hat and overcoat, with the
intention of going to his own surgeon, for an examina-
tion and a certificate, stating that his nervous system
seemed too exhausted to permit of his sustaining longer
such responsibilities and labors as were incumbent upon
the Rector of St. Simon's.

But after he should have enclosed this with his resignation, the vestry would be entitled to at least a week's
notice, and during the time he must stay in the rectory,
and be accessible as the official head of St. Simon's.

How should he meet the torrent of remonstrances, the questioning letters, the calls of astonishment, the whole battery of subtler influences **which** in that period would surely be brought to bear against **him ?**

Pondering the inextricable, inexplicable problem of his fate, Mr. Moddle made rather a silent companion, as he walked arm-in-arm with Mr. Binks up Madison avenue, ever and anon returning to himself to make suggestions or answer questions as to houses and **their** occupants.

" Who lives there ? " said Mr. Binks, pointing to what the newspapers call a brown stone palace, on the corner above.

" That's the house of Mrs. Duverney, a **widow of** wealth, who has two children, a daughter **and a son.** Both the ladies have been devoted attendants on my ministrations, **but the young man** is bitterly prejudiced. He has fought both his mother and his sister upon every act of kindness shown me. I was told by a lady friend that he had openly vilified me in society, accused me of being a Jesuit, and charged me with every scandal of the confessional."

" What did you do when you heard that ? "

" I went on my way. The young man is not worth **noticing; he is** a wild, maniacal fellow, of uncontrollable passions, but most generally drunk, **which seems, in his** case, to act as a sedative. I believe he is coming down the steps now. Yes, and drunk as usual. I'm sorry for them all to see him go on so, for there's lunacy in the family."

The street-light fell on Mr. Moddle's face and that of the person coming down the steps just as they both reached their foot. The young man gave an ugly look, and stumbled against Mr. Moddle, partly from surprise, partly of intention.

"You're the soft-handed fellow," broke forth the offender, in a hoarse, uncertain voice, "who plays old woman in gowns and petticoats behind the chancel, to make the young women take you for what you look, **and unpack their gossip in the** study to you — Holy Father!"

The intense insult of the tone with which he spoke the last words was followed by no **immediate** violence **of ac**tion. Mr. Moddle was for stopping to return stern denial, but Mr. Binks persuaded him on by reminding that the wise man never struck a drunken man or argued with a fool.

Mr. Duverney's impetus carried him nearly across the sidewalk, but he recovered himself with an "ugh" of befuddled perplexity, and began following, semi-consciously, the direction taken by the rector.

The two walked quite briskly, and for a while kept widening **the** distance between them **and** Mr. Duverney. Before five blocks were passed, however, that gentleman, brooding on his grudge against the world that had produced a Moddle and laid sidewalks zigzag, had become still drunker than when he sallied forth; so that in fact he found himself obliged to run, in order that he might maintain impetus enough to keep him perpendicular

This rate of motion soon brought him up rapidly to Mr. Moddle. As the latter, hearing him, drew out from the wall to let him pass, Duverney's eye again caught him, and another spasm of hatred concentrated all his force into his heavy cane, which he brought on the back of Mr. Moddle's head with his entire force as he rushed by. The young rector fell senseless into Mr. Binks's arms, and no policeman being within reach until the old man had tenderly disposed of that burden, the drunken bully escaped.

Mr. Binks stopped the first passer, and sent him for a carriage, in which he at once took Mr. Moddle back to the rectory.

Mr. Moddle's experience was almost painless. It began with a dull sound, and a coruscation of the entire surrounding atmosphere; this was followed by blank darkness. Now and then the darkness would part for an interval whose length he could not measure, and the faces of the Mansions, with various members of his flock besides, would peer at him out of a mist whose invariable background was the kind, honest face of old Binks. Then came a period of confused dreams,—of strange masses forever changing as to their outward form, but inwardly always cavernous, and immuring in their silent vastness Mr. Moddle himself. At last there came a fissure in the immeasurable blank; the beam of glad white light that slanted in slowly broadened; he reached forward to it; he struggled, and, with a great throe, blackness and death brought him forth into

life and the sun. He tried to lift his head, for he half
saw Binks reading by his table; but he could only
manage to give a little cry, like a waking baby. Binks
rose and came to him noiselessly, but with features **that**
could not repress their delight.

"**Thank God!**" said Binks, in a low voice. "Thank
him! I'm always havin' to thank him for something,
and I do thank him now."

When he was able to hear it, Mr. Moddle learned that
Mr. Binks had been watching by **his** bedside for six
weeks; **that he** himself had suffered brain fever from
concussion, although the skull was not **fractured ; and**
that there had been times **when the doctor considered it**
very uncertain whether he would pull through.

One of the first recollections which flashed upon him,
on his return to consciousness, was his struggle upon
the question of St. Simon's rectorship, — how to give
that up, without bringing down upon him such a demand for his inmost reasons as he could not, would not
answer; and how, not answering, to preserve intact his
reputation for strength of character, reasonableness, and
**probity. Somehow, in his weakness, this question did
not seem to trouble him as much as it normally should,
when he asked Binks, faintly,** —

" What is there left for me to do now ?"

"My dear boy !" said Binks, tenderly, sinking the
professional, and falling back on the human relation,
" you've nothing to bother ye now ! Just get well,
d'ye see ! You attend to that, and everything'll fall in
straight afterward."

"Did you tell them who did it?"

"I told 'em no such thing; for I heerd you say **the matter** was delicate. **If you** hadn't pulled through, I suppose I'd have had **to tell** 'em. But you did pull **through, d'ye see,** and so they left it at "**rowdies.**" I never see a horse that I couldn't tell anywhere if I see him ag'in; and I suppose I could tell that man Duverney; **but I** didn't want to make that row, d'ye see? Now you've identified yourself ag'in, so to speak, — got your hand right onto yerself, so you know where it is, and I reckon there wont be no need o' no other identi-fyin'. And *i-den-ti-fyin'* " (Mr. Binks made a solemn pause between his syllables to indicate the weightiness of **the act)** "**is a** right mean and sorrowful business. I done it once, when Judge Lynch sot on a bushwhacker, and I'd rather give my best gain-twist than do **it** ag'in; **for hangin' and** sich goes ag'in me smart!"

The rector clasped his wan hands, and thanked God that the ship of St. Simon's had not, through his being in **it,** foundered under the scandal which he feared.

"Can I go with you, Binks?" he added, after a few moments, in the plaintive voice of a little lost child asking to be taken home.

"That you can, **certain,**" replied Binks. "This isn't the time to hold ye to nothin'; and when ye feel better, **ye'll** remember I said how it wasn't in me **to hold ye. But if you care to go** out to Muddy along'ith me, **why** we kin hev a vacation, and **git** all right, an' see what we'll do next. There's nothin' to stop ye; ye're not *corrélled* anywhere, my dear boy!"

" But what will *they* think ? "

" They've heerd you. You don't remember, I suppose, how many times you've said you couldn't stay here; you must get right up and go to Missouri. **Mr.** and Mrs. Mansion heerd it. **There was** a large gentleman in, with a reg'ler towel round his neck, who heerd it, and said it reminded him of Paul and the Macedonian cry. **Then there was others** that heerd it. But you **told Mrs.** Mansion and me plain one night that you done wrong in coming to St. Simon's, and was a-goin' to Muddy **right** as soon as ye got up on elbow. We knew that was on'y dreamin', and didn't count nothin' **on it,** my dear boy; but it's left so you kin do anythin' you're a mind to."

" I'm glad you didn't tell them about Duverney."

" Well, I like to go easy where I do'no my way."

" You remember my reading Jonah to you ? It's almost — ah ! — last thing *I* remember. Do you know, 'tseems to me that I could not only forgive, but thank **Duverney ?** "

" **Well, I do'no. I reckon I could** forgive him, at a **pinch, but I'm** afeard **it'd** come hefty **on me, not a** kinder to **relieve Adam, if I saw him, by** takin' a crack at him."

" No, **Binks,** don't even feel *that* way. I spoke of reading Jonah, because, d'ye know, it seems to me (I **may be** light-headed from so much sickness) as if I **were** Jonah, and Duverney were the whale ? He **bolted me right** into darkness. But how should I ever have got away from St. Simon's, if it hadn't been for him? And I *must* get away from St. Simon's."

Old Binks smoothed down the young man's soft, brown hair, and hushed him, for a moment, as he would his own child, then said, soothingly, —

"Well, you shall git away; and there wont be no blame, neither. I heerd the Mansions talk together, — cryin' as they spoke, — and say as how they'd put too much anxiety and labor on the shoulders of a young man of devoted piety and noble genius. The words which they used was these," said Mr. Binks, pausing to see if he had stated the expression at once with becoming force and literalness.

"Then," continued Mr. Binks, "you told 'em to stop cryin'."

"It seems to me I remember something like that," said Mr. Moddle, mistily.

"And they answered you that they'd help you to do whatever you thought right; and they both stooped down and kissed you."

"Mr. Mansion, too?"

"Him too," said Mr. Binks, gravely.

"It seems to me I remember that now," replied Mr. Moddle, smiling faintly for the first time since he recovered his consciousness.

He was quietly nursed, and, by his physician's order, little visited for another week in his bedroom at the rectory. Then he quietly went off by boat, one evening, with Binks alone; and the envelope, which enclosed the doctor's certificate and resignation, to be handed by Mr. Mansion, *in propria forma*, to an already informally advised vestry, **was** postmarked Muddy Creek.

In Mr. Moddle's **after life Duverney** was seldom referred **to** between **himself and Mr. Binks.** But, **when** his mention was **necessary, he** was always spoken **of** smilingly, **and** as " the Whale."

12

III.

The Parish of Muddy Creek was all that fancy painted
it.   Nor was there an atom of surcharged color in the
brush of the Rev. Joseph Bowers.   Piety, like the fruit-
ful vine, did not thrive well on first-bottom land, though,
morally speaking, a looser soil was difficult to find. Back
on the bluffs, and the high-rolling prairie, Mr. Moddle
came now and then upon some untended and untrellised
saint, whose rich clusters of goodness were none the less
refreshing that they grew on a seedling stock instead of a
layer from some old ecclesiastical vineyard, — a stock
which had lost no individuality by cutting and tying to
anybody's stake.

Mr. Moddle's parish, from Muddy to Plum Creek and
Old Woman's Ranche to Pea-Soup Flats, was an area
of about twenty miles square. All hunting up the stray
sheep of his corral had to be done, like his neighbors',
in the saddle. The frame of mind in which Mr. Moddle,
as to the natural man, regarded that animal, the horse,
was, like that of most men trained in schools of abstruse
theologic study, a reminiscence of that terrible beast in
the psalms, who must be held in with bit and bridle lest
he come nigh unto thee.   Let us not dwell upon the discipline by which he was converted from this view, — the

lameness of leg, the stitches in side, the aërial vaultings,
owing to a dim conception that his animal might be ten
feet high, by which the new rector of Muddy, like ambition, o'erleaped his selle, and came down on the other
side. He had never in his life before known what it
was to be laughed at. Of that cheap, but unattractive,
novelty he now had overmuch. As he rode — often,
properly speaking, as his beast bore him captive —
through that yellow quagmire flanked by straggling,
dingy houses, which constituted the Muddy settlement's
sole claim to a street, derisive greetings daily met his
efforts to learn that noble art whose graces witch the
world. At the court-house corner, **at** the door of the
rum-and-poker den, the store, the justice's of the peace,
he was asked if his knees never knocked his teeth out,
and why he did not hitch a crank to his elbows, and let
himself out for a horse-power, with numerous other
questions of that nature, which Artemus* characterizes as
"suttle goakin." Still he pluckily stuck to his training,
and, by midsummer, had not only gained twenty pounds
in weight, as well as a vigor and a color to which he
was heretofore a stranger, but rode so well that nobody
paid the least attention to him. West of the Mississippi,
a man must ride badly to attract notice; and, in every
direction from that river, the world is only on the *qui
vive* when it finds something to censure.

As had originally been proposed, Mr. Moddle became

* Since this was written, alas! too soon immortal!

F. H. L.

an inmate of Mr. Binks's house. The plantation — more accurately the ranche, for it was but partially enclosed, and chiefly devoted to grazing purposes — covered three thousand acres of bottom and high prairie, a couple of miles from the settlement. Just under the shelter of the bluff, surrounded by a grove of elms and oaks, with a pretty view of the serpentine creek, and its fringe of cotton-woods, stood Mr. Binks's house, a structure which recorded in **itself** all the successive phases of progress through which Missouri architecture has passed since the day of Pike and the earlier Chouteaus. The first phase was represented by a good-sized wing of squared cotton-woods chinked in with mortar; the following ones by more ambitious structures of frame, batten, and **clap**-board, — two stories high, and wandering in every **di**-rection, as if they had started in life with some dissipated idea of being bowling-alleys, or a mercantile tendency to become rope-walks, **but** finally, under Binks's per-suasion, settled down to domestic bliss and the sober actualities of life. Nothing, in all their labyrinth of L's and lean-to's, would Binks permit ever to be touched by a reconstructive hand. He had a good staircase to his loft; but the rude old ladder, which had been its first access, was still his favorite means of ascent, and **he** would have pulled it down no sooner **than his king**-post. Every round **of it had been touched by dear feet**, which would walk with **him no more** in any of the world's places; and he **had** never forgotten the sweet face which used to peer from its top above the level of the loft floor, like a curly-headed sun rising over a cotton-wood horizon, to wake him into home **and** love from the buffalo-robes under which he lay asleep after a night-**hunt** in the deer covers. Many a year **ago,** that face **grew** cold, and was laid under the wavy blue grass; but Binks, though he needed no reminder of its vanished beauty, **had** one always before him **in his** playmate, his housewife, his joy and darling, his only child, Susie.

She was just twenty years old. Her eyes were large, **and** of a tender dark-blue. Her features, without being entirely regular, were full of spirit and delicacy; her color, a pure, lustrous blending of olive and rose. **Her** figure—just above woman's middle height—was round, erect, and lithe as a young huntress, and her hair, which fell in a profusion of curls upon her shoulders, was a soft, lustrous mass, black like the raven's wing. Many rural beauties disenchant admiration when they speak; but Susie's **voice** revealed a depth of womanly sweet-**ness,** kindness, and truth which were no disappointment to any man who had said, " What a lovely mouth ! " **when it was silent. She sang like a bird,** as cheerily, as deliciously, as untaught. She **played the melodeon well** enough to **lead the chants in Muddy; from some old** books, which had belonged **to** her mother, she had learned enough French not to be puzzled when she crossed a quotation in her English reading. She kept herself *au courant* in the best modern literature, and had an enthusiastic appreciation of everything beautiful in **the** nature around her, or in **the** art she had only heard

12 *

and dreamed of; there was not a subject which calls for the housewife's planning brain, overseeing eye, or skilful hand in which she was not perfectly at home. These accomplishments would have gone but very little way in the latitude of St. Simon Stylites; at Muddy they were precious. And Susie, moreover, had that disposition for whose value society has no limiting horizon; there being no place on earth where a spirit of unwearied womanly helpfulness like Susie's must not sooner or later be found the best and most enduring thing of all — the thing after every trial of time and circumstance most in demand for the use and the ornament of life.

If Mr. Moddle missed the luxury of **St.** Simon's library and the atmosphere of culture which belongs to the highest circles of metropolitan society, — if he found his professional work for the most part up-hill, and often returned from his long parochial rides or laborious and ill-attended services not only worn out with bodily fatigue but suffering still more than the average dejection belonging to every youthful enthusiast who starts forth to evangelize the world, and discovers how little it cares to be evangelized, — he found at Binks's two abundant compensations for every discouragement and disaster. For the first time since he lost his parents **and** went away to boarding-school, he **had** a home. Before the wild pecans got ripe and the cotton-wood leaves grew sere, he learned the further fact that he had a heart, and that was Susie's.

We must pass over a period of two years, and return to **Mr.** Binks's house to find it a nursery. There is **a** little girl in Mr. Binks's house. Her age is ten months, and her name is Daisy Moddle. She was baptized by that name in the Church of St. John the Beloved (locally speaking, in the court-house — the church that met **there was so** small a one that we forgot to mention its saint before), and had justified her name ever since by being the eye of day to every heart that knew her, from her old black mammy to Binks himself, who found her the image of both his Susies, and almost sang a "*nunc dimittis*" like Simeon's when she was first put into his arms. I neither can, nor need, say what she was to her mother. To her father she was an angel of unsealing, who came straight from heaven to touch all that had been rock or desert in him, and make his heart's inmost fountains gush forth with singing. When he sat writing his sermons, mother and baby must always be in the room with him. Inspiration flagged the moment that he looked up from his desk and found them gone. When he got in jaded and splashed from some long ride; when he returned from ministering to some ruined victim of the still and the gambling-table, soothing some tortured wretch on his death-bed with delirium tremens, or burying men who had murdered each other in a fight across a cock-pit; when day followed day with scarcely a visible reward for those earnest labors to which, in his boyhood, he had looked forward as the inevitable purchase **of some** great, concrete triumph, dejection never froze so deep in his heart that his baby's smile could not thaw it out again.

Mr. Moddle had preached good, faithful sermons twice on every Sunday since he came to Muddy save the three included in his buffalo-hunt on the Republican; he had held weekly services whenever it was demanded by the calendar of the church and possible to the roads of Missouri. He had frequently exchanged pulpits with the Rev. Joseph Bowers, and, wherever he preached, — in his own parish or out of it, — was regarded an able, self-denying, and zealous minister. A man approved of all the churches, however, is not necessarily one who answers the other apostolic idea, and commends himself to all them that are without. Mr. Moddle had every man's respect; but it could scarcely be expected of youth's small stock of experience that he should make all men understand or all men like him. He did not fill up the church rapidly. To be sure, in that part of Missouri, few ministers did. A great many of the rough characters of the settlement, now and then a stranger from some other " section," would drop in, drawn by curiosity to see what the service was like, or by the rector's growing reputation for preaching busters, which is the Missourian for pulpit eloquence. The curiosity satisfied and the reputation criticised, these visitors generally returned no more. The faithful few, who, with Binks at their head, had kept their lamps burning through the religious midnight of Muddy, stuck it out bravely still, — the women more especially, — and suffered from no declension.

Mr. Moddle had for several days been sorely lamenting the condition of Zion, when, on a certain morning in June, several wagon-loads of singular-looking people, followed by several wagon-loads more of equally singular-looking baggage, drove into the Muddy settlement "from up St. Louis way," just as Mr. Moddle came out of the post-office with his letters.

A small darkey, whose notions of raiment were limited to one coffee-sack and a hole to stick the head out, — having a more particular eye to the luggage, since childhood must see strange men enough every day, — remarked that the visitors were a circus; and, at first, Mr. Moddle was inclined to agree with him.

It was not long before both were undeceived. The singular-looking people drove to no tavern, but went straight, as by prearrangement, to an open, amphitheatrical spot, under the bluff, where they speedily set doubt at rest upon the nature of their baggage, by pitching it, in the shape of tents, on the sun-dried grass. But these tents had nothing either martial or histrionic about them. They bore no flags nor party-colored canopies. Their nearest approach to ornament were the large placards which were immediately hoisted high upon their sides, while several of the strange-comers went out along the street of the settlement, to distribute reduced copies of the same, to every one they met. These placards read variously, but a good idea of them may be formed from this selection:

"Come to Jesus!" "Now's the accepted time!"

"Camp-meeting every day and evening this week on Nodoway Flat."

A shiver of inexpressible disgust passed through **Mr. Moddle.** "A camp-meeting!" To him the idea had all his life-long been synonymous with superstition, credulity, and spasms. He hurried to the tie-post of the **tavern, where he** had left his horse, and got quickly into the saddle, to be beyond the reach of fanatics, repellant **to** every intellectual fibre of his religious nature. As he rode out of the inn-yard, one of the new-comers stretched out a card to him.

"No, sir!" replied Mr. Moddle, "I totally disapprove of the whole thing."

"If God agrees **with you,** we shall fail," said the man, gravely.

Mr. Moddle **bowed,** in stern conclusion of the interview, **and rode past. He had not gone many** rods before **his recollection of the man's** sober but kindly face **made him ask himself if his** manner **had** not been too **severe.** Indeed, all the singular-looking people were as singular in this, the quiet cheerfulness and good-will of their countenances and manners, as they were in the neat but somewhat austere simplicity of their dress.

Whatever feeling of regret he had was taken away as **he stopped his horse upon** the bluff and looked down into **the** settlement of Muddy. **Though, to get back to Binks'** he must eventually **return to the first bottom,** he always **took** the best and **longest road on the** top of the divide. From the bluff, Mr. Moddle could get a full view of the whole brawling, straggling, quaggy, uninteresting, and wicked street which flanked the post-office of Muddy Creek. Following this along the base-line of the bluff, his eye came to the Nodoway flats, where the recurving creek intersected it. Already those newly pitched **tents** were swarming with eager men, women, and children. Every idler in the town seemed drawn to that one magnetic focus. Already, on an open-air platform, somebody was addressing a company of upturned, inquisitive faces, and, as Mr. Moddle looked, **he** could constantly see fresh stragglers dropping in. He took out his watch; it could not yet be an **hour** since those singular-looking wagon-loads **drove in.** And he had been trying all these years to save — then only presumably — here and there **a soul.** Those ranters! Those charlatans! In one little hour they could gather a greater audience than he had, counting the entire twelve-month.

"It is enough to make one despair of the people!" **said** Mr. Moddle, bitterly, turning his mare towards home. "**I can do nothing with** them. I wish I had **stayed at St. Simon's,— no!** no! I wish, what were better yet, that I **had died.** God may save these people, but he has no **part in** the work for me."

It was in the same sad and severe spirit that he reached home. He looked in at the dining-room, kissed his wife and baby, then went up to the large, open room in the loft where he wrote, without as usual asking them to accompany him.

He threw himself down on the floor of the loft, and pondered on many things with a sore, discouraged heart. He thought of all he had left behind in the world, for the sake of duty; then called himself an ungrateful wretch for not feeling abundantly paid, even in this world's goods, by Susie and Daisy. Then his poor little lonely flock in the jury-room passed before his eyes, and the picture of the crowd hurrying to camp-meeting swiftly followed it. The contrast was too much to bear. Mr. Moddle rose to his feet unrefreshed. His eye was flashing, and his lip curled, as he said, —

"Those ranters! Those charlatans! How much better to have died than been sent to a place where all that a man can do is to preach the world right into their arms!"

Mr. Binks had never advanced to that stage of father-in-law familiarity which comes in without knocking, and it was he who now announced himself by a gentle tap on the rough deal door of the loft.

"Come in," said Mr. Moddle.

The old man helped himself to a chair, and wiped his face with his bandanna.

"I've been ridin' smart," said he. "It looks a leetle like a hail-storm to-night, and I wanted to see that the boys brought the yearlings into corral."

"Been down into the settlement?"

"Yes; and I stayed longer than I meant to, looking how those camp-meeting folks got on. One of 'em's a kinsman of mine, and I wanted to make him comforta-

ble here, but he wouldn't leave the tent. He is a young
fellow, and it's allus jist sich as never believe there's
goin' to be a hail-storm. But I've been raised round
here, and I reckon we're goin' to hev a night of it. If
so, they'll have to strike camp down there t' the flat, **and**
hold no meeting till to-morrow."

" It's well if they couldn't," replied Mr. Moddle, bit-
terly.

" Why — how — how so ? " asked old Binks, with an
air of surprise.

"Can such a devoted churchman ask that question ? "

" Well, my dear sir," replied Mr. Binks, with some
embarrassment at differing from his rector **and his son-**
in-law (Binks could not tell in which relation he most
admired him), " well, my dear sir, you and I know
they're not looked on as regular, to be sure. There's
nothing about 'em in the catechism; there's nothing
about 'em in the thirty-nine Articles; and I'm not as
well posted in such matters as I ought to be," said Mr.
Binks, at once apologetically and cautiously feeling his
way over the uncertain ground of theologic literature
like an elephant crossing a morass, " nor so well as I'd
like to be, but I think that there's nothin' fur nor agin
them in the Rubric. They're to the regular army of
salvation what the volunteers are to Uncle Sam's in war-
time. They're not so well drilled as the regulars, and I
myself like that old regulation musket, the Prayer-book,
better than I do all the odd and even sized weepons of
prayer that ye find to a camp-meetin'. When the

13

brother has a gift in prayer, I love uncommon to hear him; but 'taint every brother's got it. 'Way I say to camp-meetin' folks is this, 'There never was a free country saved without some guerilla fightin' out on the frontier; so, though you don't train in my company, all I want to know is if you're fightin' on the same side. If you are, go in. There's enough work for everybody that wants to save souls, out in this section, I can tell ye!' And, my dear sir, the more souls they save the gladder I'll be.'"

Susie, at the foot of the stairs, called them to dinner. Binks arose, glad that the conversation was turned before his earnestness led him into what might seem a preachment, and Mr. Moddle followed him moodily down to the table.

It was well that Mr. Binks hurried home to see about the shelter of his young stock; for, as he had predicted, between nine and ten o'clock in the evening the hailstorm came, — such a storm as can only be produced in a country which claims the Mississippi and Rocky Mountains of its family. It began with broad flashes of lightning, gradually increasing to a steady flame which the eyes feared to look upon, with an occasional crash and rumble which grew to one unbroken roar. It began with headlong torrents of rain, like whole lakes pouring bodily from the black and fiery heavens. It continued, with a perpetually accelerating fury of wind, until the rain became a scourge knotted with icy pebbles, and the mercury went down almost to its winter register.

Few of the oldest frontiersmen have lost their awe
for a western storm, even where that emotion partakes
much more of reverence than dread. Binks was **awake**
all night. He did not even take his clothes off. This
for several reasons. His sense of care for his stock, his
vigilance to keep everything all safe about the premises,
the loyal tendency of all pioneers to stand guard in any
emergency over women and children, and the perfect
delight which the sublimity of such **a storm** gave the
æsthetic side **of old** Binks's nature. Those Titan stair-
ways of black marble cloud, climbed in an instant and
rifted from top to base by the white foot of the lightning; the din and trembling of heaven as their masses
cracked; the unutterable spirit of power that rode in the
wind; the poetic order that ruled throughout the universal clash; these to Mr. Binks, brought up in western
Missouri, were what the opera, classic music, the stu-
dios, high art of all kinds, are to us. He would no
sooner have missed the spectacle of that storm than you
or I would go **to** bed on a Siddons night, were the tragic
queen permitted to **star it** on earth again for a limited
season.

    Long after midnight, **as he sat in his room** vigilant
for calls from the corral, but giving delighted attention
to the sky, which he could see through his western window, Mr. Moddle with a hurried rap came to beg that
he would look in and see Daisy.

    " She seems very feverish," said Mr. Moddle, very
like her in this through his terrible anxiety. " She

tosses and moans in her sleep a **good** deal, and Susie and I are troubled."

Mr. Binks's **heart leaped into his throat.** .He instantly started **up and followed his son-in-law to** the bedroom, where Susie's **face looking into his over her restless** little armful made him the mute appeal of a young mother's first fear, the moment he opened the door.

" **Father dear,**" said Mr. Moddle with a trembling lip, " **can you tell us what is the matter** with her ? **Her** breathing **seems so distressed** " —

Mr. Binks took the candle and looked with tender scrutiny into the weary eyes which seemed to know him and ask help **of** him; saw how hard Daisy found **it** to breathe, and **was about** to pronounce the case croup, when **it occurred to him** to examine the **child's throat,** as he **had seen doctors do, with a spoon-handle.** Mr. Binks **read the papers enough to know how** diphtheria **showed itself, and with one glance at the** thickening **white patches which lined the little throat,** saw what made **him set** down **the** candle, and turn to hide his dismay from Susie by looking out of the window.

But there was no time to be lost. He could think of no medicine fitter for the case than the Hives' syrup they had **been** using. **He** had heard that steam eases **the** breathing of **a** diphtheritic patient and keeps the membrane **from becoming** consistent. **He had heard that the faculty gave** stimulants, **and there ended all** the wisdom which he **had** to help **steer** that all-precious little bark through this terrible exigency. No wonder the cold drops stood on his forehead ! But something must be done at once; it would do to wait for no doctor. So he controlled himself, and with a hopeful voice told the parents what ailed their Daisy. His courage made them brave. In less than five minutes they had replenished their fire, and had a teakettle steaming vigorously through a stable-hose over Daisy's face. They had prepared a mild milk-punch, and Susie was giving it at short intervals, a teaspoonful at a time. Binks rapidly imparted to them all the counsel he could, and hastened to the stable to ride to the settlement for a doctor. When they spoke to him about the night, he told them that it was the kind of weather he loved, and cheerily bade them take heart, and told them that his horse and he knew every foot of the road in the dark. With a lantern at his pommel he went off bravely into the pelting night, as he would have gone into a battle to serve any whom he loved.

As soon as the thunder hid the clatter of his hoofs, his son-in-law sat mutely down by the fire, gazing into his wife's face and Daisy's. The vapor seemed beginning to make the baby's breathing easier, but the stimulants had yet done little for her evident languor and pain.

"Husband," spoke Susie, when the silence of the watchers got unendurable, "will you read a little in the Bible to me ? I feel so afraid, dear, — and my heart aches so."

He kissed her tearful eyes and tremulous mouth, and

13 *

went and brought his **own** old Family Bible from the spot where Susie had set a cushion for it **when she was** first married. He sat **down** by the lamp, and, in the mechanical way of one stupefied with anxiety, slowly spread the book open on his knees.

What always had happened, from the first day its pages held Binks's letter, happened now. The leaves separated at the prophecy of Mr. Moddle's namesake. In the same mechanical way **with** which he opened the book his eye glanced down the column, and as it went the following passages past **it** in review **like** some sketchy but powerfully-drawn panorama:

" And the Lord God prepared a gourd, and made it to come up over Jonah, that it might be a shadow over his head to deliver him from **his** grief. So Jonah was exceeding glad of the gourd.

" But God prepared a worm . . . . and it smote the gourd that **it withered.**

" And it came to **pass . . . . that Jonah said, 'It is** better for me to die than to live.'

· · · · " Then said the Lord, thou hast had pity on the gourd, for the which thou hast not labored, neither madest it grow.

· · · · " And should not I spare Nineveh ? "

" O dear wife ! " said Mr. Moddle, kneeling **down at** the lap where his little Daisy lay, **" I have been an un-** grateful, hard-hearted sinner."

" Husband ! " said Susie, half-reproachfully. Though she knew in a general way that all mankind are sinners, her husband seemed to her a man who could never be ungrateful or hard-hearted.

"Yes, Susie, not to you, **nor** to Daisy, nor to dear father, but to **God. I have** quarrelled with his mercy and compassion, — been angry with his largeness, — been angry that much good is done **in** the world by **men widely** other than myself. I have quarrelled with his creation of me, — with the places where he has put me in life. I have been restive and impatient. *I* restive ! *I* impatient ! to whom he gave you and Daisy as a lovely bower to grow up over me while I sat in the desert of my life crying God's warning to a world no worse than I. Not because I had any right to command, but because I was to be spoken through from above. I impatient ! when perhaps even to-morrow more souls may be saved out of Muddy by those Methodists than I have saved with my whole three-years' work ? *That* did make me impatient. It was for a moment. I abhor myself for that moment ! How can I wonder that, to call **me** back from such **a** black spirit, he, who sent me the sweet plant to be my cover from the heat, will not hesi- **tate, if need be, to smite it ! But, O Lord, the lesson is learned. I have seen my sin. I am** glad thy **work is** done by *anybody !* Give me any part of it, — only spare this dear, dear shelter ! "

In the intensity of his emotion, he clasped his arms around his wife and child, and kissed them, — all three face to face.

Daisy opened her lovely eyes, knew her father, and

stretched out her little arms to go to him. This first conscious effort brought on an immediate spasm of distressed breathing. The young father leaped up in despair.

"O God! I have killed my child!" he thought, heartbrokenly, as **he** brought the steam nearer to Daisy's **face.**

She gave a convulsive grasp, — the veins in her forehead grew purple while the blood was slowly settling back into her parents' hearts, and then Life drove out Death with one great throe. Something like a little delicate cartridge-paper was all that separated between the foes; and when the fiercest combat raged for the possession of Daisy, Life broke that through with a cough. A little delicate cast of a little delicate windpipe — to think that the dividing width between Life and Death may be less than a line! — that the decision between them may be an ounce or so surplus of pneumatic pressure, inherited from a strong-lunged race!

The false membrane ejected, the baby's breathing was perceptibly easier at once. Mr. Moddle sat till dawn, feeding her milk-punch as she lay in her mother's lap, and keeping up the steam above her face. Gradually her face lost its bloated look and sank toward the sweet, natural roundness of childhood; her pulse became evener and fuller; and, at intervals, she appeared to be getting good, natural sleep. When she awoke, she would pat their cheeks, take a teaspoonful of her punch, lie curiously regarding them for a while, then draw a

pleasant little sigh, as if the inspection had proved satisfactory, and go to sleep for half an hour more.

The day broke cold and murky. The hail had ceased,
but the wind was savage, booming in and out through
the deep ravines of the bluff, making havoc with all **the**
dead cotton-woods, whirling **great sheets** and tangled
skeins of bark into the air, like a crazy rag-man out
on holiday; snapping off from the dismantled skeletons
entire limbs at once; and trying the stanchness of
everything along Muddy Creek, **as a** man's hour of sor-
row tries the loyalty of his friends.

There was one institution along the bank of this
Epic's sacred river, which stood the test as well as if it
had been rooted three feet in the soil, instead of lifted
that height above it by a swift-galloping horse, — Daisy's
grandfather, to wit, — who, with his long grey hair streaming from under his slouch, the ends of his grizzled mustache floating back to his ears, his buffalo collar dang-
ling **loose on his** back, his throat open and his face full
of a whole life's faith and patience concentrated into one
hour, — did not seem to know it was cold, **and** rode as
the Pride of the Border should, whether it blow or no.
Beside him came another man, — a rough-looking fellow,
in his great bear-skin coat, — whom Mr. Moddle would
scarcely have taken for the person accosting him yesterday with a tract, unless he looked closely in his
face, and saw the grave refinement, simplicity, and kind-
liness there was there. As they both rode silently, Mr.
Binks thought over the matter of his night's errand. He

had found the only two doctors of the settlement off long distances on midwifery cases.

"Well," said Mr. **Binks,** "**God** save the little babies that are goin' to **be born.** O Lord, if ye could, save Daisy, too !"

He had caught hold of God with such a desperate faith that he was quite at peace.

" If it had been best for Daisy, the doctors would have been here. The angels that take care of little children, always behold my father's face."

The thought occurred to him, as by an inspiration arising out of this peace, that he had heard his cousin talk of a missionary announced to speak at the camp-meeting, who was also a very able practitioner of medicine. The hail had long ago broken up the camp; for though one may put up with lying out in a hail-storm on the Plains, not even an Indian does it when he can get shelter. The camp-folk were dispersed among various houses along the street, and thus it happened that Mr. Binks could not gain clue to the missionary, wake him and get him on the road home with him, until dawn was breaking in upon the watchers by Daisy.

"Sunrise !" said Binks. " Don't you think there's *some* leetle chance still, brother Linn ? "

" I hope so."

For a moment it seemed as if the old man's heart would break; but he drew himself straight in his seat. "I wasn't there when she died, — my Susie's Susie's Daisy ! "

Daisy was slumbering very quietly, when a clatter of hoofs in the front-yard brought Mr. Moddle instantly down to the door.

"Well ? " said Mr. Binks.

"Daisy seems better," said Mr. Moddle.

The old man's stern, grave face melted away at once into the look of a thankful little child, and clasping his son-in-law's neck, he hid his face in his breast and wept aloud.

"Come, come," said he, resolutely, " I mustn't break down *now !* I'm forgettin' my manners, brother Linn — this is my dear son, — my Susie's husband and my Daisy's father, — Mr. Moddle, brother Linn.

"I have seen you before, — you offered me something yesterday which I too churlishly refused. I am sorry for it. Though there may be many things we disagree upon, I've gone through during the past night, with enough to show me that I've been wrong in quarrelling about our shares in the work of the world. Now, I ask you only this, — what work do you want in this world "—

"To help make the world better," said the missionary, opening to the young man's scrutiny as kind and honest a pair of eyes as ever belonged to a soul true to its inmost conviction.

Mr. Moddle stretched out his hand, and took the missionary cordially.

"That is my work, also, brother Linn."

The next day in camp-meeting brother Linn publicly thanked God for the recovery of Daisy, and there was

not a dry eye in the tent when the people heard for the
first time at once of the sickness and recovery of fine
old Binks's grandchild.   **From** that hour the tender
layer **of** the Muddy Creek nature seemed to have been
reached. The raging drunkards, the quarrelsome bullies,
the card-sharpers, and the irreclaimable loafers, all began
flocking into the tents, seemingly for no other reason
than that a simple little story had been told of a popular
favorite's baby-grand-daughter, who had been given
back from death **in** answer to agonizing prayer. I know
people who think this a most ridiculous reason for making such a stir; but I have to deal with facts as they
universally are among mankind, — in this particular instance among the Missourians of Muddy Creek. They
were powerfully moved by the incident, so that great,
shaggy fellows, whose appearance **at** the window of a
drawing-room **would have thrown all** the women into
hysterics, were **to** be seen sobbing like children. They evidently believed it was an answer to prayer, for they fell to
praying immediately. The result, while the camp-meeting
stayed in Muddy Creek, was a settlement freer from its
worst vices than old Binks himself had ever seen.

And after the camp-meeting went, what ?

Not the millennium. It is no one-dose remedy which
will ever cure the world. Muddy Creek settlement, sharing with the world in this respect, did not become so good
that there was not much left for Mr. Moddle. Nothing
was absolutely perfect; there was no day when trench-
ing was not as **large** a part **of** the Christian soldier's

work as psalm-singing; the best people in the parish were not so good but they could conceivably be better; but Mr. Moddle had become a changed man, who could tolerate the world as it is, and do his share in it.

Not that the change in the place was imperceptible. There was a shutting up of all the worst dens, the restoration of peace in families to which it had been a **stranger for** years, the addition **to Mr.** Moddle's church **of many whom the** camp-folks had **reclaimed. For as old** Binks said,—

" **There are lots of people who could** take real comfort **with their heads, if they only got their** hearts saved first." Perhaps, also, the preaching of the rector is more to the hearts of men than it used to be; for many more people than he ever found before, now feel a sincere affection for him. Old Binks has now two desires of his heart — an able man for Muddy Creek and a house to praise God in. The latter is an unpretending frame structure, with a small organ, a cross on the spire and no mortgage anywhere.

Daisy and Susie shall paint a little picture to close this view of Mr. Moddle's experience. As he sits at twilight among the Michigan **roses which climb on his** porch, the baby, grown **to be a lovely** little girl of **six,** and Susie, changed only by the deepening of her eyes' constant expression of wifely and maternal love, lean over him, until he is embowered upon both sides in curls.

" See, mamma, we're making a little summer-house over papa."

14

And that moment there came into Mr. Moddle's mind a text, which has dropped out of the canonical version of his namesake's prophecy:

"And Jonah said, 'I have **sinned.**' Wherefore the Lord rebuked the blight, and the gourd sprang again, **and** its shelter was sevenfold. And Jonah sat under the shadow of the gourd and thanked the **Lord exceedingly.**"

LITTLE BRIGGS AND I.

LITTLE BRIGGS AND I.

'M going to give you a bit of autobiography, and when I say that, I don't mean the usual kind. Most people who write their own lives make up for themselves an ideal of perfect living, to which they square their facts. The Rev. Mr. Rhodomontade does not tell how he pulled all the hairs out of his Greek professor's horse's tail, and the Hon. Simon Pure gives us no reminiscences of the day when he cheated at marbles. I've no doubt that Payson got tight, and James Brainerd Taylor stole sweetmeats off the top shelf of his mother's closet ; that Benjamin Franklin played hookey, and General Scott cried when he got thrashed. Read their memoirs, and you wont find a stagger or a stained apron, a black mark or a blubber, in the whole of them. If memoirs are meant for a personal puff, this is all very well. If they're for the generation to come after us, it couldn't be worse. Many a trembling saint gets demoralized by contemplation of such inaccessible excellence. He feels

14 *   (197)

as if he were reading about another man's having got to
Newport without ever having passed through Massachu-
setts or Connecticut, Narraganset Bay or Long Island
Sound.   His idol has **the fruits of experience without**
the experience itself ; and, naturally considering him an
exceptional case, he gives up the insoluble problem of re-
sembling him.   I don't think   Rousseau's . Confessions
exactly the kind of book for boarding-school reading,
but for instruction **in** the conduct of human life it's
worth a dozen memoirs of **any Mr.** Optimus Paragon,
written **by** himself.   Let's **know where** the reefs are, if
you *did* get that ugly bump on your keel !   So far as we
have steered, there's no remarkably plain sailing ; if
you've had it all the way, very well ; you're in port now ;
hand your log **over to** the **owners. We,** who **have**
plenty of foul weather, are busy with charts, and, when
there's a fair spell, find livelier reading in Robinson
Crusoe. If you don't like to tell how many mistakes
you've made, how rash you've been, how mad, even how
mean, — why, you've etymology on your side, for modern autobiography is derived from the fact that it's a
man's life as it ought-to-be, and not as it was.   In **that**
sense I'm ruled out of your company, for this sketch is
no ought-to-be-ography at all.

My name **is Ben** Thirlwall, and I am **the son of rich**
but honest parents.   I never had a wish ungratified until I **was twelve** years **of age.   My wish** then was to
stay on a two-year-old colt which had never been
broken.   He did not coincide with me, and a vast revela-

tion of the resistances to individual will of which the universe is capable, also of a terrestrial horizon bottom upward, burst upon me during the brief space which I spent in flying over his head. Picked up senseless, **I was carried to the bosom of my family on a wheelbarrow, and** awoke to the consciousness that my parents **had decided** on sending me to boarding-school, — a remedy to this day sovereign in the opinion of all well-regulated parents for all tangential aberrations from the back of a colt or the laws of society.

The principal's name was Barker ; and my only clue to his character consisted in overhearing that he **was an** excellent disciplinarian. I was afraid to ask what that meant, but on reflection concluded it to be a geographical distinction, and, associating him with Mesopotamia or Beloochistan, expected to find him a person of mild manners, who shaved his head, wore a tall hat of dyed sheep's wool, and did a large business in spices with people who visited him on camels in a front-yard surrounded by sheds, and having a fountain that played in the middle.

Having read several books of travels, I was corroborated in my view when I learned that Mr. Barker lived at the east, and still further, when, going around Point Judith on the steamboat with my father, I became very sick at the stomach, as all the travellers had done in their first chapter.

I need not say that the reality of Mr. Barker was a very terrible awakening, which contained no lineament

of my purple dream save the bastinado. Without distinction of age or season the youths who, as per **circular**,
enjoyed the softening influences of his refined Christian
home, rose to the sound of the gong at five A. M., which
may have been very nice in a home for the early Chris-
tians, but was reported among the boys to have entirely
stopped the growth of Little Briggs. This was a child,
whose mother had married again, and whose step-father
had felt his duty to his future too keenly to deprive him
of the benign influences of Barker any time in the last
six years. After rising, we had ten minutes to wash
our faces and hands, — a period by the experience of
mankind demonstrably insufficient, where the soap is of
that kind very properly denominated cast-steel (though
purists have a different spelling), and you have to **break**
an inch of ice to get into the available region of your
water-pitcher.   Chunks, who has since made a large
fortune on war-contracts, kept himself in pea-nuts and
four-cent pies for an entire winter session, by selling an
invention of his own, which consisted of soap, dissolved
in water on the stove during the day-time, put in bottles
hooked from the lamp-room by means of a false key, to
be carried to bed and kept warm by boys, whose pocket-
money and desire for a prompt detergent in the morning were adequate to the disbursement of half a dime a
package. I myself **took several violent colds from hav-**
ing the glass next my skin during severe nights ; but
this was nothing so bad as the case of Little Briggs, who,
from lack of the half-dime, often came down to prayers

with a stripe of yesterday's pencil-black on one side of
his nose, and a shaving of soap, which, in the frenzy of
despair, he had gouged out of his stony cake, on the
other. The state of mind consistent with such a condition of countenance did not favor correct recitation of
the tougher names in Deuteronomy ; so, it can be a
cause of surprise to no one, that, when called on at
prayers and prompted by a ridiculous neighbor, little
Briggs sometimes asserted Joshua to have driven out
the Hivites and the Amorites, and the Canaanites and
the Jebusites, and the Hittites and the Perizzites, and the
Moabites and the Musquito-bites, for which he was regularly sent to bed on Saturday afternoon, as **he had no**
pocket-money to stop, his papa desiring him to learn
self-denial young, as he was intended for a missionary;
though goodness knows that there wasn't enough of him
to go round among many heathen.

From this specimen of discipline may be learned the
entire Barkerian system of training. I was about to
say, " ex uno disce omnes," but, as it's the only Latin I
remember from the lot which got rubbed into — or
rather over — me at **Barker's, I'm rather sparing** of it,
not knowing but I can bring it in somewhere else with
better effect. As with the Word of God, so with that
of man, — the grand Barkerian idea of how to fix it in a
boy's memory was to send him to bed, or excoriate his
palm. If religion and polite learning could have been
communicated by sheets, like chicken-pox, or blistered
into one like the stern but curative cantharides, Mr.

Barker's boys would have become the envy of mankind
and the beloved of the **gods; but not** even Little Briggs
died young from the latter or any other cause, which
speaks volumes for his constitution.

Even at Barker's, boys grew up, somehow; and in
process of time I became fourteen years of age. I recollect that epoch well, for it was marked by my first sor-
row. I learned to sympathize, at least half way, with
Little Briggs. I lost a good and indulgent father, though
I did not get one of an opposite character, nor indeed
any at all. When I came back to Barker's, a few weeks
after the funeral, little Briggs looked at me with peculiar interest, and made me a timid offer of baked
chestnuts.

"I **had on as good clothes as that, when** I was in
mourning, — real bombazine with jet buttons," said Little
Briggs, waxing confidential during second recess. "I
wish I was in mourning now. Do you feel very bad?"

My heart rose in my throat.

"Of course you do. But *I* wouldn't. I'm different,
you know; my dad's not the real thing, — only imita-
tion. If he should die I wouldn't cry — no more — no
more than — than" — Little Briggs cast about for some
particularly stern and tearless comparison, and finally
hit on the not very felicitous one of **"that pump,"**
which just **at the moment was yielding water freely**
to the solicitations **of Mr. Barker's hired man,** Yankee.
Yankee was pumping for the cook, between whom and
himself there were supposed to be still more romantic

love-passages, wide credence having been given among
Barker's boys to the theory that she was the daughter
of a man with countless millions, who had turned her
out of doors on account of her love for a pedler of humble birth ; upon which she and the pedler, not to be separated, had come to take service at Barker's. Maturer
selfishness than ours would have propitiated her with
reference **to** her post-obit expectations, but the blandishments of Barker's boys were directed solely to the
more immediate particular of pies. As we passed Yankee and the cook, the latter glanced at Little Briggs's
threadbare knees, and said compassionately to her **companion,**—

"Poor thing ! he don't look as if he was much sot on
by his family ! "

"Wall, naow," replied Yankee, with a drawl and
twinkle, "I should say, to look at him, that they'd all on
'em sot on him to once, and tol'ble heavy tew ! "

Little Briggs heard him, and made what within my
experience was his first self-assertion. He rushed at
the pump, with his face as pale as death and his lip quiv-
ering, drew back his foot, paused, **and**—

"See here, you old hog," said Little Briggs, "if that
wasn't the cook's pail, I'd — I'd kick it over ! "

"They're all hogs," he added, as he walked away with
me, leaving Yankee petrified by his exceptional demonstration, "everybody's hogs at Barker's. Barker's the
biggest; he haint got any more feeling than a bedpost.
When your father died, the fellers all signed a paper

asking for a half-holiday, and Pete Gilbert took it up to him; and he went right on with school just the same. Don't I wish I was big enough to break his head! I'd run away this minute — if I'd only got anywhere to run to!"

Whether, as a result of his first bold stand, or from the expansive influence of having found in me something like a common ground of human sympathy, Little Briggs, to the surprise of everybody, began growing; — so rap- **idly, in fact,** that within a few months he confided to me as many as three letters, signed, "Yours, T. Mixer," and written in a stiff, invoicy hand, to complain of an extension of legs which had defeated all T. Mixer's cal- culations regarding the annual family demand for pep- per and salt cassimere; and, moreover, if the mind might yield fond credence to T. Mixer as a representa- tive of Briggs's mamma's opinions, given that lady great **solicitude** from being an indication of the "tuberculous diathesis." "If I've got to have that," said Briggs, "I'd rather stay short — what is it?" I confessed my ignorance, and advised him to ask Barker, in which I did him an unintentional unkindness, that worthy invit- ing him to examine the dictionary, which might have **suggested** itself in the first instance, and assisting him to fix it in his mind by writing it on a slate three hun- dred times after school-hours.

In spite of **all (I am not** sure but this may be a mix- ture of metaphors), Briggs's legs turned a deaf ear to parental remonstrance, his upper frame at the same time filling out to a degree which, taken in connection with the stern simplicity of Barker's table, was a corroboration of the nutritive properties of oxygen, which must have satisfied the most sceptical physiologist. By the **season that we** were both fifteen, he lacked but an inch of the five feet six on which I prided myself ; and six months after, when I began to talk of going to college, he was quite up to me, and, but for a certain unmistakable air of never having any pocket-money, one of the wholesomest looking boys in school.

It was about this latter period, that an astonishing innovation was introduced at Barker's. The two Misses Moodle came to establish a young ladies' seminary **in** the village of Mungerville, on whose outskirts our own school was situated, bringing along with them, as the county paper stated, "that charming atmosphere of refinement and intellectuality in which they ever moved ;" and, what was of more consequence, a capital of twenty girls to start with. Professional politeness inspired Mr. Barker to make **a** call on the fair strangers, which the personal fascinations of the younger Miss Moodle in**duced him to repeat. The** atmosphere of refinement and intellectuality gradually acted on him in the nature of an intoxicating gas, until at length, after twenty-five years of successfully intrenched widowhood, he laid his heart in the mits of the younger Miss Moodle, and they two became one Barker.

As a consequence of this union, social relations began to be established between the two schools. Mrs. Bar-

15

ker, of an occasional evening, wished to run down and
visit her sister.   If Mr. Barker was engaged in quarry-
ing a page of Cicero out of some stony boy in whom nature had never made any Latin deposit, or had just put
a fresh batch of offenders into the penal oven of untimely
bed, and felt compelled to run up now and then to keep
up the fire under them, by a harrowing description of
the way their parents would feel if they knew of their
behavior — an instrument dear to Mr. Barker as a favorite poker to a boss-baker in love with his profession
— then, after a clucking noise, indicative of how much
he would like to chuck her under the chin, but for the
presence of company, Mr. Barker would coo to Mrs.
Barker, "Lovey, your pick, sweet!" waving his hand
comprehensively over the whole school-room; or "Dear,
suppose we say Briggs, or Chunks, or Thirlwall," as
the case might be.   The only difficulty about Briggs
was clothes.   That used to be obviated by a selection
from the trunks of intimate friends; and Briggs was
such a nice boy, that it was a real gratification to see
him with your best jacket on.   Many's the time the old
fellow has said to Chunks or me, "What a blessing that
I grew!   If I hadn't, how could I ever wear your trousers?"   In process of time these occasional visits, as
escort to Mrs. Barker, expanded into an attendance of
all the older boys (when not in bed for moral baking
purposes) upon a series of bi-monthly soirées, given by
the remaining Miss Moodle, with a superficial view to
her pupils' attainment of ease in society; and a material

substratum of sandwiches, which Miss Moodle preferred to see, through the atmosphere of refinement and intellectuality, as "a simple repast." To this was occasionally added a refreshment, which I have seen elsewhere only at Sunday-school picnics, — a mild tap of slightly sweetened water, which **tasted as** if lemons had formerly been kept **in the pail** it was made in ; — only for Sunday schools they make it strong at the outset, and add **water** during the hymns, with **a vague,** but praiseworthy expectation that, in view **of the** sacredness of **the** occasion, there **will be some miraculous interposi**tion, as in the case of the widow's cruse, to keep the beverage up to proof ; while **Miss Moodle's liquor pre**served throughout the evening a weakness of which generous naturès scorned to take advantage beyond the first tumbler.

At this portion of my career I was dawned upon by Miss Tucker. From mature years, I look back with a shudder upon the number of parchmenty sandwiches which I ate, **the reservoirs of lemony** water which I drank, in order to be **in that** lovely creature's society. I experienced agonies **in thinking how much longer it** might **be before I got a coat** with tails, **when I calcu**lated how soon she would be putting up her back hair. Her eyes were as blue as I was when I thought she liked Briggs ; and she had a complexion compared with which strawberries and cream were nowhere. When she was sent to the piano, to show people what the Moodle system could do in the way of a musical education,

I fell into a cataleptic state, and floated off upon a flood of harmony. Miss Moodle and her mits, self and lemon kids, even the sleepless eye of Barker, watching for an indiscretion, upon the strength of which he might defensibly send somebody to bed the next Saturday afternoon, all vanished from before me, swallowed up in a mild glory, which contained but two objects, — an angel with low neck and short sleeves, and an insensate hippopotamus of a piano, which did not wriggle all over with ecstasy when her white fingers tickled him. At such moments, I would gladly have gone down on all fours, and had a key-board mortised into my side at any expense of personal torture, if Miss Tucker could only have played a piece on me, and herself been conscious of the chords she was awakening inside my jacket. I loved her to that degree that my hair never seemed brushed enough when I beheld her ; and I quite spoiled the shape of my best boots through an elevation of the instep, caused by putting a rolled-up pair of stockings inside each heel, to approximate the manly stature, at our bi-monthly meetings. Even her friend, Miss Crickey, — a mealy-faced little girl, with saffron hair, who had been pushed by Miss Moodle so far into the higher branches, that she had a look of being perpetually frightened to death with the expectation of hearing them crack and let her down from a great height, — seemed beautiful to me from the mere fact of daily breathing the same air with such an angel, sharing her liquorice-stick, and borrowing her sweet little thimble.

I had other reasons for prejudice in Miss Crickey's favor. She was the only person to whom I could talk freely regarding the depth of my passion for Miss Tucker. Not even to the object of that tremendous feeling could I utter a syllable which seemed in any way adequate. With an overpowering consciousness how ridiculous it was, and not only so, but how far from original, I could give her papers of lemon Jackson-balls, hinting simultaneously that, though plump as her cheeks, they were not half so sweet ; and through a figure, whose correct name I have since learned to be periphrasis, I could suggest how much my soul yearned to expire on her ruby lips, by asking if she had ever played door-keeper ; regretting that the atmosphere of refinement and intellectuality did not admit of that healthful recreation at Moodle's, and begging her to guess whom I would call out if I were door-keeper myself. When she opened her blue eyes innocently, and said, "Miss Crickey ?" the intimation was rejected with a melancholy dissatisfaction, which would have been disdain but for the character of my feelings to its source. And when, on my pressing her for the name of the favored mortal whom she would call out if she were door-keeper, she slyly dropped her eyes and asked if Briggs sounded anything like it, I savagely refused to consider the proposition at all, and for the rest of the evening ate sandwiches to that degree I wonder my life was not despaired of, and fled for relief to the lemony bowl. The result of this mad vortex having been colic and calomel, after my

15 °

return to Barker's on that evening, I forswore such
dangerous excesses at the next bi-monthly ; but putting
a larger pair of stockings in each boot-heel, to impress
Miss Tucker with a sense of what she had lost, I devoted myself during the earlier part of the evening to a
growing young woman, of the name of Wagstaff, considerably older than myself and running straight up and
down from whatever side one might contemplate her.
Her conversation was not entertaining, unless from the
Chinese point of view, which, I understand, distinctly
favors monosyllables, and she giggled at me so persist-
ently that I feared Miss Tucker would think I must be
making myself ridiculous ; but, on her being sent to the
piano, I stood and turned over her music with a consciousness that if I ever looked impressive it was then.
All this I did in the effort to seem gay, although my
heart was breaking. I had no comfort on earth save
the thought that I had been brutal to Briggs, and that
he sat in an obscure corner of the room among some little girls in Long Division, hiding, behind an assistant
teacher's skirts, the whitey-brown toe which my blacking-
brush had refused to refresh, while I bore my grief upon
a pair of new boots plentifully provided with squeak-
leather. When Miss Tucker slipped a little piece of paper into my hand, as I made a hollow show of passing
her the sandwiches, I came very near dropping the
plate ; and when I had a chance to open it unobserved,
and read the words, " Are you mad with me ? " I could
not occupy my cold and dreary pinnacle a moment lon-

ger, but sought an early opportunity of squeezing her hand two seats behind the voluminous asylum of Briggs's toes, and whispering, slightly confused by intensity of **feeling,** that if I had done anything **I** was **sorry for, I was willing to be forgiven.** From that moment I was **Miss Tucker's slave. Oh, woman,** woman ! The string **on which you play us** is as long as life; it ties your baby-**bib; it laces your queenly** bodice; and on its slenderest **tag we** dangle everywhere !

The **next term at** both Moodle's and Barker's ran from **May to October. The blessed discovery of long sum**mer vacations had **not yet dawned upon the educational mind. Mr. Barker or Miss Moodle would** have regarded such a thing very much as a kitchen-gardener would have received a proposition to give holiday through the warm weather to his early cauliflowers. What was the use of such nice long days, except to get the whole of the rule for cube root at one lesson ? As for passing a Saturday afternoon **in** bed, what month could compete **with July in its opportunities of** salutary irritation ? **So all the boys and girls of my day, melted through the dog-days into the moulds of classic eloquence, discovered** the value of x while their own flesh took **its place** as an unknown quantity ; **solved** the square of the hypothenuse and the rotundity of their own solids with the same process, and exuded on the other side of the French irregular verbs as an insensible perspiration. When I think **what we** endured, I am all the more set in my conviction of the **hypocrisy of** autobiographies; for I know that no man could ever have struggled through to worldly eminence in this day, who did not freely play hookey in that ; while distinguished piety would be too much strain on any mature modern constitution which in boyhood had not relieved itself by going out into the middle of a ten-acre lot for, at least, a quarterly swear.

When I returned for the summer session, I had two comforts, which were not granted to every boy at Barker's — a kind and neighboring ma and a coat with tails. The latter in several newspapers, and a trunk perceptibly marked with my name and address in full upon three several cards, to provide against the contingency of its miscarriage, which I could not think of on the steamboat without being indescribably moved, came with me to my little coop at Barker's. The former, having **been** recommended by her physician to try sea-air during the summer, took a pretty little cottage, with ample grounds and a stable, to which she brought down her own horses, at a quiet though favorite watering-place, preserving, after a deservedly admired usage, its old romantic Indian name of Squash-ke-bosh. Squash-ke-bosh was situated at a distance of but fifty miles, by a good post road, from the village of Mungerville. It was considered by Mr. Barker very injurious to his pupils' future prospects to allow them to see their parents in term-time. **He** thought **it made them** dissatisfied when they got back to school. Nor was he far out of the way, when we consider that even Buffum, the least impressible boy in school, was moved to tears whenever he got a letter from his mother, and made inadequate to any decent amount of Latin grammar for the rest of the afternoon solely by the reflection of what a hand she was for chicken pot-pies. Nevertheless, the feeling of sympathy toward an invalid for whom sea-air was recommended, and the thought that Mrs. Barker might also like to become an invalid of the same kind at a cheap rate sometime during the summer, made it impossible for Mr. Barker to refuse a lady, with such a nice house and grounds, the request that her darling might pass an occasional Sunday with her and have a week for the same purpose about the Fourth of July.

A boy with such a kind ma and a coat with tails was naturally expected to be very good during the entire term. It is astonishing how insufficient basis these mercies proved for the proper style of behavior on my part, and when I now look back on what I went and did in spite of them, I appreciate the struggles of the sincere autobiographer as I never did before. I went and took a ride without asking Barker. Perhaps it was because I did this that he said, " There's no use in granting a boy **pleasures, — if** you give him an inch **he** takes **an ell;** " perhaps it **was** because I had heard him say it before, and reflected that the witness of that previous tail-coat would rise to bar my having any further swing of wild hilarity, that I didn't ask him if I might.

It was a bright Saturday in June, — neither too cold nor too warm, — and three P. M. At a bi-monthly during the preceding week I had seen Miss Tucker, and was still her slave. She had put her back hair up, and looked beautifully presented **in that** way ; but I thought what a contrast there would **have been to** my existing heavenly serenity **of** mind, had **I a** ma like some boys' mas and a coat without tails. I also saw Miss Crickey, who, having grown mealier during vacation and adhered to the fashion of queues tied on her back with blue ribbons, looked more than ever like a mote floating in the radiance of that back hair. I had long ago made up with Briggs, for whom I was now ready to do anything, from the particular of blacking upward, which could be any comfort to a person not the object of preference by **Miss** Tucker. The singular accident of his having known what to do with your participle in *dus,* when you wanted to be a peg more elegant than was compatible with your gerund **in** *dum,* **had, on this** particular Saturday, de**prived Mr.** Barker of any pretext for putting an extra brown upon his slack-baked mind in the oven of the dormitory; and an amount of self-control, arguing rapid growth toward manhood's worldly astuteness, had prevented him from whistling with ecstasy over his unusual luck before he left the school-room, and being called back to write the noun descriptive of his act five hundred times upon a slate. So Briggs and I, at three P. M., as aforesaid, stood untrammelled **by aught save** guilty **fear** in the little stably-smelling pen, **shared** by the whips, ledgers, and buffalo-robes of Mr. Greescels, the liveryman.

"I want a conveyance," I began boldly.

" In the nature o' wot ? " returned Mr. Greeseels, eying us suspiciously from under a fell left eyebrow, which needed the singeing lamp more than any hack's coat in his stud.

" I think Mr. Barker prefers a four-seated rockaway," interposed Briggs, with a prompt acuteness, which showed that his tussle with the gerund in *dum* had done wonders for his intellectual discipline.

At the same time I pulled out a gold watch, which my mother had given me during vacation, stated the time, and asked that the vehicle might be got ready immediately; also, drawing out a wallet which contained my entire savings for the term, and demanding how much it would be for the whole afternoon, with a first-rate horse let him take notice, turned around so as to show Mr. Greeseels that he was not dealing with one of your jacket sort of characters by any means. So much opulence, assurance, and tails were too much for Mr. Greeseels, who succumbed without another word. In five minutes the rockaway and a big, long-stepping gray stood at the mounting-block. I paid the price in advance, motioned Briggs to the back seat, grasped the reins, jumped up in front, and drove away. To favor the impression left upon the cautious hippodromic mind, yet with fear and trembling lest Barker should meet us, we kept the road toward the school till a turn shut the stables out of sight, then cut down a side street to the retired candy store, at which, during Miss Moodle's last bi-monthly, we had appointed a clandestine meeting with Miss

Tucker and Miss Crickey. We found those young ladies chilling their consciences with ice-cream in a back-room, and quite unable, through preoccupation in watching for a **momently** possible Miss Moodle, to say whether it was lemon or vanilla. They were prettily attired in Marseilles basquines and dresses of sprigged muslin; **and the** novel position of committing an impropriety **had** imparted an interesting flush to the cheek of Miss Crickey, which I could not but observe with satisfaction, as I definitely intended her and Briggs for each other, — a purpose additionally furthered by putting the two together on the back seat. The direction in which I should drive was perplexed by several harassing conditions. Miss Tucker was not quite sure whether the honest peasant, who accommodated Miss Moodle in the matter **of** milk, lived **upon the** Pratt's Corners road or the Tinkerville **turnpike, and he** was familiar with her beautiful countenance, having sold her sour buttermilk **for** its sunburns, had a long memory and a communicative tongue. A day-boarder, who objected to Miss Crickey from the fact of her always answering first for the men who built stone walls in a given number of days, or the boys who had apples to distribute in mental arithmetic, would probably be swinging on the parental **gate** all **the afternoon,** three miles out of town in the direction **of North** Jenkins; and nothing would give her greater pleasure than the solution of the question, if two girls went out riding, unbeknownst, on Saturday, P. M., how many would get put on bread and water the

next Monday morning. Briggs's step-father had **an**
aunt with piles of money, on still another road, but **as**
he knew the boss (such was his unfilial expression)
would never go to see her unless **she** died, **and there**
was no danger of her doing that, for all the family had
a way of hanging on like thunder, he didn't care a row
of pins whether we took that road or not. As that road
happened to be the one leading to Squash-ke-bosh, and I
felt a natural interest in seeing how it looked since my
mother was at the other end of **it, I** decided that we
should take it. It was a very pleasant one, with snug
farms and patches of beech **and oak forest** upon either
hand, enlivened here and there by more ambitious
grounds, trim lawns with stately Palladian residences
shining through bowers of ash, larch, althea, and smoke-
tree in the back-ground, and the *fermes ornées* of retired merchants, who had a passion for skipping away
their hard dollars on the bottomless pond of fancy cat-
tle-breeding. **A** pretty little brook kept us company all
the way, — now running alongside the straight old turnpike, now dodging **under it to come** gleefully **singing
out of the umber bridge-shadows on the other side, like**
a coquettish child gambolling about the knees and duck-
ing between **the legs of some** staid ancient gentleman.
Everything in the gift of bountiful nature was received
with such thankful joy by the four escaped criminals
who freighted the rockaway, that only the eye of an ex-
pert in natural depravity, like Barker or Moodle, could
have pierced the thick veil of deception and gloated on

16

the depths of iniquity which lay hidden in the compass of the one-horse vehicle. As for myself, I can say that I was full of a fearful happiness. I drove in a dream of bliss. I was already married to Miss Tucker ; the big, raw-boned grey was my own team of thorough-breds ; we were making an original honey-moon tour by easy stages, stopping at rural inns over night, hav-ing our coffee as strong as we liked, and sugaring it ourselves, in the morning ; unrestricted as to pancakes, gravy, bedtime, anything ; paying large bills with easy nonchalance out of an inexhaustible cheque-book carried under the back-seat ; having our groom and bridesmaid behind us already engaged and driven to tantalizations of rapture by **the** consummated hymeneal example in front ; while, adding **an** intoxicating zest to all this sweetness, **like the spirituous** soupçon which tingles through the siropy flavors of an arrack punch, came that masculine smack of the illicit — that thought of all this being in spite of the Barker and the Moodle. Many a time since then have I trundled behind my own two-forty trotter ; but there was nobody to stop me, and I found it, oh, how tame !

We came to a place where, under drooping alders, the little brook paused in a quiet pool, like **a** frolicsome pilgrim, **turning** aside and sitting out of the noontide **brightness to ponder demurely on** reflections of the leaves and sky. Steeped **in** coolness to their dewlaps, — the whole problem of worldly anxiety reduced to flies, a few square feet of tawny back, and a whisking tail, —

a group of cattle lifted their great brown eyes vacantly toward us, as we rolled over the twentieth bridge upon our journey. I had halted the gray for Miss Tucker to admire a lovely little calf, with a white star on his forehead, and the most incapable legs ever vouchsafed an immature vertebrate. On her expressing a wish that she had him, I was submitting to my mind the insane proposition whether it would not be possible to tie his legs with a pocket-handkerchief, carry him back with us between the seats, and get Briggs to help me build a cage for him, that he might be hung up in Miss Tucker's room, when the sound of rolling wheels behind us **waked** me from my trance, and, looking back, I beheld Barker and Mrs. Barker, Boens the mathematical teacher, and Miss Moodle, coming on in a rockaway like unto our own.

A dreadful moment! The eye of Barker had marked me; the voice of Barker was already calling on me to **stop. I** simply gasped his name, when Miss Tucker uttered a piteous little **cry** like **a wounded fawn. I** added that of Moodle; she hid her **face in my bosom,** and **I was strong. The entire force of my character** came to a point at **the end of my whip. The** gray struck out manfully ; and, looking through the back-glass, Briggs reported that the old 'un was a going it likewise. Miss Crickey, having a mathematical mind, became our strong pillar of consolation, — first suggesting to us the thought if four grown people behind Barker's fat mare could go a certain distance in a given

time, how far could as many light weights go, with our
gray, in the same time ? I do not recollect that I analyzed
the problem according to the method of Colburn; but
what I do know is, that it gave me the only comfort I
ever got out of mental arithmetic. **The** voice of Barker
grew fainter and fainter, and at last died away like some
spectral **echo of the** dead schoolmasters who flogged
mankind **in the** days of the Seleucidæ; then sank to
nothing, as their remorseful cries have gone down into
hades and oblivion. Looking back from the top of
every hill, we could still see Barker pressing on. But
a stern-chase is a long chase; weight and age were
both against him; and, at every **view, fat Kitty** showed
increasing bellows **to** mend. At length, going **up a**
long rise, Briggs reported from the rear that the enemy
had abandoned pursuit; and, for the first time venturing
to look out, I beheld him, at the distance of half a mile
turn Kitty's head and start for home. It was before
the **day** of universal telegraphs, or he would have been
abundantly adequate to set the rural police on **us**
throughout the county; there was no railway communication in the direction we were travelling, or he would
not have hesitated a moment to hire a special engine for
our capture, **and** charge **it on my** ma's quarterly bill.
What he might do was to return, and, selecting the
fleetest courser in Mungerville, resume the scent in the
saddle **or a** sulky. There **was no** time to lose. Without thinking whither we went, I pressed the big gray,
until a solemn-faced stone at the wayside warned us

that we had strayed a distance of sixteen miles from
the refining and intellectual atmosphere of Moodle's.
Miss Tucker was sobbing bitterly. Briggs, plunged in
gloom and his own pockets to the elbow, was uttering
grim reflections upon the liveliness of a future eternity
of Saturdays in bed. I was suffering agonies of remorse
at the misery in which I had involved the lovely and
uncomplaining but heart-broken creature at my side.
Miss Crickey alone was calm. Retiring into the fastnesses of a mind strengthened by the compound frac-
tions, and, unlike Miss Tucker, having no back hair
to come down in the distraction of the exigency, she
was something to admire, and I could not but hope
that Briggs would do it. She never uttered a syllable
until that youth ungenerously threw the whole responsibility upon me by saying, —

"Well, here's a pickle! Now what do *you* mean to
do?"

Before I could reply, Miss Crickey returned from her
fastnesses to the actual situation with the words, —

"I think Mr. Thirlwall once remarked that he had a
ma living at Squash-ke-bosh. This is the road to
Squash-ke-bosh. Sixteen from fifty leaves thirty-four
miles. Let us go and throw ourselves upon the compassion of Mr. Thirlwall's ma."

Miss Tucker looked up radiantly, bid farewell to every
fear, and wiped her weeping eyes.

"That was the way George Washington did," said
Miss Tucker, in a moist voice, "the time he had been
and done it with his little hatchet."

"He had immediate recourse to his pa," said Miss Crickey, supplying the exact details with a commendable desire for historic accuracy.

"And a ma's a darned sight better than a pa," quoted Briggs from the stores of his own experience.

I myself could think of nothing better to do than Miss Crickey proposed ; for I would as soon, under the circumstances, have changed places with Regulus, and gone back to Carthage for a ride down hill in a nail-keg, as to have returned to Barker's and Moodle's. Fortunately, just after sunset, there came up a heavy thunder-shower, which gave us an excuse for turning a mile down a cross-road, and taking shelter for the night in a farm-house, where we were hospitably taken care of in the character of a family of cousins, on their way to visit an aunt; had a splendid time eating strawberries and cream, and realized the long ideal ecstasy of "doorkeeper." Memory still chronicles, with a thrill, that under that humble roof I kissed Miss Tucker for the first time. Avaunt, thou spectral recollection, that Briggs similarly improved the opportunity !

The big gray, having been equally refreshed, after his fashion, took us cleverly into Squash-ke-bosh by one o'clock the next afternoon. As my ma was a newcomer to that pleasant seaport, I expected considerable trouble in finding her cottage ; but was saved that by the occurrence of another awkwardness, — meeting her just as she came out of church, upon the principal street, and startling her, by my apparition, to that degree she dropped her handsome prayer-book and forgot whether the text had been in Revelation or Job. Explanation being impossible, where people discuss a subject from such different grounds as a rockaway and the sidewalk, I took her up on the front seat with Miss Tucker, and gave her a sketch of our recent adventures, in that spirit of frankness which characterized the before-cited memorable interview between Mr. Bushrod Washington and his boy G. The grandfather of his country could not be more lenient than was that dear mother. Her chiding was of the gentlest; tears and laughter contended for the possession of her eyes; when she got **us** into **the** house she took us all literally to her heart and kissed us, beginning with me, and promised us an asylum until mediation could let us down easily into the stern but placated bosoms of Barker and Moodle. The ensuing evening she spent in writing letters to those authorities, and to the mammas of my three fellow-convicts.

Monday and Tuesday must necessarily pass before she could receive any reply to the Barker and Moodle **letters, which went out** by **the** early stage **on** Monday **morning.** The **big gray** was sent back in charge of a trusty messenger, **who** also bore behind him **in** the rockaway two hampers of choice hot-house fruit as a propitiatory offering to the offended Moloch of education. While we were waiting, the hours passed in a perfect trance of delight. We played every game of which human ingenuity is capable. We bathed in the surf and we boated on the bay. We drove out in the carriage

with my mother to visit a Hanging Rock, and a Lover's
Leap. When Miss Crickey said that the former was in
only apparent danger **of falling because a line drawn**
through **its** centre of gravity would not strike outside
the base, **I** was pained to see Briggs manifest less admiration at the statement than its scientific accuracy de-
served, and regretted that he could not experience those
emotions which thrilled my bosom when, standing on the
edge of the latter, I imagined Moodle and Barker
coming up behind **to tear Miss** Tucker from my arms,
put my arms tenderly around **her** waist, and calculated
the distance between us and the fathomless deep. My
mother's sympathy for Briggs was of a nature which
constantly affected him to **tears.** She had heard of his
family circumstances from me, and took extra pains to
show him those delicate little attentions which are so
missed by the homeless boy. If she drew him caress-
ingly to her side, or gave **him a** particularly large slice of
marmalade **at lunch, he was** certain to be missing al-
most immediately after, and to turn **up in** some unexpected corner violently blowing his nose.

On Wednesday afternoon we received our replies from
Mr. Barker and Miss Moodle, couched very much in such
terms as might be expected from a pair of Turkish
pashas **sparing the lives of** a batch of political offenders
at the intercession of some **powerful foreign** government.
Briggs alone was **made an exception to** the amnesty.
With a terseness which left so much for the imagination
as to prove that Mr. Barker would have achieved great

eminence in dramatic literature had he chosen that career, the letter said that Master Briggs' case was now
under consideration of his pa, who would doubtless act
wisely under the circumstances, and needed **no** suggestions from the writer.

About an hour after the letters **came,** while we sat in
the parlor in deep gloom, discussing the honorableness
of going back to Mungerville without Briggs, the maid
brought in a card to my mother's sitting-room from a
gentleman in the front parlor.

"Lard and bacon ! Pork packed and shipped!" exclaimed my mother. "**He** really can't think I deal in
any such articles. **Do you** know any such name **as that,**
Ben ?"

I glanced at the card, and my involuntary exclama-
tion of "By jingo !" brought Briggs to my side. "T.
Mixer! O Lord !" said the poor boy ; and with something very like a howl of anguish, he jumped out of the
back window to the verandah and fled into the shrubbery.

"**Go you after** him, **Ben,**" spoke my **mother.** "**I'm
afraid he'll run away to sea.** Tell him *I'm* going **in to
see Mr. Mixer, and comfort him.**" My mother's **man-**
ner prevented any misconstruction of the equivoque. It
was plain enough that she was not going in to be any
comfort to Mixer, and I gladly rushed out to do that
office for Briggs. I found him in the hay-loft, leaning
against a stringer, and apparently trying to kick all the

pegs out of his left heel, which in moments of despera-
tion was his **favorite method of** making up his mind. .

"You see that beam ?" asked Briggs, huskily.

"Yes ! what of that ? " said I.

"Has your ma got a spare clothes-line, — a strong one,
— one she wont want to use till to-morrow ? "

"I suppose so; but what do you want of that now ?"

"Just get it for me, will you, please, then leave me
alone for a few minutes. If anything happens before
you **come back, cut a** lock of hair off the back of my
head ; that's where my mother — used — to be —
fondest of brushing — it; it don't stick out so stiff as
it does in front. Tell her I didn't blame her ; enclose it
in a little note, and say — I — I — I loved her to the
last." Here his voice choked with emotion ; he buried
his face in a bale of hay and groaned alond.

I threw myself upon Briggs's neck, combed the hay-
seed out of his hair, and besought him to weigh the matter well before he hanged himself. I implored him to
remember what nice times we might have gathering
chestnuts in the fall; to think of his mother (he shut
his eyes doggedly) — of me (he did not stir) — of Miss
Crickey (he made a perceptible sign of disdain) — of —
of — I hesitated but a moment and added, "Miss Tucker."
A pang shot through **me, though I did not wish him to
hang himself, when** I beheld a remarkable change come
over him at the mention of that lovely name. He shut
his teeth, clenched his fists, shook himself like a New-
foundland, and stood up to his full stature of five feet

seven. It was undeniable that Briggs was a very stout, manly looking boy.

" Well," said he, grimly, after a moment's reflection, " there's one thing I can do. I can go off to China, and come back, when I'm a man, with a cargo of silks and teas."

" Be a man now, Briggs," said I, encouragingly; " let's go out and walk in the air ; you'll feel better for it. Bless me ! Don't you suppose we'll stand by you, old fellow ? "

We were wandering, arm in arm, toward a rustic sum- mer-house in the back-grounds, when we perceived my mother coming down the gravel walk from the verandah, accompanied by a stranger, whom it was not difficult to divine as Mixer. The problem of his objection to Briggs's growth was solved immediately, for nature had been a stern creditor with him in the matter of legs, and after letting them run for the first twelve years of his life, inexorably refused him any further extension, so that he was scarcely, if any, taller than Briggs was when I first knew him. He had a small, lumpy head, with strands of a peculiar greenish-brown shade of hair plas- tered on it at wide intervals, like ribbons of half-dry sea- weed ; a diffused slippery nose, that looked as if it had been boned and larded as some fearful delicacy, and a flat, doughy face shoved under it to serve for bottom crust. His thin, vulgarly cut lips wore an expression of pert criticism, which might have sprung from the habit of testing the strength of pork-brine, and his reddish-brown eyes had all the mean truculence of a snapping cur's.

Briggs turned deadly pale when he saw him, but kept on his way toward him.

" Mr. Mixer wished to walk out and **look for you**," said **my** mother, **in a** voice where kindness to **Briggs** struggled with poorly-concealed disgust for **the** object at her side.

" **Yes**," spoke **Mixer**, with a smack of malignant satisfaction ; " yes–s–s ; happening through this flourishing seaport on business, and accidentally having heard from Mr. Barker, with whom **I** chanced to spend last evening, that a young friend of mine was passing the summer here very pleasantly, I naturally felt a desire to **call and see how he was getting on ; also, to see** if there **was** anything **I could do for him. And** I think — **very decidedly** — I think there is. Your son, ma'am, I suppose " (turning **his hang-dog eyes** from Briggs to me), — " **and a nice boy he is** — yes–s–s, **really, a very nice boy. Master Briggs, if** this **lady and** your agreeable young friend will excuse us, suppose you oblige me with a few moments' conversation in the shrubbery ? "

Briggs's lip quivered for a moment, and then he said, " Well." " We shan't go far," he added to me, with a **most expressive glance, that meant that my mother and I should not.** We understood **him, and, as** he strolled off **toward the stables again with Mixer by** his side, kept out of sight, but conveniently near to afford him the sense of our moral support. At first we could hear nothing but the shrill hiss of Mixer's satirical affirmatives, answering every quiet, low-voiced explanation which Briggs made.' Presently, however, Briggs's key rose, and he was quite audible when he told Mixer that he had bullied his mother almost into her grave, and was trying to shove her son in after her. "But you shan't!" added Briggs, "you shan't! and *she* shouldn't stay with you another day if I were only a man and had any place to take her to."

"So ho!" replied T. Mixer, unconsciously speaking louder, but still in a tone of satanic coolness. "Mr. Barker has failed with you too, has he? You have a peculiarly depraved and stiff-necked nature, young man, but we'll make one more effort to save you. You can take that jacket off, and be quick about it, too."

They had come to a pause under a big linden, and for a moment Briggs stood irresolutely, eying his step-father.

"Come—do you hear me?—off with that jacket!" repeated Mixer, and at the same time passing his hand inside a loose travelling-sack which he wore, produced a stout, red raw-hide about three feet long.

"Damn the brute!" said I, involuntarily, and my mother did not check me, for the blood was mounting into her gentle face till it crimsoned her very temples; and the next instant, dashing her garden-flat to the greensward, she burst from behind the shrubbery, and made her way toward Mixer at a pace which looked either very unlike an invalid for whom sea-air had been recommended, or like one to whom the prescription had been remarkably salutary. Before she reached him, the cowhide had descended once upon the head of Briggs, and made two angry red wales across his upheld hands.

" Give me that whip, sir," said my mother, between her clenched teeth.

Mixer cast at her one look of savage amazement, then lifted the raw-hide again.

" *Give me that whip*," repeated my mother, in a still lower tone ; her brows coming down to a point over eyes which pierced Mixer through. The cur dropped his hand, and unresistingly suffered my mother to take the rod out of it. She flung it out into the tall grass as far as she could throw; then with flashing eyes addressed Briggs,—

" I don't want you to hurt this — *man* — you know; but you can turn him out of my premises just as soon as **you like. You're a good** stout boy, and you might make mincemeat of him, if you put out your strength; so don't knock him down, or pound him, or anything of that sort. I leave him to you ; be careful of him."

" Now's the time to oblige him ! " I cried. " Off with your coat, Briggs ! "

So saying, I was about to come in for my share of the fun, but Briggs stopped me.

" No, no, Ben ! Two to one's **not fair play** ; besides, he's up to having you **put in** the lock-up for assault and battery, and calling your own mother to swear on you; I'm able for him alone I guess."

With these words Briggs let fly a neat left-hander, and threw his shoulder after it, bringing up against his substitute for a parent in the region just above the cravat-tie. Mr. Mixer went in pursuit of his balance spirally for a few yards, and, failing to overtake it, sat suddenly **down.** The distance between his sedentary and upright posture was not so great as in the case of a person more **liberally blessed** with legs; but even this little he was unable to make up before Briggs was once more upon him. Catching his ancient tyrant by the collar with his left hand, and taking as firm a hold of his nose as that broad and slippery member admitted of, with his left, he elevated him to his feet, and asked him which side he should let go of, back or front; "for out you go one way or t'other, you know," added Briggs, considerately, "and you can take your choice; so say now — push or pull ? "

T. Mixer, thoroughly cowed, began whining that he preferred to have his nose let go of, but added, in a nasal voice, which marred the moral dignity of the senti-ment, **that he hoped** that Briggs would " rebebber his filial **duty, if it was odly for his Ba's sake."**

"**Don't you talk to me of my ma, you sneak !** " roared Briggs, giving the nose one final tweak before he abandoned it; "don't you dare to mention her, you hypo-crite ! " he repeated, shaking Mixer as a terrier would shake a rat, "unless you want to sit on the ground again without anything to put your feet on ! " Then, propelling him before him by the nape of the neck as

fast as his legs would carry him, Briggs trundled the de-
throned despot to the front gate, and, while I held it open
for him, dismissed Mr. Mixer into the outer world with
a parting kick, which sent him half-way across the road.
For a moment he turned round and showed symptoms
of relieving himself in a torrent of abuse; but, seeing
his castigator ready to perfect his lesson, contented
himself with shaking his fist, and departed down the
road toward Squash-ke-bosh. Briggs returned silently
from the gate, and, sitting down on a rustic seat in the
grounds, gave way to the reaction of his feelings. He
struggled bravely to repress his excitement; but as
he buried his face in his hands, the words came out
sobbingly, —

" And now — I'm all—a-a-alone in the world."

My mother came out of the shrubbery behind him,
stole one arm tenderly around his neck, and said, —

" No, you aren't, my child; if this has lost you all
the home you had, you can have your share of Ben's."

So the long and the short of it was, that Briggs
spent all his vacations after that under my mother's
roof ; and as for his school-days, she herself personally
saw to the arrangement by which he was received back
at Barker's. T. Mixer, upon reflection, concluded that he
would do himself no credit by appearing further on the
scene.

My history here makes a Hanlon Brothers' leap
across the chasm of seven years. Briggs had thrown
away all his early experience of self-denial by refusing

to go out as a missionary, and accepting a confidential
position in the Wall-street house, of which I was junior
partner. We occupied a suite of rooms together in Clinton Place, and Miss Tucker, now a belle in society, **was**
at home with her parents, a few blocks above us on the
avenue. Miss* Crickey had married a widower, and
having a large capital of ready-made children to start
the mental arithmetic business **with,** had gone to Ger-
many to **consult the** newest lights of education. My
mother's attachment to the old homestead where my
father had first brought her, kept her from selling the
place and she stayed there during the greater part of
the year, **I** spending **all the time with** her that **I could**
spare from my business in summer, and promising myself the pleasure of having her under my own roof during the winter, as soon as I could get married and keep
house. How soon that might be was very uncertain. I
was of a singularly constant nature, and still Miss Tucker's slave. My mother's letter to her ma, written on her
behalf when she eloped with me from Moodle's, had led
to an intimate acquaintance between the families, **and
now, living in New York, I visited her one and often
two evenings in the week.** Briggs's friendship **was no**
less sedulous, and I spared myself the possibility of
pain by refraining from the inquiry how much deeper
feeling he entertained toward the object of my adoration.
I knew that this state of uncertainty could not last always. I felt a daily increasing reticence toward my old
school-mate, and saw that if something definite were not

17 *

done soon, an incurable jealousy and coolness would be
established between us. **For** the sake of our intimacy,
to say nothing of my own peace of mind, I must bring
matters to a decision by speaking definitely **to Miss**
Tucker. The result might be as painful as an heroic
surgical operation to either Briggs or myself; but **it**
would stop the gangrene of our friendship.

I came to this conclusion one evening when Briggs
had gone up to call on Miss Tucker, and I sat by a
small sea-coal fire (for, though spring, the weather was
still chilly) smoking my cigar at eleven o'clock, and
wondering how in the world any man could have the
thoughtlessness to keep a private family up till that
hour. It must have been still later when he left the
Tuckers, for he did not get back to our lodgings until
twelve. When he did come, he kicked off his boots as
soon as he entered our parlor, and went to his bedroom
without saying a word beyond good-night.

The next afternoon, as Briggs stood by a desk at the
window, deep in some abstruse stock calculation, and **I**
sat before the office-grate reading business letters just
brought in by the mail-boy, we heard the whole street
thrown into an uproar outside us, by the sonorous cry of
" Extra ! " Partners, clerks, and loungers ran to the
door **at once, to discover that** History had opened her
iron account-book with the nation, **and** made her first
entry in the fall of Sumter. That revelation closed
our own trivial business for the day. The next day's
wild excitement, slowly but surely settling into the

strength of inexorable loyal purpose, who needs that I
recall? Briggs was absent from his desk, but I never
noticed the fact till it was time for me to go up town.
Just then he entered the office. If his conduct was
strange to me on the night of his last return from the
Tuckers, it was stranger now. He vouchsafed me noth-
ing but a cold nod, then entered into animated conversa-
tion with a knot of business men who were discussing
the great question of the day in our back office. Hav-
ing fifteen minutes to spare, I presently joined them.
The talk ran upon volunteering. Several, who already
belonged to municipal organizations, expressed their intention of sharing **the** fight, and one of them suddenly
turned to me with the question, —

"Are *you* going?"

I thought of the hostage I might be leaving to Fortune, in the person of Miss Tucker, and hesitatingly re-
plied that there seemed to be plenty going for the
present without me, and I didn't know.

Briggs said, as if speaking, incidentally to a third
person, that there were also plenty of cowards staying .
behind.

Our old jealousies culminated in an instant. "Do you
mean to apply that term to me?" I asked, fiercely, with
my cheeks crimson.

"If the shoe fits, wear it," answered Briggs, noncha-
lantly. The kind of autobiography that I write compels
me to own that I struck him. I was sorry for the act
the moment after. I ought to have been patient with

him and made allowance for some hidden source of irritation. I ought not **to have** given serious weight to a
sneer which I **was conscious of not deserving, and of**
which I might know that another mood would make him
ashamed. But these thoughts only came with the reaction from my anger, and the blow **was struck.**

Briggs turned on me at once, but **some of the others**
jumped between us to prevent a fight, telling him **that
he had** given the first offence, and trying to persuade
him to walk away soberly. I **returned into the front**
office, **and tried to absorb myself in the** afternoon
news, that I might get quiet enough to walk up town,
but my heart was too full. I **thought of** Briggs's unhappy boyhood, of the many hard and happy times we
had been through together, **of the almost** brotherly relations which had so long existed between us, of the
rivalry which **had been** disturbing them, and of the
bitterness of spirit which he must have endured **in
silence before he** could become so changed toward me.
The current **of my** reflections was suddenly broken by
the entrance of Briggs, the other gentlemen following
him.

" Ben," said he, addressing me in a husky voice, " you
might have known me well enough **to be sure that I**
didn't mean to call **you a coward; and yet"** — his
voice trembled so he could scarcely speak — " and yet,
you struck me — struck me in **the** face. You know the
way we look upon those insults, — they're things to be
atoned for; and if you were not who you are, and we

what we've been to each other, I'd call you out to-
morrow. But this is a time which forbids men to throw
away their blood on private quarrels; so I challenge
you another way, — I challenge you to go with me into
the fight for our country. . There is a meeting at eight
o'clock to-night at Ralston and Crosby's warehouse, of
young men who wish to organize a volunteer regiment
for immediate service under Colonel Crosby. I shall be
there to enroll myself. Will you accept ? "

I looked into his face for a moment, and then answered
" I will."

I kept my word, and left the warehouse at nine that
evening a member of the Crosby regiment. From that
place, I rode at once to the residence of Mr. Tucker. I
stayed longer there than I had at the warehouse, and on
coming away was member of still another organization,
— an organization of two. A fortnight afterward,
Briggs and I were on our way to Washington.

Again my autobiography makes a leap. The regiment had several times seen active service. Briggs and
I had risen to the captaincies of our several companies.
On the eleventh day of December, 1862, we had crossed
the Rappahannock, and now, where this narrative re-
sumes its thread, were fighting our way under a mur-
derous fire from every cover, from street to street,
through Fredericksburg.

As I was engaged in posting advanced skirmishers
along the line on which brave Arthur Fuller had just
fallen but forty rods further to the eastward, a body of

one hundred rebels rose with yells from behind a low board-fence across the way, and poured a volley into our little squad. We looked about in vain for support. It was a necessity bitter as death; but we were compelled to fall back to the cover of an old stable on the next street. Slowly and in good order, firing steadily as we retired, we got within a pistol-shot of shelter, **and,** looking back, saw Briggs's company coming at the double-quick up a lane on the right to reinforce us, when I felt a sudden shiver of pain, as if a sharp icicle had run into my thigh; my feet went from under me; my eyes grew misty; and then all was darkness.

When I next came to myself, it was late twilight. I was lying alone, in maddening thirst and agony,—the air about me stifling with smoke, and still singing with bullets. Two detachments of the opposing forces were contending for the space on which I lay; and, as the balls whistled over me, I momently expected the final quietus to my pain. In an interval between the volleys on our side, I saw a man leave the ranks, and come crawling on his hands and knees toward me. Little by little he approached the place where I lay, without attracting the aim of the opposite combatants. It was too dark to distinguish his uniform; but I supposed him **some reckless rebel, coming to rob me** of my watch and side-arms; and, having heard of the practice, occasionally indulged in by our foes, of putting wounded men beyond the future trouble of claiming such little trinkets,

feigned death, with eyes tight-shut and breath close-
held. But he bent over me only an instant; then lifted
me upon his back, with my face over his shoulder and
my arms hanging down, and began returning with me,
on his hands and knees, as he had come. When he was
about half-way home to his comrades, the enemy evidently caught sight of him ; for a shout ran along their
front, and a dozen shots followed, unpleasantly close to
my ears. My carrier lay down for a moment, slid me
off his back, wound one arm around my waist, and,
covering me with his own body, crept on his knees **and**
the remaining hand until **he had** dragged me within his
own lines. Just as he got in, the pain of my **wounded**
leg reached such a pitch, through the irritation of movement, that I heard only the burst of cheers with which
his friends received him, and the rattle of the volley
which his return left them free to fire, then once more
became dead to all the world.

When I again awoke, I found myself lying on a bed
of army-blankets, with a pillow of the same material
rolled up under my head; and two men stood near me,
talking **in a repressed voice, under the shadow of a high**
stone-wall.

"I'm afraid he can't possibly last through the night,"
said one of them; "he has lost so much blood that
there's nothing left to rally. He may revive again for a
moment, but hardly."

"Well, doctor," answered the other, in a voice of deep

sadness, "don't let me keep you any longer; I'll stay and watch with him till the stretcher comes."

It was my old school-mate who spoke. I tried to call on him ; but, in my intense weakness, my tongue failed me.

He brought a lantern from the shadow of the wall, and, tucking the blankets tenderly about my feet, threw the light upon his lap, and took out of his pocket a little bundle tied up in his handkerchief. When he undid the knots, I recognized in their enclosure the precious little remembrances which I had carried next my breast and taken into every fight with me since the war began. One by one he held them in the light of the lantern, and soliloquized over them bitterly.

" *She* gave me a home; *she* stood up for me when I hadn't a defender in the world; *she* did a mother's best for me when mine couldn't help me. That's her dear face, with the eyes looking just as if she expected Ben; and there lies all that will ever get home to her. And *I* brought him here — *I*, I ! O God ! why couldn't they have shot me, too ? Why didn't I fall dead on him while I was dragging him out of fire ? How can *I* send him back to her, *so ?*

" Here are the letters, — ' Captain Ben Thirlwall '; he'd have been a general if he'd lived. How proud his mother'd have been. How proud *she'd* have been too. And here's *her* picture. Oh, sweet, sweet ! how I've loved those eyes — ever so long ago — ever since I was a little boy ! — and I'd no right — they were *his* — they

always looked **dearly** at him, and I was a vain, presump-
tuous, passionate fool. They were to have been married the first time he got furlough. Lovely face ! all **my**
life far off and darling as heaven, how can I ever look
into **you any** more ? Let **me be** forgiven; let me **kiss
you once, as if we were** children again in the old farm-
house; no one can see it — **even** you can't know: it
will do you no wrong; once — **the only,** the last time
my beloved, widowed, *sister.*"

He pressed **his lips to the** photograph; his sorrowful
eyes **grew wet; and, hearing a** measured noise of feet,
he **thrust the articles back** into his pocket, drew **his cuff**
across his face, and stood up with a stern " **Who goes**
there ? "

" Men with the stretcher, captain," answered a cor-
poral, saluting.

My school-mate raised me tenderly in his arms and
laid me on the stretcher. I made one desperate effort,
patted his cheek and whispered, " Dear old boy ! " then
swooned once more with **his cry of** delight ringing in
my ears, and never woke again till the sun was shining
brightly into my hospital tent on the northern side of the
Rappahannock.

The moans of **wounded men, sinking to** their final **rest,**
mingled around me with the outcries of those who were
fighting their battles over again in the frenzy of delirium. Inflammation had set in, and I was suffering great
pain and fever; but my reason was left me, and my first
thought **was of** the friend who **had borne** my bleeding

18

body and his own broken heart out of last night's hellish hail-storm.

" Briggs ! " I cried, faintly.

A kind fellow in employ of the Sanitary Commission, who was watching in the tent, came softly to my side with a canteen of cool spring water and a cup of brandy.

" No — not that — not that ! " said I; " where's Captain Briggs ? "

He moistened my lips, and told me he would look about in camp and see. He had not been gone five minutes when I heard a bustle outside the tent and some one say, —

" Where did you find him ? "

" He was shot from behind a fence last night, while he was gathering in the wounded," said another voice.

" No — not in there ! " exclaimed a third, hastily; " take it to the next tent — Captain Thirlwall lies in this, badly wounded."

Take *it.* Who was it that had been *he* last night, and was only *it* this morning ? A terrible strength came into me; I crawled off my ground-spread blankets, and pulled myself on my elbows to the door. When they saw my deathly face in the gap of the tent, they hurriedly closed up in front of me, making as if they would conceal from me something which lay still and ghastly on a stretcher. Too late, — I had seen the well-known forehead with its clustering brown curls matted in blood, and one ragged, blue hole in the centre — and seeing that saw no more. My next four weeks were past in raving delirium.

When my wife and I sit in the evening by our bed-room fire, our eyes sometimes fall on a worn, little daguerrotype, which has been removed from its morocco case and put on the mantle-piece, in an open frame of black walnut. It represents a bluff-faced, pleasant-eyed school-boy; it was taken during the days of fearful happiness which we spent all together at my mother's cottage by the sea. My mind glances on to another time when a full-grown man bore me under his own body's cover, out of the fire at Fredericksburg. I clasp my wife's hand closer, and as neither can see the other for tears, we know that we are both thinking of Little Briggs.

A BRACE OF BOYS.

A Brace of Boys.

AM a bachelor uncle. That, as a mere fact, might happen to anybody; but I am a bachelor uncle by internal fitness. I am one essentially, just as I am an individual of the Caucasian division of the human race; and if, through untoward circumstances,— which Heaven forbid!—I should lose my present position, I shouldn't be surprised if you saw me out in the *Herald* under "Situations Wanted — Males." Thanks to a marrying tendency in the rest of my family, I have now little need to advertise, all the business being thrown into my way which a single member of my profession can attend to.

I suppose you wont agree with me; but do you know sometimes I think it's better than having children of one's own? People tell me that I'd feel very differently if I did have any. Perhaps so; but then, too, I might be unwise with them. I might bother them into mischief by trying to keep them out. I might be avaricious of them,— might be tempted to lock them up in my own stingy old nursery-chest instead of paying them out to meet the bills of humanity and keep the Lord's business moving. **I might** forget, when I **had** spent my life in fining **their gold and polishing their graven-work,** that they were still vessels for **the Master's use, — I** only **the** butler, — the sweetness and the spirit **with** which they brimmed all belonging to His lips **who** **tasted bitterness for me.** **Then,** if seeking **to drain** another's wine I raised the chalice to my lips and found **it gall, or** felt it steal into my old veins to poison the heart and paralyze the hand which had kept it from the Master, what further good would there be for me in the world ? Who doesn't know in some friend's house a closet containing that worst of skeletons, — the skeleton which, in becoming naked, grim, and ghastly, tears its way through our own flesh and blood ?

To be an uncle is a different kind of thing. There you have nothing of the excitement of responsibility to **shake** your judgment. That's **what makes** us bachelor uncles so much better judges of what's good for children than their fathers and mothers. We know that nobody will blame us if our nephews unjoint their knuckles or cut their fingers off; so we give them five-bladed knives and boxing-gloves. This involves getting thanked at the time, which **is pleasant; and** if **no** catastrophe occurs, when **they have grown stout and ingenious,** with what calm satisfaction **we hear people say,** " **See** what a pretty wind-mill the child's **whittled out** with Uncle Ned's birthday present ! " or " That boy's grown an inch round the chest since you set him sparring ! " Uncles never get stale. They don't come every day like parents and plain pudding; they're a sort of holiday relative, with a plummy, Christmas flavor about them. Everybody hasn't got them; they're not so rare as the meteoric showers, but as occasional as a particularly fine day, and whenever they come to a house they're in the nature of a pleasant surprise.

I meander, **like** a desultory, placid river of an old bachelor as I am, through the flowery mead of several nurseries. I am detained by all the little roots that run down into me to drink happiness, but I linger longest among the children of my sister Lu.

Lu married **Mr. Lovegrove.** He is a merchant, retired with a fortune amassed by the old-fashioned, slow processes of trade, and regards the mercantile life of the present day only as so much greed and gambling Christianly baptized. For the ten years elapsing since he sold out of Lovegrove, Cashdown, & Co., he has devoted himself to his family and **a** revival of letters, taking up again the Latin and Greek which he had not looked at since his college days until he dismissed teas and silks **to adorn** a suburban villa with the spectacle of a prime Christian parent and Pagan scholar. **Lu** is my favorite sister; Lovegrove an usually good article of brother-in-law; and I cannot say that any of my nieces and nephews interest me more than their two children, Daniel and Billy, who are more unlike than words can paint them. They are far apart in point of years; Daniel is twenty-two, Billy eleven. I was reminded of this fact the other day by Billy, as he stood between my legs, scowling at his book of **sums.**

"'A boy has eighty-five turnips, and gives his sister thirty,'—pretty present for a girl, isn't it?" said Billy, with an air of supreme contempt. Could *you* stand such stuff,—say?"

I put on my instructive face and answered,—

"Well, my dear Billy, you know that arithmetic is necessary to you if you mean to be an industrious man and succeed in business. Suppose your parents were to lose all their property, what would become of them without a little son who could make money and keep accounts?"

"Oh!" said Billy, with surprise. "Hasn't father got enough stamps to see him through?"

"**He has now,** I hope; but people don't always keep **them.** Suppose they should go by some accident, when **your** father was too old to make any more stamps for himself?"—

"You haven't thought of brother Daniel"—

True; for nobody ever had, in connection with the active employments of life.

"No, Billy," I replied, "I forgot him; but then, you know, Daniel is more of a student than a business man, and"—

"O Uncle Teddy! you don't think I mean he'd support them? **I meant I'd** have to take care of father and mother, and him too, when they'd all got to be old people together. Just think! I'm eleven, and he's twenty-two; so he is just twice as old as I **am.** How old are you?"

"Forty, Billy, last August."

"Well, you aren't so awful old, and when **I get to be as old as you** Daniel will be eighty. Seth **Kendall's grandfather isn't more than that, and he** has to be fed **with a spoon,** and a nurse puts **him to** bed, and wheels **him round in a chair** like a baby. That takes the **stamps,** *I* bet! **Well, I'll tell you how** I'll keep my accounts: I'll have a stick, like Robinson Crusoe, and every time I make a toadskin I'll gouge a piece **out of** one side of the stick, and every time **I spend one I'll** gouge **a piece out of** the **other."**

"Spend a *what?*" said the gentle and astonished **voice of** my sister Lu, who, unperceived, had slipped into the room.

"A toadskin, ma," replied Billy, shutting up Colburn with a farewell glance of contempt.

"**Dear, dear!** Where does **the boy** learn such horrid words?"

"Why, ma! Don't you know what a toadskin is? Here's one," said Billy, drawing a dingy five-cent stamp from his **pocket.** "**And don't** I wish I had lots **of** 'em!"

"Oh!" sighed his mother, "to think I should have a child so addicted to slang! How I wish he were like Daniel!"

"Well, mother," replied Billy, "if you wanted two **boys** just alike you'd oughter had twins. There aint any use of my trying to be like Daniel now, when he's got eleven years the **start**. Whoop ! There's a dog-fight; hear 'em ! It's Joe **Casey's dog, — I know** his bark ! "

With these words **my** nephew snatched his Glengarry bonnet from the table and bolted downstairs **to** see the fun.

" **What** will become **of him ? "** said Lu, hopelessly; " **he has no** taste for anything **but** rough play; and then such language as he uses ! Why *isn't* he like Daniel ? "

" **I** suppose because his Maker never repeats himself. Even twins often possess strongly marked individualities. Don't you think it would **be** a good plan to learn Billy better before you **try to teach** him ? **If you do, you'll** make something as **good of him as Daniel; though** it will be rather **different from that model."**

" Remember, **Ned,** that **you never did like Daniel as well as you do** Billy. But **we all know** the proverb about old maids' daughters and **old bachelors' sons. I** wish you had Billy **for a month, — then you'd see."**

" **I'm not sure that I'd do any** better than **you. I** might err as much **in** other directions. **But I'd try to** start right by acknowledging that he was a new problem, not to be worked without finding out the value of *x* in his particular instance. The formula which solves one boy **will no more solve the next one than the rule-of-three will solve a question in calculus, — or, to rise** into **your sphere, than the receipt for** one-two-three-four cake **will** conduct **you to a** successful issue through plum-pudding " —

I excel in metaphysical discussion, and was about giving further elaboration to my favorite idea, when the door burst open. Master Billy came tumbling in with a torn jacket, a bloody nose, the trace of a few tears in his eyes, and the mangiest of cur dogs in his hands.

"Oh my! my! ! my! ! !" exclaimed his mother.

"Don't you get scared, ma!" cried Billy, smiling a stern smile of triumph; "I smashed the nose off him! He wont sass me again for nothing *this* while! Uncle Teddy, d'ye know it wasn't a dog-fight, after all? There was that nasty, good-for-nothing Joe Casey, 'n Patsy Grogan, and a lot of bad boys from Mackerelville; and they'd caught this poor little ki-oodle and tied a tin pot to his tail, and were trying to set Joe's dog on him, though he's ten times littler "—

"You naughty, naughty boy! How did you suppose your mother'd feel to see you playing with those ragamuffins?"

"Yes, I *played* 'em! I polished 'em, — that's the play I did! Says I, 'Put down that poor little pup; aint you ashamed of yourself, Patsy Grogan?' 'I guess you don't know who I am,' says he. That's the way they always say, Uncle Teddy, to make a fellow think they're some awful great fighters. So says I again, 'Well, you put down that dog, or I'll show you who *I* am;' and when he held on, I let him have. Then he dropped the pup, and as I stooped to pick it up he gave me one on the bugle."

"*Bugle!* Oh! oh! oh!"

22

"The rest pitched in to help him; but I grabbed the pup, and while I was trying to give as good as I got, — only a fellow can't do it well with only one hand, Uncle Teddy, — up came a policeman, and the whole crowd ran away. So I got the dog safe, and here he is!"

With that Billy set down his "ki-oodle," bid farewell to every fear, and wiped his bleeding nose. The unhappy beast slunk back between the legs of his preserver and followed him out of the room, as Lu, with an expression of maternal despair, bore him away for the correction of his dilapidated raiment and depraved associations. I felt such sincere pride in this young Mazzini of the dog-nation that I was vexed at Lu for bestowing on him reproof instead of congratulation; but she was not the only conservative who fails to see a good cause and a heroic heart under a bloody nose and torn jacket. I resolved that if Billy was punished he should have his recompense before long in an extra holiday at Barnum's or the Hippotheatron.

You already have some idea of my other nephew, if you have noticed that none of us, not even that habitual disrespecter of dignities, Billy, ever called him Dan. It would have seemed as incongruous as to call Billy William. He was one of those youths who never gave their parents a moment's uneasiness; who never had to have their wills broken, and never forgot to put on their rubbers or take an umbrella. In boyhood he was intended for a missionary. Had it been possible for him to go to Greenland's icy mountains without catching

cold, or India's coral strand without getting bilious, his
parents would have carried out their pleasing dream of
contributing him to the world's evangelization. Lu and
Mr. Lovegrove had no doubt that he would have been
greatly blessed if he could have stood it. They brought
him up in the most careful manner, and I cannot recollect the time when he was not president, secretary, or
something in some society of small yet good children.
He was not only an exemplar to whom all Lu's friends
pointed their own nursery as the little boy who could
say most hymns and sit stillest in church, but he was a
reproof even unto his elders. One Sunday afternoon,
in the Connecticut village where my brother-in-law **used**
to spend his summers, when half the congregation were
slumbering under the combined effect of the heat, a
lunch of cheese and apples, and the sermon, my nephew,
then aged five, sat bolt upright in the pew, winkless as
a deacon hearing a new candidate suspected of shaki-
ness on " a card'nal p'int," and mortified almost to death
poor old Mrs. Pringle, who, compassionating his years,
had handed him a sprig of her " meetin' seed " over the
back of the seat, **by saying, in a loud and stern voice,—**
" I don't eat things in church."

I should have spanked the boy when I got home, but
Lu, with tears in her eyes, quoted something about the
mouths of babes and sucklings.

Both she and his father always encouraged old manners in him. I think they took such pride in raising a
peculiarly pale boy as a gardener does in getting a nice

blanch on his celery, and so long as he was not absolutely sick, the graver he was the better.   He was a sensitive plant, a violet by a mossy stone, and all that sort
of thing.   But when in his tenth year he had the measles, and was narrowly carried through, Lu got a scare
about him.   During his convalescence, reading aloud
a life of Henry Martyn to amuse him, she found in it
a picture of that young apostle preaching to a crowd of
Hindoos without any boots on.   An American mother's
association of such behavior with croup and ipecac was
too strong to be counteracted by known climatic facts;
and from that hour, as she never had before, Lu realized that being a missionary might involve going to
carry the gospel to the heathen in your stocking-feet.

When they had decided that such a life would not do
for him, his training had almost entirely unfitted him
for any other active calling.   The strict propriety with
which he had been brought up had resulted in weak
lungs, poor digestion, sluggish circulation, and torpid
liver.   Moreover, he was troubled with the painfulest
bashfulness which ever made a mother think her child
too ethereal, or a dispassionate outsider regard him too
flimsy, for this world.   These were weights enough to
carry, even if he had not labored under that heaviest of
all, a well-stored mind.

No misnomer **that last to any one who** has ever fre-
quented the Atlantic Docks, or seen storage in any large
port of entry.   How does a storehouse look?   It's a
vast, dark, cold chamber, — dust an inch deep on the

floor, cobwebs festooning the girders, — and piled from
floor to ceiling, on the principle of getting the largest
bulk into the least room, with barrels, boxes, bales,
baskets, chests, crates, and carboys, — merchandise **of
all** description, from the roughest raw material to **the
most** exquisite *choses de luxe.* **The** inmost layers are
inextricable without pulling down the outer ones. If
you **want** a particular case of broadcloth you must clear
yourself an alley-way through a hundred tierces of
hams, and last week's entry of clayed sugars is inaccessible without tumbling on your head a mountain **of**
Yankee notions.

In my nephew's unfortunate youth such storage **as**
this had minds. As long as the crown of his brain's
arch was not crushed in by some intellectual Furman-
street disaster, those stevedores of learning, the schoolmasters, kept on unloading the Rome and Athens
lighters into a boy's crowded skull, and breaking out of
the hold of that colossal old junk, The Pure Mathe-
matics, all the formulas **which could be** crowded into
the interstices between his Latin a**nd Greek.**

At the time I introduce Billy both **Lu and her hus-**
band were much changed. They had **gained** a great
deal in width of view and liberality of judgment: They
read Dickens and Thackeray with avidity; went now
and then to the opera; proposed to let Billy take a quarter at Dodworth's; had statues in their parlor without
any thought of shame at their lack of petticoats, and did
multitudes of things which, in their early married life,

22 *

they would have considered shocking. Part of this change
was due to the great **increase** of travel, the wonderful
progress in art and refinement which **has** enlarged this
generation's thought and corrected its ignorant **opinions;** infusing cosmopolitanism into our manners by a
revolution so gradual that its subjects were a new peo-
ple before their combativeness became alarmed, yet so
rapid that a man of thirty can scarcely believe his birthday, and questions whether he has not added his life up
wrong by a century or so when he compares his own
boyhood with that of the present day. But a good deal
of the transformation resulted from the means of gratifying elegant tastes, **the comfort, luxury, and** culture
which came with Lovegrove's retirement **on a** fortune.
They had mellowed on the **sunny shelves** of prosperity
like every good thing which has **an** astringent skin when
it is green. They would greatly have liked to see Daniel
shine in society. Of his erudition they were proud even
to worship. The young man never had any business,
and his father never seemed to **think of giving him any,**
knowing, as Billy would say, that he had stamps enough
to " see him through." If Daniel liked, his father would
have endowed a professorship in some college and given
him the chair; but that would have taken him away from
his own room and the family **physician.**

Daniel knew how **much his parents** wished him to
make a figure in the world, and only blamed himself for
his failure, magnanimously forgetting that they had
crushed out the faculties which enable a man to mint the

small change of every-day society, in the exclusive cultivation of such as fit him for smelting its ponderous ingots. With that merciful blindness which alone prevents **all our lives from** becoming a horror of nerveless self-reproach, his parents were equally unaware of their share in the harm done him, when they ascribed to delicate organization the fact that, at an age when love runs riot in all healthy blood, he could not **see a** Balmoral without his cheeks rivalling the most vivid stripe in it. **They** flattered themselves that he would outgrow his bashfulness; but Daniel had no such hope, **and frequently** confided **in me** that he thought he should never marry at all.

About two hours after Billy's disappearance under his mother's convoy, the defender of the oppressed **returned** to my room bearing the dog under his arm. His cheeks shone with washing like a pair of waxy spitzenbergs, and other indignities had been offered him to the extent of the brush and comb. He also had a whole jacket on.

" Well, Billy," said I, " what are you going **to** do with **your dog ?** "

" I don't **know** what I am a-going to do. I've **a great** mind to be a bad, disobedient boy with him, and *not* have my days long in the land which the Lord my God giveth me."

" O Billy ! "

" **I can't help it.** They wont be long if I don't mind ma, she says; and she wants me to be mean, and put

Crab out in the street to have Patsy catch him and tie
coffee-pots to his tail. I — I — I " —

Here my small nephew dug his fist into his eye and
looked down.

I told Billy to stop where he was, and went to inter-
cede with Lu. She was persuaded to entertain the
angels of magnanimity and heroism in the disguise of a
young fighting character, and accept my surety for the
behavior of his dog. Billy and I also obtained permission to go out together and be gone the entire afternoon. We put Crab on a comfortable bed of rags in an
old shoe-box, and then strolled hand in hand across that
most delightful of New York breathing-places, Stuyve-
sant Square.

" Uncle Teddy ! " exclaimed Billy, with ardor, " I
wish I could do something to show you how much I
think of you for being so good to me. I don't know
how. Would it make you happy if I was to learn a
hymn for you, — a smashing big hymn, — six verses,
long metre, and no grumbling ? "

" No, Billy; you make me happy enough just by being a good boy."

" Oh, Uncle Teddy ! " replied Billy, decidedly, " I'm
afraid I can't do it. I've tried so often, and I always
make such an awful mess of it."

" Perhaps you get discouraged too easily " —

" Well, if a savings-bank wont do it there aint any
chance for a boy. I got father to get me a savings-
bank once, and began being good just as hard as ever I

could for three cents a day. Every night I got 'em, I put 'em in reg'lar, and sometimes I'd keep being good three whole days running. That made a sight of money, I tell you. Then I'd do something, ma said, to kick my pail of milk over, and those nights I didn't get anything. I used to put in most of my marble and candy-money, too."

" What were you going to do with it ? "

" It was for an Objeck, Uncle Teddy. That's a kind of Indian, you know, that eats people and wants the gospel. That's what pa says, any way; I didn't ever see one."

" Well, didn't that make you happy, — to help the poor little heathen children ? "

" That's just it, Uncle Teddy; they never got a cent of it. One time I was good so long I got scared. I was afraid I'd never want to fly my kite on the roof again, or go anywhere where I oughtn't, or have any fun. I couldn't see any use of going and saving all my money to send out to the Objecks, if it was going to make good boys of 'em. It was awful hard for me to have to be a good boy, and it must be worse for them 'cause they aint used to it. So when there wasn't anybody up-stairs I went and shook a lot of pennies out of my chimney and bought ever so much taffy, and marbles, and pop-corn. Was that awful mean, Uncle Teddy ? "

The question involved such complications that I hesitated. Before I could decide what to answer, Billy continued : —

" Ma said it was robbing the heathen, and didn't I get it ! I thought if it was robbing, I'd have a cop after me."

" What's a ' cop ? ' "

" That's what the boys call a policeman, Uncle Teddy; **and** then I should be taken away and put in an awful **black** place under ground, like Johnny Wilson, when he broke Mrs. Perkins's window. I was scared, I tell you ! But I didn't get anything worse than a whipping, and having my savings-bank taken away from me with all that was left in **it.** I haven't tried to be good since, much."

We now got into a Broadway stage going down, and being unable, on account of the noise, to converse further upon those spiritual conflicts of Billy's which so much interested me, amused ourselves with looking out until **just as we** reached the Astor House, when he asked me **where we were going.**

" Where do you guess ? " said I.

He cast a glance through the front window, and his **face** became irradiated. Oh, there's nothing like the simple, cheap luxury of pleasing a child, to create sunshine enough for the chasing away of the bluest adult devils !

" **We're going to** Barnum's ! " **said** Billy, involuntarily **clapping his hands.**

So we were; and, much as stuck-up people pretend to look down on the place, I frequently am. Not only so, but I always see that class largely represented there when I do go. To be sure they always make-believe that they only come to amuse the children, or because they've country cousins **visiting** them, and never fail to refer to the vulgar set **one finds** there, and the fact of the animals smelling like anything but Jockey Club; yet I notice that after they've been in the hall three minutes they're as much interested as any of the people they come to poh-poh, and only put on the high-bred air when they fancy some of their own class are looking at them. I boldly acknowledge that I go because I like it. I am especially happy, **to** be sure, if I have a child along to go into ecstasies, and give me a chance, by asking questions, for **the** exhibition of that fund of information which is said to be one of my chief charms in the social circle, and on several occasions has led that portion of the public immediately about the Happy Family into the erroneous impression that I was Mr. Barnum ex-**plaining his five** hundred thousand curiosities.

On the present occasion we found several visitors of the better class in the room devoted to the Aquarium. Among these was a young lady apparently about nineteen, in a tight-fitting basque of **black velvet, which** showed **her** elegant **figure to fine advantage, a skirt of** garnet silk looped up **over a** pretty Balmoral, and the daintiest imaginable pair of kid walking-boots. Her height was a trifle over the medium; her eyes a soft expressive brown, shaded by masses of hair which exactly matched their color, and, at that rat-and-miceless day, fell in such graceful abandon as to show at once

that nature was the **only maid** who crimped their waves
into them. Her **complexion was rosy** with health and
sympathetic **enjoyment;** her mouth was faultless, her
nose **sensitive, her manners** full of refinement, and her
voice musical as a **wood-robin's,** when she spoke to the
little boy of six at her side, to whom she was revealing
the palace of the great show-king. **Billy and I were**
flattening our noses against the abode of the balloon-
fish, and determining whether he looked **most** like a
horse-chestnut **burr** or a ripe cucumber, **when** his eyes
and **my** own simultaneously **fell on the child** and lady.
In a moment, **to Billy, the** balloon-fish was as though he
had not been.

"That's a **pretty** little boy!" said I. **And then I**
asked **Billy one of** those **senseless routine** questions
which **must make children** look at us, regarding the
scope **of our** intellects **very** much as we look at Bush-
men.

"How would **you like to** play with **him?"**

"Him!" replied **Billy, scornfully,** "that's his first
pair of boots; see him pull up his little breeches to
show the red tops **to** 'em! But, crackey! **isn't** *she* a
smasher!"

After that we visited the **wax** figures and the sleepy
snakes, the learned **seal and the** glass-**blowers.** When-
ever we passed **from one room into another,** Billy could
be caught **looking** anxiously **to** see **if** the pretty **girl**
and child were coming, too.

Time fails me to describe how Billy was lost in astonishment at the Lightning Calculator, — wanted me to
beg the secret of that prodigy for him to do his sums
by, — finally thought he had discovered it, and resolved
to keep his arm whirling all the time he studied his
arithmetic lesson the next morning. Equally inadequate
is it to relate in full how he **became** so confused among
the wax-works that he pinched the solemnest showman's
legs to see **if he was real,** and perplexed **the** beautiful
Circassian to the verge of idiocy by telling her he had
read all about the **way** they **sold** girls like her in his
geography.

We had reached the stairs to that subterranean chamber in which the Behemoth of Holy Writ was wallowing
about without a thought of the dignity which one ex-
pects from a canonical character. Billy had always
languished upon his memories of this diverting beast,
and I stood ready to see him plunge headlong the moment that he read the sign-board at the head of the
stairs. When **he** paused and hesitated there, not seeming at all anxious to go **down** till he **saw** the **pretty
girl and the child following after,** — a sudden intuition
flashed across **me. Could it be possible that** Billy was
caught in that vortex which whirled **me** down at ten
years, — a little boy's first love ?

We were lingering about the elliptical basin, and
catching occasional glimpses between bubbles of a vivi-
fied hair trunk of monstrous compass, whose knobby
lid opened at one end and showed **a** red morocco lining,

23

when the pretty girl, in leaning over to point out the rising monster, dropped into the water one of her little gloves, and the swash made by the hippopotamus drifted it close under Billy's hand. Either in play or as a mere coincidence the animal followed it. The other children about the tank screamed and started back as he bumped his nose against the side; but Billy manfully bent down and grabbed the glove not an inch from one of his big tusks, then marched round the tank and presented it to the lady with a chivalry of manner in one of his years quite surprising.

"That's a real nice boy,— you said so, didn't you, Lottie ?— and I wish he'd come and play with me," said the little fellow by the young lady's side, as Billy turned away, gracefully thanked, to come back to me with his cheeks roseate with blushes.

As he heard this, Billy idled along the edge of the tank for a moment, then faced about and said, —

"P'raps I will some day, — where do you live ? "

" I live on East Seventeenth street with papa, — and Lottie stays there, too, now, — she's my cousin: where d'you live ? "

" Oh, I live close by, — right on that big green square, where I guess the nurse takes you once in a while," said Billy, patronizingly. Then, looking up pluckily at the young lady, he added, " I never saw you out there."

"No, Jimmy's papa has only been in his new house a little while, and I've just come to visit him."

"Say, will you come and play with me sometime?" chimed in the inextinguishable Jimmy. "I've got a cooking-stove, — for real fire, — and blocks and a ball with a string."

Billy, who belonged to a club for the practice of the great American game, and was what A. Ward would call the most superior battist among the I. G. B. B. C., or "Infant Giants," smiled from that altitude upon Jimmy, but promised to go and play with him the next Saturday afternoon.

Late that evening, after we had got home and dined, as I sat in my room over Pickwith with a sedative cigar, a gentle knock at the door told of Daniel. I called "Come in!" and entering with a slow, dejected air, he sat down by my fire. For ten minutes he remained silent, though occasionally looking up as if about to speak, then dropping his head again to ponder on the coals. Finally I laid down Dickens, and spoke myself.

"You don't seem well to-night, Daniel?"

"I don't feel very well, uncle."

"What's the matter, my boy?"

"Oh — ah — I don't know. That is, I wish I knew how to tell you."

I studied him for a few moments with kindly curiosity, then answered, —

"Perhaps I can save you the trouble by cross-examining it out of you. Let's try the method of elimination. I know that you're not harassed by any economical considerations, for you've all the money you want; and I know that ambition doesn't trouble you, for your tastes are scholarly. This narrows down the investigation of your symptoms — listlessness, general dejection, and all — to three causes, — Dyspepsia, Religious Conflicts, Love. Now, is your digestion awry ? "

" No, sir, good as usual. I'm not melancholy on religion, and " —

" You don't tell me you're in love ? "

" Well — yes — I suppose that's about it, Uncle Teddy."

I took a long breath to recover **from my** astonishment at this unimaginable revelation, then said, —

" Is your feeling returned ? "

" I really don't know, uncle. **I don't believe it is. I** don't see **how it can be. I never did anything to** make her love me. **What is there in me** to love ! **I've** borne nothing for her, — that is, nothing that could do her any good, — **though** I've endured on her account, I may say, anguish. So, look at it any way you please, I neither **am, do,** nor suffer anything that can get a woman's love."

" Oh, you man of learning ! Even in love you tote your grammar along with you, and arrange a divine passion under the active, passive, and neuter ! "

Daniel smiled faintly.

" **You've** no idea, Uncle Teddy, **that you are** twitting on facts; but you **hit** the truth there; indeed you do. If she were a Greek or Latin woman I could talk Anacreon or Horace to her. If women only understood the philosophy of the flowers as well as they do the poetry " —

" Thank God they don't, Daniel ! " sighed I devoutly.

" Never mind; — in that case I could entrance her for **hours,** talking about the grounds of difference between Linnæus and Jussieu. Women like the star business, **they say, — and** I could tell her where all the constellations are; but sure as I tried to get off any sentiment about them, I'd break down and make myself ridiculous. But what earthly chance would the greatest philosopher that ever lived have with the woman he loved, if he depended for her favor on his ability to analyze her bouquet or tell her **when she** might look out for the next occultation of Orion ? I can't talk bread-and-butter talk. I can't do anything that makes a man even tolerable to a woman ! "

" I hope you don't mean that nothing but bread-and-butter talk is tolerable to a woman ! "

" No; but it's necessary to some extent, — at any rate the ability is, — in order to succeed in society; and it's **in society men first meet and** strike **women.** And O Uncle Teddy ! I'm such a fish out of water in society ! — such **a** dreadful floundering fish ! When I see her dancing gracefully as a swan swims, and feel that fellows, like little Jack Mankyn, who " don't know twelve times," can dance to her perfect admiration; when I see that she likes ease of manners, — and all sorts of men without an idea in their heads have that, — while I turn all colors when I speak to her, and am clumsy, and

23 *

abrupt, and abstracted, and bad at repartee, — Uncle Teddy! sometimes (though it seems so ungrateful to father and mother, who have spent such pains for me) — sometimes, do you know, it seems to me as if I'd exchange all I've ever learned for the power to make a good appearance before her!"

"Daniel, my boy, it's too much a matter of reflection with you! A woman is not to be taken by laying plans. If you love the lady (whose name I don't ask you, because I know you'll tell me as soon as you think best), you must seek her companionship until you're well enough acquainted with her to have her regard you as something different from the men whom she meets merely in society, and judge your qualities by another standard than that she applies to them. If she's a sensible girl (and God forbid you should marry her otherwise!), she knows that people can't always be dancing, or holding fans, or running after orange-ice. If she's a girl capable of appreciating your best points (and woe to you if you marry a girl who can't!), she'll find them out upon closer intimacy, and, once found, they'll a hundred times outweigh all brilliant advantages kept in the show-case of fellows who have nothing on the shelves. When this comes about, you will pop the question unconsciously, and, to adapt Milton, she'll drop into your lap ' gathered — not harshly plucked.'"

"I know that's sensible, Uncle Teddy, and I'll try. Let me tell you the sacredest of secrets, — regularly every day of my life I send her a little poem fastened round the prettiest bouquet I can get at Hanft's."

" **Does she** know who sends them ? "

" She can't have any idea. The German boy that takes them knows not a word of English except her **name and** address. You'll forgive me, uncle, for not **mentioning her name** yet ? You see she may despise **or hate me** some day when she knows who it is that has paid her these attentions; and then I'd like to be able to feel that at least I've never hurt her by any absurd con-**nection with** myself."

" Forgive you ? Nonsense ! The feeling does your heart infinite credit, though a little counsel with your head would show you that your only absurdity **is self-**depreciation."

Daniel bid me good-night. As I put out my cigar and went to bed, my mind reverted to the dauntless lit-tle Hotspur who had spent the afternoon with me and reversed his mother's wish, thinking, —

" **Oh, if** Daniel were more like Billy ! "

It was always Billy's habit to come and sit with me while I smoked my after-breakfast cigar, but the next morning did not see him enter my room till St. George's hands pointed to a quarter **of nine.**

" Well, Billy Boy **Blue, come blow** your horn; what haystack have you been under till this time of day ? We sha'n't have a minute to look over our spelling to-gether, and I know a boy who's going in for promotion **next** week. Have you had your breakfast, and taken care of Crab ? "

" Yes, sir; but I didn't feel like getting up this morn-ing."

" Are you sick ! "

" No-o-o — it isn't **that;** but you'll laugh at me if I tell you."

" Indeed I wont, **Billy** ! "

" Well," — his voice dropped to a whisper, and he stole close to my side, — " I had such a nice dream about *her* just the last thing before the bell rang; and when I woke up I felt so queer, — so kinder good and **kinder bad,** — and I **wanted to** see her so much, that if I hadn't been a big boy I believe I should have blubbered. I tried ever so much to go to sleep and see her again; but the more I tried the more I couldn't. After all, I had to get up without it, though I didn't want any breakfast, and only ate two buckwheat cakes, when I always **eat** six, you know, Uncle Teddy. Can you keep a secret ? "

" **Yes, dear, so you** couldn't get it out of me if you **were to shake me upside-down** like a savings-bank."

" Oh, aint **you** mean ! That was when I was small I **did** that. I'll tell you the secret, though, — that girl and I are going to get married. I mean to ask her the first chance I get. Oh, isn't she a smasher ! "

" My dear Billy, sha'n't you wait a little while to see if you always like her as well **as you** do now ? Then, too, you'll **be older."**

" I'm old enough, Uncle Teddy, and I love her dearly ! I'm as old as the kings **of** France used to be when **they got** married, — I read it in Abbott's histories. But there's the clock striking nine ! I must run or I shall get a tardy mark, and, perhaps, she'll want to see my certificate sometime."

So saying, he kissed me on the cheek and set off for school as fast as his legs could carry him. O Love, omnivorous Love, that sparest neither the dotard leaning on his staff nor the boy with pantaloons buttoning on **his** jacket, — omnipotent Love, that, after parents and teachers have failed, in one instant can make Billy try to become a good **boy** !

With both of my nephews hopelessly enamored, and myself the confidant of both, I had my hands full. Daniel was generally dejected and distrustful; Billy buoyant and jolly. Daniel found it impossible to overcome his bashfulness; was spontaneous only in sonnets, brilliant only in bouquets. Billy was always coming to me with pleasant news, told in his slangy New York boy vernacular. One day he would exclaim, — "Oh, I'm getting on prime ! I got such a smile off her this morning as **I** went by the window !" Another day he wanted counsel how to get a valentine to her, — because **it was too big** to shove in a lamp-post, and she might catch **him if he left it on** the steps, **rang the** bell, and ran away. Daniel wrote his own valentine; but, despite its originality, that document gave him no such comfort as Billy got from twenty-five cents' worth of embossed paper, pink Cupids, and doggerel. Finally, Billy announced **to** me that he had been to play with Jimmy, and **got** introduced to his girl.

Shortly after this Lu gave what they call "a little

company," — not a party, but a reunion of forty or fifty people with whom the family were well acquainted, several of them living in our immediate neighborhood. There was a goodly proportion of young folk, and there was to be dancing; but the music was limited to a single piano played by the German exile usual on such occasions, and the refreshments did not rise to the splendor of a costly supper. This kind of compromise with fashionable gayety was wisely deemed by Lu the best method of introducing Daniel to the *beau monde*, — a push given the timid eaglet by the maternal bird, with a soft tree-top between him and the vast expanse of society. How simple was the entertainment may be inferred from the fact that Lu felt somewhat discomposed when she got a note from one of her guests asking leave to bring along her niece, who was making he' a few weeks' visit. As a matter of course, however, she returned answer to bring the young lady and welcome.

Daniel's dressing-room having been given up to the gentlemen I invited him to make his toilet in mine, and, indeed, wanting him to create a favorable impression, became his valet *pro tem.*, tying his cravat, and teasing the divinity student look out of his side-hair. My little dandy Billy came in for another share of attention, and when I managed to button his jacket for him so that it showed his shirt-studs "like a man's," Count d'Orsay could not have felt a more pleasing sense of his sufficiency for all the demands of the gay world.

When we reached the parlor we found Pa and Ma

Lovegrove already receiving. About a score of guests had arrived. Most of them were old married couples, which, after paying their devoirs, fell in two like unriveted scissors, — the gentlemen finding a new pivot in pa and the ladies in ma, where they mildly opened and shut upon such questions as severally concerned them, such as " the way gold closed," and " how the children were."

Besides the old married people there were several old young men of distinctly hopeless and unmarried aspect, who, having nothing in common with the other **class,** nor sufficient **energy of** character to band themselves for mutual protection, hovered dejectedly about the arch pillars, or appeared to be considering whether, on the whole, it would not be feasible and best to sit down on **the** centre-table. These subsisted upon such crumbs of comfort as Lu could get an occasional chance to throw them by rapid sorties of conversation, — became galvanically active the moment they were punched up, and fell flat the moment the punching was remitted. I did all I could for them, but, having Daniel in tow, dared not sail too near the edge of the **Doldrums, lest he should** drop into sympathetic stagnation **and be** taken preternaturally bashful, with his sails all aback, just as I wanted to carry him gallantly into action with some clipper-built cruiser of a nice young lady. Finally, Lu bethought herself of that last plank of drowning conversationists, the photograph album. All the dejected young men made for it at once, some reaching it just as they were about to sink for the last time, but all getting a grip on it somehow, and staying there in company with other people's babies whom they didn't know, and celebrities whom they knew to death, until, one by one, they either stranded upon a motherly dowager by the Fire-place Shoals, or were rescued from the Sofa Reef by some gallant wrecker of a strong-minded young **lady,** with a view to taking salvage out of them in the German.

Besides these were already arrived a dozen nice little boys and girls, who had been invited to make it pleasant for Billy. I had to remind him of the fact that they were his guests, for, in comparison with the queen of his affections, they were in danger of being despised by him as small fry.

The younger ladies and gentlemen, — those who had fascinations to disport, or were in the habit of disporting what they considered such, were probably still at home consulting the looking-glass until that oracle should announce the auspicious moment for their setting forth.

Daniel was in conversation with a perfect godsend of a girl, who understood Latin and had begun Greek. Billy was taking a moment's vacation from his boys and girls, busy with "Old Maid" in the extension-room, and whispering, with his hand in mine, "**Oh, don't** I wish *she* were here ! " **when a fresh** invoice of ladies, just unpacked from the dressing-room in all the airy elegance of evening costume, floated through the door. I heard Lu say, —

" Ah, Mrs. Rumbullion ! Happy to see your niece,
too. How d'ye do, Miss Pilgrim ? "

At this last word Billy jumped as if he had been shot,
and the bevy of ladies opening about sister Lu disclosed
the charming face and figure of the pretty girl we had
met at Barnum's.

Billy's countenance rapidly changed from astonishment to joy.

" **Isn't that splendid, Uncle** Teddy ? Just as I was
wishing it ! It's just like the fairy books ! " and, rushing up to the party of new-comers, " My dear Lottie ! "
cried he, " if I'd only known you were coming I'd have
gone after you ! "

As he caught her by the hand I was pleased to see
her soft eyes brighten with gratification at his enthusiasm, but my sister Lu looked on naturally with astonishment in every feature.

" Why, Billy ! " said she, " you ought not to call a
strange young lady ' *Lottie !* ' Miss Pilgrim, you must
excuse my wild boy " —

" And you must excuse my mother, Lottie," said Billy, affectionately patting Miss Pilgrim's rose kid, " for
calling you a strange young lady. You are not strange
at all, — you're just as nice a girl as there is."

" There are no excuses necessary," said Miss Pilgrim,
with a bewitching little laugh. " Billy and I know each
other intimately well, Mrs. Lovegrove; and I confess
that when I heard the lady aunt had been invited to
visit was his mother, I felt all the more willing to in-

24

fringe etiquette this evening by coming where I had no previous introduction."

"Don't **you care!**" said Billy, encouragingly. "**I'll** introduce you to **every one of our** family; **I know 'em** if you don't."

At this moment I came up **as Billy's reinforcement,** and fearing lest in his enthusiasm he might forget the **canon** of society which introduces a gentleman to a lady, not **the lady** to him, I ventured **to suggest it delicately** by saying, —

" Billy, will you grant me the favor of a presentation to Miss Pilgrim ? "

" In a minute, Uncle Teddy," answered Billy, considerably lowering his voice. "The older people first; " and after this **reproof I was left to** wait in the cold until he had **gone through the ceremony** of introducing to **the young lady his father** and his mother.

Billy, **who had now** assumed entire guardianship of Miss Pilgrim, with an air of great dignity intrusted her to my care and left us promenading while he went in search of Daniel. I myself looked in vain for that youth, whom I had not seen since the entrance of the last comers. Miss Pilgrim and I found a congenial common ground in Billy, whom she spoke of as one of the most delightfully **original boys she had** ever met; in fact, altogether the most fascinating young gentleman she had seen in New York society. You may be sure it wasn't Billy's left ear which burned when I made **my** responses.

In five minutes he reappeared to announce, in a tone
of disappointment, that he could find Daniel nowhere.
He could see a light through his keyhole, but the door
was locked and he could get no admittance. Just then
Lu came up to present a certain — no, an uncertain —
young man of the fleet stranded on parlor furniture
earlier in the evening. To Lu's great astonishment
Miss Pilgrim asked Billy's permission to leave him. It
was granted with all the courtesy of a *preux chevalier*,
on the condition, readily assented to by the lady, that
she should dance one Lancers with him during the
evening.

"Dear me!" exclaimed Lu, after Billy had gone back
like a superior being to assist at the childish amusement
of his contemporaries. "Would anybody ever suppose
that was our Billy?"

"I should, my dear sister," said I, with proud satisfaction; "but you remember I always was just to
Billy."

Left free I went myself to hunt up Daniel. I found
his door locked and a light showing through the keyhole, as Billy had stated. I made no attempt to enter
by knocking; but going to my room and opening the
window next his, leaned out as far as I could, shoved up
his sash with my cane, and pushed aside his curtain.
Such an unusual method of communication could not fail
to bring him to the window with a rush. When he saw
me he trembled like a guilty thing, his countenance fell,

and, no longer able to feign absence, he unlocked his door and let me **enter** by the normal mode.

"Why, Daniel Lovegrove, my nephew, what does this mean? Are you sick?"

"Uncle Edward, I am not sick,—and this means that I am a fool. Even a little boy like Billy puts me to shame. I feel humbled to the very dust. I wish I'd been a missionary and got massacred by savages. Oh that I'd been permitted to wear damp stockings in childhood, or that my mother hadn't carried me through the measles! If it weren't wrong to take my life into my own hands, I'd open that window, and — and — sit in a draught this very evening! Oh, yes! I'm just that bitter! Oh, oh, oh!"

And Daniel paced the floor with strides of frenzy.

"Well, **my dear fellow, let's** look at the matter calmly a minute. What brought on this sudden attack? You seemed doing well enough the first ten minutes after we **came down. I was only out of** your **sight long** enough to speak to the Rumbullion party who had just come in, and when I turned around you were gone. Now you are in this fearful condition. What is there in the Rumbullions to start you off on such a bender of bashfulness as this which I here behold?"

"Rumbullion indeed!" said Daniel. "**A** hundred Rumbullions could not make me feel as I do. But *she* can shake me into a whirlwind with her little finger; and *she* came with the Rumbullions!"

" What !   D'you ← Miss Pilgrim ? "

" Miss Pilgrim ! "

I labored with Daniel for ten minutes, using every encouragement and argument I could think of, and finally threatened him that I would bring up the whole Rumbullion party, Miss Pilgrim included, telling them that **he** had invited them to look at his conchological cabinet, unless he instantly shook the ice out of his manner and accompanied me downstairs. This dreadful menace had the desired effect. He knew that I would not scruple to fulfil it; and at the same time that it made him surrender, it also provoked him with me to a degree which gave his eyes and cheeks as fine a glow as I could have wished for the purpose of a favorable impression. The stimulus of wrath was good for him, and there was little tremor in his knees when he descended the stairs. Well-**a-day !**   So Daniel and Billy were rivals ! .

The latter gentleman met us at the foot of the stair-**case.**

" Oh, there you are, Daniel ! " said he, cheerily.   " I was just going to look after you and Uncle Teddy. We've wanted you for the dances. We've had the Lancers twice and three round dances; and I danced the second Lancers with Lottie. Now we're going to play some games, — to amuse the children, you know," he added, loftily, with the adult gesture of pointing his thumb over his shoulder at the extension-room. " Lottie's going to play, too; so will you and Daniel, wont **you,** uncle ?   Oh, here comes Lottie now ! This is my

24*

brother, Miss Pilgrim, — let me introduce him to you.
I'm sure you'll like him. There's nothing he don't
know."

Miss Pilgrim had just come to the newel-post of the
staircase, and, when she looked into Daniel's face,
blushed like the red, red rose, losing her self-possession
perceptibly more than Daniel.

The courage of weak warriors and timid gallants
mounts as the opposite party's falls, and Daniel made
out to say, in a firm tone, that it was long since he had
enjoyed the pleasure of meeting Miss Pilgrim.

"Not since Mrs. Crameroud's last sociable, I think,"
replied Miss Pilgrim, her cheeks and eyes still playing
the tell-tale.

"Oho! so you don't want any introduction!" exclaimed Master Billy. "I didn't know you knew each
other, Lottie.?"

"I have met Mr. Lovegrove in society. Shall we go
and join in the plays?"

"To be sure we shall!" cried Billy. "You needn't
mind, — all the grown people are going to."

On entering the parlor we found it as he had said.
The guests being almost all well acquainted with each
other, at the solicitation of jolly little Mrs. Bloomingal,
sister Lu had consented to make a pleasant Christmas
kind of time of it, in which everybody was permitted
to be young again, and romp with the rompiest.
We played Blindman's-buff till we were tired of
that, — Daniel, to Lu's great delight, coming out splen-

didly as Blindman, and evincing such "cheek" in the style he hunted down and caught the ladies, as satisfied me that nothing but **his** eyesight stood **in** the way of his making an audacious figure in the world. Then a pretty little girl, Tilly Turtelle, **who seemed** quite a premature flirt, proposed " Door-keeper," — a suggestion accepted **with** great *éclat* **by** all the children, several grown people assenting.

To Billy — quite as much **on** account **of** his shining prominence in the executive faculties as of his character as host — was committed the duty of counting out the first person to be sent into the hall. There were so many of us that " Aina-maina-mona-mike " would not go quite round; but, with that promptness of expedient which belongs to genius, Billy instantly added on, " Intery-mintery-cutery-corn," and the last word of the cabalistic formula fell upon me, — Edward Balbus. I disappeared into the entry amidst peals of happy laughter from both old and young, calling, when the door opened again to **ask** me **whom** I wanted, for the pretty lisping flirt who **had** proposed the game. After giving me a a coquettish little **chirrup** of a kiss, and telling me my beard scratched, she **bade me,** on my return, send out to her " Mithter Billy Lovegrove." I obeyed her; my youngest nephew retired; and after a couple of seconds, during which Tilly undoubtedly got what she proposed the game for, Billy being a great favorite with the little girls, she came back, pouting and blushing, to announce that he wanted Miss Pilgrim. That young lady showed no mock-modesty, but arose at once, and laughingly went out to her **youthful** admirer, who, as I afterward learned, **embraced her ardently,** and told her he loved her **better than any** girl in the world. **As he turned to** go back, she told him **that he** might **send to her one of her juvenile** cousins, Reginald **Rumbullion. Now,** whether because on this youthful Rumbullion's **account** Billy **had suffered the** pangs of that **most terrible passion,** jealousy, **or from** his natural enjoyment **of** playing practical jokes destructive **of** all **dignity in his** elders, B.lly marched into the **room,** and, having **shut the** door behind him, paralyzed the crowded parlor **by an announcement that Mr. Daniel Lovegrove was wanted.**

I was standing at his side, and **could feel him tremble,** — see him turn pale.

" Dear me ! " he whispered, in **a choking voice;** " can she mean me ? "

" Of course she does," said I. **" Who else ?** Do you **hesitate ? Surely you** can't refuse such an invitation from a lady."

"No, I suppose not," said he, mechanically. **And** amidst much laughter from the disinterested, while the faces of Mrs. Rumbullion and his mother were spectacles of crimson astonishment, **he made his exit from the room. Never in my life did I so** much long **for that** instrument **described by** Mr. Samuel Weller, — a pair of patent double-million-magnifying microscopes of hextry power, to see through a deal door. Instead of this, I had to learn what happened only by report.

Lottie Pilgrim was standing under the hall burners with her elbow on the newel-post, looking more vividly charming than he had ever seen her before at Mrs. Cramcroud's sociable or elsewhere. When startled by the apparition of Mr. Daniel Lovegrove instead of the little Rumbullion whom she was expecting, — she had no time to exclaim or hide her mounting color, none at all to explain to her own mind the mistake that had occurred, before his arm was clasped around her waist, and his lips so closely pressed to hers, that through her soft thick hair she could feel the throbbing of his temples. As for Daniel, he seemed in a walking dream, from which he waked to see Miss Pilgrim looking into his eyes with utter though not incensed stupefaction, — to stammer, —

" Forgive me ! Do forgive me ! I thought you were in earnest."

" So I was," she said, tremulously, as soon as she could catch her voice, " in sending for my cousin Reginald."

" Oh, dear, what shall I do ! Believe me, I was told you wanted me, — let me go and explain it to mother, — she'll tell the rest, — I couldn't do it, — I'd die of mortification. Oh, that wretched boy Billy !"

On the principle already mentioned, his agitation reassured her.

" Don't try to explain it now, — it may get Billy a scolding. Are there any but intimate family friends here this evening ?"

" No — I believe — no — I'm sure," replied Daniel, collecting his faculties.

"Then I don't mind what they think. Perhaps they'll suppose we've known each other long; but we'll arrange it by-and-by. They'll think the more of it the longer we stay out here, — hear them laugh ! I must run back now. I'll send you somebody."

A round of juvenile applause greeted her as she hurried into the parlor, and a number of grown people smiled quite musically. Her quick woman-wit showed her how to retaliate and divide the embarrassment of the occasion. As she passed me, she said in an undertone, —

" Answer quick ! Who's that fat lady on the sofa that laughs so loud ? "

" Mrs. Cromwell Craggs," said I, as quietly.

Miss Pilgrim made a satirically low courtesy, and spoke in a modest but distinct voice, —

" I really must be excused for asking. I'm a stranger, you know; but is there such a lady here as Mrs. Craggs, — Mrs. *Cromwell* Craggs ? For if so, the present doorkeeper would like to see Mrs. Cromwell Craggs."

Then came the turn of the fat lady to be laughed at; but out she had to go and get kissed like the rest of us.

Before the close of the evening, Billy was made as jealous as his parents and I were surprised to see Daniel in close conversation with Miss Pilgrim among the geraniums and fuschias' of the conservatory. " A regular flirtation," said Billy, somewhat indignantly. The conclusion which they arrived at was, that after all no great harm had been done, and **that** the dear little fellow ought not to be peached on for his fun. If I had known at the time how easily they forgave him, I should have suspected that the offence Billy had led Daniel into committing was not unlikely **to be** repeated on the offender's **own** account; but so much as **I** could see showed me that the ice was broken.

Billy's jealousy did not outlast the party. He became more and more interested in "his girl," and often went in the afternoon, after getting out of school, ostensibly to play with Jimmy. **Daniel's** calls, according to adult etiquette made in the evening, did not interfere with my younger nephew's, and as neither knew that the other, after his fashion, was his most uncompromising rival, my position as the confidant of both was one of extreme delicacy. But the matter was more speedily settled than **I** expected.

Billy came to me one day and told me that he intended to get married immediately; that he was going to speak to his Lottie that very afternoon. He was prepared to meet every objection. He had asked his father if he might, and his father said **yes, if he had** money enough to support a wife, — and Billy thought he had. He'd saved up all the money his Uncle Tom and Aunt Jane had sent him for Christmas; and besides, if he were once married, his father wouldn't see him want for stamps, he knew. Then, too, he was going to leave school and be a merchant next year, — and I'd help him now and

then, if he got hard up, wouldn't I ? If he were driven
to it, he could **be a good boy** again, and save up the
money to buy Lottie dresses instead of giving it to
nasty old " **Objecks.**" He was so much older than when
he had the savings-bank, that he ought to have at least
ten cents a day now for being good: didn't I think that
was fair ? As to his age, if Lottie loved him he didn't
care, — any way he'd be lots bigger than she was before
long, — and he'd often heard **his** ma say she approved of
early marriages; her's and pa's was one. So he ran off
up Livingston **Place,** the most undaunted lover that
ever put extra shine on his proposal boots, or spent half
an hour **on the** bow of his popping neck-tie.

Shortly after Daniel went into the street. Not meaning **to** call upon his *inamorata,* but, drawn by the irresistible fascination of passing her house, he strolled in
the direction that Billy had gone. As he came to the
Rumbullions' something suddenly **bade** him enter, — a
whim he called it, but not his own, — one of the whims
of Destiny, which are always gratified.

" **Yes,** sir," said the servant, " Miss Pilgrim is in. I
will call her."

His step was always light. He passed noiselessly into
the front-parlor, and sat down among the heavy brocatelle curtains which shadowed a recess of one of the
windows. **He supposed** Miss Pilgrim to be upstairs,
and while his heart fluttered, expecting her footfall at the
parlor-door, he heard an earnest, boyish voice in the
extension-room. Looking from his concealment, he be-

held Miss Pilgrim on a sofa in the pier, and sitting by her side, with her hand clasped in his, his brother Billy. Before he could avoid it, he became aware that Billy was unconsciously but eagerly forestalling him.

"Now, Lottie, my dear Lottie! I wish **you** would! I'll do everything I can to make you happy. **If** you'll only marry me, I'll be good all the **time**! Come, now! Say yes! Father's got a real nice **place over** the stable, — they only use it for a tool-room now; **we could** clear it out and have it scrubbed, and go **to** house-keeping right away. Ma 'd let us have all **her old set of china;** I've got a silver mug Uncle Teddy **gave me, and a** napkin-ring and four spoons. **As soon** as I make **my** money I'll buy you a nice carriage and horses, any color you want 'em. Oh, my darling, darling Lottie, I do love you so much, and we could have such a splendid time! Do say yes, Lottie, — please, *do* please!"

Miss Pilgrim looked at the earnest little suitor with a face in which tender interest and compassion quite over-rode any sense of the whimsicality of the situation which might lurk there. Daniel's astonishment at **the** sight was so great that he realized **the entire state of the** case before he could recover himself **sufficiently to** rise and go into the back-room.

Billy jumped up and looked defiantly at the intruder. Miss Pilgrim blushed violently, but turned away her head to avoid the exhibition of a still more convulsing emotion than embarrassment.

"I must beg your pardon, Miss Pilgrim, — and yours

too, Billy," began Daniel in a hesitating way, hardly knowing how to treat the posture in which he found things; "but — you see — the fact is — the servant said she'd go to announce me — and really, when I came in, I hadn't any idea you were here, or Billy either."

"Then," said Billy, moderating the defiant attitude, "you truly weren't dodging around and trying to find out what Lottie and I were about on the sly? Well, I'll believe you. I'm sure you couldn't be as mean as that when I'm the only brother you've got, that always brings you oranges when you're sick, and never plays ball on the stairs when you've got a headache. Now, then, I'll trust you. I've been asking Lottie to marry me, and I want you to help me. Ask her if she wont, Daniel, — see if she wont do it for you!"

Miss Pilgrim had been trying to find words; but her face was too much for her, and she was obliged to seek retirement in her handkerchief. As she drew it from her pocket a well-worn piece of paper followed it and fell upon the floor. Billy picked it up before she noticed it, and was about to hand it to her, when his jealous eye fell upon a withered rosebud sewed to its margin. As he looked at it, with his little brows knit into a precocious sternness, he recognized his brother's handwriting immediately beneath the flower. It was one of the daily anonymous sonnets of which Daniel had told me, and the bud a relic of the bouquet accompanying it. Still Daniel was silent. What else could he be?

"Very well, very well, Master Daniel!" exclaimed

Billy, in a voice trembling with grief and indignation; "there's good enough reason why you wont speak a word for me! You want her yourself,—here it is in your own writing. No wonder you wont tell Lottie to be my wife when your trying to take her away from me. O Lottie, dear Lottie! I love you just as much as he does, though I don't know everything, and can't write you poetry like it was out of the Fifth Reader! Daniel, how could you go and write to my Lottie this way: 'my churner,'—no, it isn't churner, it's 'charmer,'—'let me call thee mine?'"

Forgetting the sacredness of private MS. in that of private grief, he would have gone on, with a pause here and there for certainty of spelling, to the conclusion of the poem, had not Lottie sprung up with her imploring face suffused by her discovery, for the first time, of the identity of her secret lover and the escape of his sonnet from her pocket. It was too late! There he stood before her unmistakably proved, and himself unmistakably proving in what estimation she held his verses and bouquets.

"O Billy, dear Billy! if **you do love** me don't do so!" So exclaiming, she held out her hand, and Billy put the MS. into it with all the dignity of a wounded spirit.

"Mr. Lovegrove," said Miss Pilgrim, "I don't know what to say."

"I feel very much that way myself," said Daniel.

"*I* don't!" said Billy, now in command of his voice.

"I'll tell you what it is: perhaps Daniel didn't know how much I wanted **you**, Lottie,— and perhaps he wants you 'most **as bad as I do**. But whatever way it is, I **want** you to choose between **us** fair and square and no dodging. Cóme now! You can take just whichever one of us you please, and the other wont lay up any **grudge**, though I know if that's me or like **me** he'll feel **awful**. **You can** have **till** to-morrow morning to make up your mind between me and Daniel; and if he wont say anything **about it to pa and** ma till then *I* wont. Good-by, *dear* **Lottie** !"

He drew **her face** down to his, kissed her most affectionately, and then marched out of the door, feeling, as he afterwards told me, as if he'd blacked his boots all for nothing. Ah me! my dear Billy, **how** many times we do that **in** this world! **Of** what followed when Daniel and Miss Pilgrim were left **alone** I have never had full details.

But I do know that the young lady obeyed Billy and **made** her choice. Six months after that both my nephews stood up in Mrs. Rumbullion's parlor to **take** their several shares in a ceremony of which Miss Pilgrim was the central figure when it began, and **Mrs. Daniel Lovegrove when it concluded. Time and the** elasticity of **boyhood had so closed the sharp** but evanescent wound in Billy's heart **that** he could **stand** the trial of being groomsman where he had wanted to be groom, — more especially since he was supported through the emergency by a little sister of Lottie's, who promises to be wondrously like her by the time Billy can stand up in the more enviable capacity. Neither Daniel nor Lottie would listen to any objection to such a groomsman on the score of his extreme youth; for, as they said, Billy had been quite as instrumental in bringing them together as any agent save the Divinity shaping all the ends and tying all the knots in which there are heart-strings concerned as well as white ribbon.

Since then Lu has stopped wishing that Billy were like Daniel, for she sees that, if he had been, there would never have been any Mrs. Daniel Lovegrove in the world.